'My dear, t̸̶... st provocative nightg̸̶... I have ever seen.'

His voice was a growl dipped in honey, and his weight on the bed next to her angled the mattress so that her hip touched his flank. His skin was hot.

'You forgot the candles.' The room seemed bright as day.

'Oh, no, I haven't.' Justin's fingers were tangling with the ribbons at her neckline, not with any apparent urgency, but with the leisurely pleasure of someone trailing wool for a kitten. 'I love looking at you, Mari. I love it when you blush. I love it when you drop your lashes like that to try to hide the expression in your eyes.'

She gasped again as his fingers brushed the line of her collarbone. *Focus on how it feels. Do not think…* How hard that was to do. Her mind ran off along its own unhappy path. *He loves all those things about me, but he does not love me. He does not trust me. He will not share his life or his worries or his secrets with me. His secrets.*

Louise Allen has been immersing herself in history, real and fictional, for as long as she can remember, and finds landscapes and places evoke powerful images of the past. Louise lives in Bedfordshire and works as a property manager, but spends as much time as possible with her husband at the cottage they are renovating on the north Norfolk coast, or travelling abroad. Venice, Burgundy and the Greek islands are favourite atmospheric destinations.

Recent novels by the same author:

ONE NIGHT WITH A RAKE
THE EARL'S INTENDED WIFE
THE SOCIETY CATCH
A MODEL DEBUTANTE
THE MARRIAGE DEBT
MOONLIGHT AND MISTLETOE
  (in *Christmas Brides*)
THE VISCOUNT'S BETROTHAL

MILLS & BOON®

The *Regency*
LORDS & LADIES
COLLECTION
*Two glittering Regency
love affairs in every book*

2 Books
and a surprise gift!

We would like to take this opportunity to thank you for reading this Mills & Boon® book by offering you the chance to take TWO more specially selected titles from the Historical Romance™ series absolutely FREE! We're also making this offer to introduce you to the benefits of the Mills & Boon® Reader Service™—

- ★ **FREE home delivery**
- ★ **FREE gifts and competitions**
- ★ **FREE monthly Newsletter**
- ★ **Exclusive Reader Service offers**
- ★ **Books available before they're in the shops**

Accepting these FREE books and gift places you under no obligation to buy, you may cancel at any time, even after receiving your free shipment. Simply complete your details below and return the entire page to the address below. You don't even need a stamp!

YES! Please send me 2 free Historical Romance books and a surprise gift. I understand that unless you hear from me, I will receive 4 superb new titles every month for just £3.69 each, postage and packing free. I am under no obligation to purchase any books and may cancel my subscription at any time. The free books and gift will be mine to keep in any case.

H6ZEF

Ms/Mrs/Miss/Mr ....Initials..............................

Surname .... BLOCK CAPITALS PLEASE

Address...

....

....Postcode ....

Send this whole page to:
UK: FREEPOST CN81, Croydon, CR9 3WZ

THE BRIDE'S SEDUCTION

Louise Allen

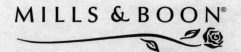

MILLS & BOON®

First published in Great Britain 2006
Harlequin Mills & Boon Limited,
Eton House, 18-24 Paradise Road, Richmond, Surrey TW9 1SR

© Melanie Hilton 2006

ISBN-13: 978 0 263 84668 3
ISBN-10:   0 263 84668 7

Set in Times Roman 10½ on 12½ pt.
04-0906-85912

Printed and bound in Spain
by Litografia Rosés S.A., Barcelona

THE BRIDE'S
SEDUCTION

Prologue

⌒⌒⌒⌒⌒⌒

June 6 1817

'With this ring I thee wed, with my body I thee worship…'

Marina was thankful for the protection of her veil as the blood surged hot in her cheeks. *What am I doing? How did I let it come to this? If only I had more resolution.* She resisted the temptation to look up at the tall figure standing next to her and made herself concentrate as the ceremony took its course. Finally,

'I now pronounce you man and wife.'

A soft murmur went round St George's. Relief? Marina wondered, or surprise that the old maid of the Winslow family had found herself such an eligible husband? Or perhaps it was simply a sentimental sigh. Her distraction was cut short by Justin raising the edge of her veil and setting it back from her face. She looked up at him and saw the look in his eyes that had convinced her to accept his proposal: kindness and honesty that had made her trust him, had made her feel safe and able to set aside all her doubts and scruples. Suddenly her nervousness seemed foolish.

Then, as he bent to touch his lips to hers, she saw a spark in his eyes, which turned their hazel to green. *Not so safe*, a panicky little voice whispered as their lips met. She returned the pressure until another murmur, this time an unmistakably sentimental one, brought her to herself. She was standing almost on tiptoe, one hand raised to rest against her new husband's chest, and there was the strange fluttering through her veins that she was coming to expect whenever he touched her. Whatever she did, she must not betray her true feelings, not to this man she had just married.

Blushing in real earnest now, and without her veil to protect her, Marina let Justin place her hand on his arm as they turned. Slowly they began to walk back down the aisle and she made herself behave as her position now required. Nodding and smiling from side to side, the new Countess of Mortenhoe was conscious of genuine smiles, of her mother unashamedly weeping into her lace handkerchief, of some speculative looks and one or two less friendly glances.

Well may they stare and wonder, she thought as they emerged on to the steps of St George's overlooking Hanover Square. *They probably find it as hard to believe as I do that Justin Ransome should marry Charlie Winslow's sister, a woman who has been on the shelf these four years past.*

And what possessed me to agree? she wondered as she had done almost every waking hour since Justin's proposal, the panic rising in her breast again. *Whatever made me think I could make a success of a marriage to a man I have known only eleven weeks and who makes no pretence of the fact he does not love me?*

As the animated, chattering guests thronged out of the church into the bright sunshine, she turned, catching their mood all of a sudden. She threw her bouquet with a laugh into the mass of young ladies who reached and jostled for it.

Beside her Justin laughed too, amused by the sight of ladylike behaviour abandoned for a few moments, and she glanced up at him again.

And why did he ask me? she queried for the hundredth time. *Why should one of the most eligible men in London wish to marry* me? She had gone over his words again and again, had dreamed them, analysed them to the point of exhaustion. It was too late to wonder now, she realised as Justin helped her into the waiting carriage. Far too late.

Chapter One

Eleven weeks earlier—3 April 1817

Take a deep breath. Justin Ransome stood on the upper step of the double-fronted house in Cavendish Square with his life in the balance. Today, after twenty years, if he could keep his temper in check and his wits about him, he was going to achieve the ambition that had driven him since he was eight years old.

He found his right hand was in his coat pocket, the thumb and forefinger rubbing the small crystal lustre that had been a talisman for all of those years. The sharp edges had become dulled with handling, the ball of his thumb had a callus from the habitual, unthinking gesture.

Now. He raised his hand, let the knocker drop with a thud that echoed the knocking of his own heart against his ribs. Almost immediately he heard faint footsteps from inside the house. They were expecting him, of course. He stepped back slightly as the door opened, a fortunate move; for, instead of the impassive figure of the family butler, a small boy erupted out of the opening pursued by a frantically barking dog almost the same size.

At the sight of the tall man on the step the hound skidded to a halt and regarded him hopefully, head on one side. Justin braced himself to repel a leap, but the creature simply dealt his highly polished Hessians a swipe with a slavering tongue and bounded after its young master.

So much for working oneself up into a state of high drama: fate had a sure way of bringing one down to earth.

'Giles! Hector! Oh, sir, I can only apologise for my brother.'

Justin looked up from the rueful contemplation of his footwear to find himself being regarded with anxiety by a fine pair of silver grey eyes.

'Which is which?' he enquired of the owner of these admirable features, smiling as the anxiety in them was replaced with something closer to amusement. The lady was dressed for walking, presumably in the wake of the harum-scarum child.

'Giles is my little brother. Hector is the abominable hound. I am Miss Winslow and my brother—my elder brother—is Charles Winslow. Just so you know how to direct the account from your bootmaker.'

'Good morning, Miss Winslow.' Justin, by now diverted by the situation, held out his hand. The gesture was met with a warm smile and a confident handshake in return. 'I am Justin Ransome. I am sure only the most superficial damage has been done: a wipe will put it to rights.'

'Lord Mortenhoe.' Miss Winslow nodded. 'I recall Charlie said you would be calling. I cannot conceive where Bunting has vanished to. Ah, there he is. And I should not be keeping you standing here on the doorstep—you must think you have arrived at Bedlam, not a respectable home. Bunting, here is Lord Mortenhoe to see Lord Winslow, but first, please see if Kyte can do something with his lordship's Hessians—that hell hound of Master Giles's has been slobbering all over them.'

'Of course, Miss Winslow. My lord, if you would care to

step into the salon, I will fetch Lord Winslow's valet to you immediately. One trusts no lasting damage has been done.' The butler relieved Justin of hat, gloves and cane and opened the door into the front reception room as another young lady came down the stairs.

Justin bowed slightly to the new arrival, succeeding in reducing her to blushing confusion. She was a pretty child of perhaps fifteen, still childishly plump but with wide blue eyes, a pert little nose and abundant blonde ringlets emerging from under her somewhat plain bonnet.

'My lord, this is my sister Elizabeth. Lizzie, Lord Morten-hoe has called to see Charlie and unfortunately has encountered Giles and Hector.' Miss Winslow held out her hand. 'My lord, I can only apologise once more and leave you to the care of Bunting and Charles's valet. If I delay much longer, I shudder to think what havoc will have been wrought upon the gardens in the Square.'

'Miss Winslow, good day. I trust you have an uneventful walk.'

She smiled up at him, drawing on her gloves. 'No hope of that, my lord. Good day to you. Come, Lizzie.'

Justin was left with the impression of amused tranquillity, a pleasing sensation. Not a beauty, the elder Miss Winslow, with her soft brown hair, oval face and wide grey eyes, but a soothing presence, which was very much in tune with his needs just now.

The valet descending upon his Hessians with a cry of distress distracted him from further thoughts of the Misses Winslow. 'The merest dabbing with a little warm water, my lord, then a buff with my own polish and a chamois cloth, and all will be restored. If your lordship will permit me to remove both boots…'

Justin submitted and was therefore at the disadvantage of

standing in his stockinged feet when his host sauntered in. 'Mortenhoe.' They shook hands and the younger man peered at Justin's feet. 'Raining, is it?'

'No, my lord,' the butler hastened to intervene. 'That Dog, my lord.'

'Oh. Enough said. Is Kyte fixing things? Good. Do you want to borrow some slippers? No? Then let's make ourselves comfortable in my study.'

Winslow led the way across the hallway and waved his guest to a chair. As Justin sat he found he had an admirable view out over the Square to where young Master Winslow was engaged in hot pursuit of his dog while his sisters, parasols unfurled, looked on.

'Brandy?' Lord Winslow was unstopping a decanter.

'Not for me, thank you. But please—'

His host needed no encouragement, pouring a good measure into his glass before dropping into the chair opposite. Justin regarded him thoughtfully. Having now, he assumed, seen all the brothers and sisters, he could see the likeness between Charles and his younger sister, despite Charles's dark brown hair and Lizzie's blonde curls.

But in the brother the good looks were already blurred at only twenty-seven by what, from his reputation, was a mixture of late nights and strong drink. The elder Miss Winslow with her well-bred, pleasant face seemed to have missed out; she would never have been an Incomparable, which he suspected Lizzie one day might be. Young Giles was still blessed with the chubby features of any small boy; too early to tell how he would turn out.

'We'll wait until Kyte brings your boots,' Winslow announced. 'We don't want to be interrupted while we talk business.'

'No, indeed,' Justin agreed equably, hiding the stab of impatience he felt. *Calm*, he told himself. *This is the most significant piece of business you will ever have to do, just keep calm.* Without conscious thought his eyes strayed again to the window from whence Miss Winslow could be seen. She was fending off a now filthy hound, which had decided it wanted nothing more than for her to throw its ball. She was laughing out loud, he could see, and felt a sudden curiosity to hear what her laughter sounded like.

Marina's laughter was, in fact, nearer a series of breathless and indignant gasps as she did her best to keep Hector's large paws off her skirts. 'Sit, sir!' she ordered, more in the hope than the expectation of being obeyed. 'Giles, come and get hold of this animal at once. It defeats me,' she added to Lizzie, who was giggling, 'how this creature manages to get muddy on a fine day like today. Thank you, Giles. Now *please* put a cord through his collar and let us attempt to present the appearance of a normal family out for a walk and not a group of wandering circus performers.'

Giles, finding this vastly humorous, captured Hector and allowed himself to be towed off around the flower beds that edged the curving paths in the centre of the Square. Lizzie fell in beside her sister and the two began to pace more decorously.

'Who was that gentleman?' she demanded.

'Lord Mortenhoe. I did introduce you, Lizzie, you must make a push to remember introductions. It will present a very off impression when you come out if you cannot recall people's names. A true lady takes an interest in other people.'

Lizzie, sublimely confident that her come-out would be a great success and nothing but a pleasure from start to finish, ignored this good advice. After all, poor Marina had been out for three Seasons and had quite failed to catch a husband, so really, fond though one was of her, her advice could safely be disregarded.

'I *am* taking an interest, I just could not recall his name. And why is Lord Mortenhoe visiting Charlie?'

'I have no idea,' Marina said repressively. 'A matter of business, no doubt, and no concern of ours.'

'You mean that one of them owes the other some money?' Lizzie deduced pertly. 'Let us hope Lord Mortenhoe owes Charlie, for that would be a great comfort to poor Mama.'

'We have no reason to suppose Lord Mortenhoe is a card player,' Marina pointed out, giving up the effort to turn her sister's thoughts to a more seemly topic.

'It might be anything,' Lizzie countered. 'Racing, cards, hazard—anything. Someone told me Charlie would even bet on which of two flies would land upon a window first. When I am out in society and playing cards I will be like dear Papa and always win. I do not know why Charlie never does.'

Marina contemplated a lecture on how fatally fast it would be to be seen gambling and decided it was pointless just now. There were two more years before Lizzie came out—if the money lasted that long. Time enough to instil some decorum.

'He is very good looking, is he not?' Lizzie observed. 'Is he an earl?'

'Lord Mortenhoe is an earl, yes. As for looks, I am sure he presents a most amiable and gentlemanlike appearance.' She was certainly not going to agree that the breadth of Lord Mortenhoe's shoulders, his classically moulded features or the flexible, deep voice were more than enough to flutter any lady's pulse. They had certainly fluttered hers, an unusual occurrence in a well-regulated existence. It was a surprisingly pleasant sensation. 'That,' Marina added firmly, more to herself than to her sister, 'is all a lady should be concerned with.'

'Poppycock,' Lizzie announced reprehensibly. 'I think

how a gentleman looks is very important. After all, fancy being married to someone with bad teeth like Mr Percival or to a man who looks like a codfish.'

Much struck by this, Marina swallowed a laugh and demanded, 'Whoever do we know who looks like a codfish?'

'Sir Willoughby Cavendish. Have you not noticed?'

Now it was pointed out, Marina could easily see the likeness. 'Certainly not. And what are you about, young lady, thinking of gentlemen at all, let alone about marrying one?'

'Well, I will have to, will I not?' Lizzie pointed out. 'A rich one, because of not having any dowry. So it would be nice if he was handsome too, I think.'

Kyte returned the now gleaming Hessians and assisted Justin into them with much play of gloved hands and soft polishing leather.

'I venture to say, my lord, that your man will be unable to detect the slightest defect. We must be thankful that the Animal did not paw at them.'

Justin had a strong suspicion that Shepton would be distinctly put out that another valet had so much as touched the boots, especially since the finish obtained was so fine, but he smiled and thanked the man. With a final pat at the tassels, Kyte bowed himself out.

His host did not immediately take advantage of their privacy, fidgeting around the room and pouring himself another brandy before finally returning to his seat.

'I suppose you find it strange that I should decide to sell Knightshaye after all this time,' he said abruptly.

'Considering that I have offered to purchase it on at least a dozen occasions since I came of age seven years ago, and first your father, and then you, has always refused to even discuss it, then, yes, you may say I am surprised.' Justin kept his tone even. He had no reason to distrust the young baron, no reason to suppose that, however rackety his reputation, he took after his father in any way. To project his loathing for the late Lord Winslow on to his son would be both unfair and counterproductive.

'My father always swore he would never sell to you, and he would never sell to anyone else either, in case you approached them. He told me I must do the same thing. Damned if I know why.'

'You do not?' Despite his control, the words sounded sceptical to Justin's own ears.

'And you do know? Something to do with a quarrel between our respective fathers, that is all I could ever gather.' Charlie shrugged. 'Ancient history now, and whatever it was, I can't afford to cut off my own nose just to prolong some pointless feud.'

'Then you definitely intend to sell?' Justin was conscious of a tightness in his chest and switched his gaze from the face opposite him to the scene outside. Feigning indifference was pointless, but pride forced him to at least an appearance of calm. Miss Elizabeth threw the ball for her brother and an ecstatic hound to race after while Miss Winslow stood gracefully, watching. She had a calm poise, which suggested not only that she was past her green years but that, despite her single state, she had acquired much of the style of a young married lady. He found his lips had curved into a smile; she seemed to have that effect on him.

'Fact is, I'm going to hell in a handcart,' his host announced abruptly, startling his attention back.

'I beg your pardon?'

'I drink too much, game too much and, unlike my revered Papa, I lose too much. I've tried reforming my way of life, and it don't last above a week or two, mostly.' Winslow shifted uneasily in the high-backed chair. 'But I'm not so far gone I can't see what effect it's going to have on the family if I don't do something about it. So I've spoken to the lawyers and what I'm going to do is sell Knightshaye to you, put the whole lot in a trust and that will look after Giles's education, Lizzie's dowry and set Mama up comfortably in the Dower House, which is where she'd rather be most of the time anyhow. I won't be able to touch a penny, even if I wanted to.'

'An admirable plan,' Justin said drily. 'I am honoured by your confidence.' Odd he had made no reference to Miss Winslow, but perhaps she would be expected to become her mother's companion. Or perhaps there was a respectable suitor in the background.

'You do still want it?' Lord Winslow looked anxious.

'Yes,' Justin admitted, suddenly wary. 'Considering it is my family home and I have been intending to retrieve it for twenty years, you may be confident that I still wish to buy it back from you.'

'Twenty years? But you must only have been, what, six, seven…?'

'Eight. I was eight when my father lost Knightshaye to your father in a card game and eight when he…died three months later.' And he had been ten when his mother died, apparently of no other cause than a broken heart.

'Why do you question whether I still want it?'

'Well, I, er… Have you been there recently?'

'No. I have never been back.' As the carriage had pulled away, his mother weeping, his father with a face set like stone, he had vowed never to set foot on Knightshaye land until it was his again. But he saw no reason to confide that to the son of the man who had taken it from the Ransomes. 'Why do you ask? Is something wrong there?'

'Shouldn't think so,' Charlie said with a somewhat suspicious carelessness. 'Never been there myself. The tenanted farmland's all in good enough heart—the rents are fine, so my steward tells me. The house is shut up. My father left instructions for its maintenance, so I just told our steward to get on with everything in the same way as before.'

So, the late Lord Winslow had taken Knightshaye entirely for revenge, not because he wanted it for itself. If spite had not been the reason, then surely the family would have used it: it was a far finer mansion that their own small estate. It was as Justin had always suspected, and he knew the reason why, even if apparently old Winslow's heir did not.

'Why not name your price?' Justin suggested, unclenching his left hand, which had fisted until the nails cut into the palm.

Charlie Winslow got to his feet and began to pace again, finally coming to rest by the window where he stood watching his brother and sisters. 'There's a price—and a condition,' he said finally.

Justin raised his eyebrows. He had been willing to buy back Knightshaye without negotiation and without insisting on examining the books. Winslow had him over a barrel as far as striking a bargain was concerned; it was not possible to conceal his interest, not after seven years of persistent requests to buy the place. 'What condition?'

'That you marry my sister.'

'What?' Justin found himself on his feet, staring at the baron.

'That you marry Marina,' Charlie said stubbornly. 'Or I won't sell. There won't be enough for a dowry for her as well as for Lizzie and she doesn't deserve to dwindle into a spinster aunt or my mother's unpaid companion. I'm dashed fond of my sister,' he added, 'and I am damned sure my reputation and the lack of the readies is what scuppered her chances on the Marriage Mart.'

'So you hit on this idea to provide for her,' Justin observed coldly. 'And what does Miss Winslow have to say to it, might I ask?'

'She knows nothing about it. And that's another thing, you must not tell her, not a word, or she will never agree.'

'You flatter me.'

Charlie flapped a hand, dismissing his own tactlessness. 'Don't mean you're not as eligible as they come—title, fortune and all that—and now that other matter with Miss Henslow has blown over, there's no reason why—' He broke off in the face of the hard glint in Justin's eyes. 'Well, no need to go into that, all a hum, I dare say, but you aren't involved with anyone now, are you? You're not engaged—if you ever were, that is…' He found himself in the mire again, took a deep breath and restarted. 'Thing is, Marina's dashed proud and she wouldn't like it if she thought I was fixing something up, do you see?'

'I think I do,' Justin said grimly, trampling firmly on thoughts of his former love's golden beauty and avaricious little heart. The two men sat down again, eyeing each other warily. It was as though they were sitting over the opening hand of a game of cards, sizing up the odds, deciding their wagers. 'And what is the price—beside your sister's hand, that is?'

Lord Winslow named a sum that was at the top end of Justin's expectations and sat there, looking hopeful.

'I will pay that and add another two thousand—but I will not marry your sister.'

'Thought you might say that,' Charlie said equably. 'But it's the money and Marina, or nothing. If you won't buy on my terms, I'll sell to someone else and I will get the lawyers to put a clause in the deeds so it can never be sold to you or your heirs.'

Justin felt the anger surge up hot and powerful and was surprised to find himself still sitting down, hands calmly clasped. His self-control must be better than he thought.

'So, like your father, you have a talent for blackmail,' he observed evenly.

'Damn it—' the younger man looked hurt, but not insulted '—I'm doing it for my sister.' He frowned. 'What do you mean about my father?'

'That there was no reason why my father, had he wished to gamble with yours, could not have met any money stake, however high. He wagered Knightshaye because he was blackmailed into it.'

'Why?' Charlie demanded bluntly. 'He was a hard devil, my father, I'm not denying that, but blackmail? What did he know about your father that could force him to that risk?'

'He had nothing on Father, but it was a matter that concerned two other people, one dead now, one still alive. It is not something I can speak of. You will just have to take my word for it.'

The younger man grimaced. 'Very well. But you can call it what you like, you won't insult me—take Marina or the deal is off.'

'And if your sister does not wish to marry me?' Even as he spoke, Justin knew he was giving way simply by letting himself consider the proposition. There was something about Charlie Winslow's demeanour that warned him the younger man was absolutely determined on this plan. He might be weak, but that very weakness made him stubborn when he was driven into a corner. If Justin wanted Knightshaye, he was going to have to dance to Winslow's tune.

'If you give me your word of honour you will do your best to attach her interest and she still won't take you, then we'll call it quits. Damn it, I can't blame you if she turns down a chance like that. But I want your pledge you'll give it your best effort for two months—and that you won't ever breathe a word of this arrangement to her.'

Justin got to his feet and walked to the window. The Winslow family were making their way back to the house: young Giles was more or less in control of a muddy, panting Hector; Miss Elizabeth was talking vehemently and using her hands to describe what appeared to be an elaborate hat. And Miss Winslow—Marina—was listening attentively. As they reached the steps she glanced up at the window, saw him— and smiled.

It was a flash of friendly goodwill in a face distinguished more by pleasant symmetry and colouring than beauty. And it conjured up a vivid opposite in his mind. Golden hair, blue eyes, a perfect little nose and red lips always trembling on the edge of a calculated pout.

He turned back, holding out his hand. 'Very well. I agree to your price and your condition. You have my word on it.'

Chapter Two

❦

'Take Hector down to the scullery and do not dare to bring him back up until he is completely clean and dry,' Marina ordered firmly, as Giles with his hound bundled through the front door behind his sisters.

'Charlie should engage another tutor for Giles,' Lizzie said crossly, twisting to examine the hem of her walking dress, which had been trodden on by large paws.

'It seems such an extravagance when I can teach him; besides, recall how distracted he made poor Mr Livingstone. When he is older, of course, and needs to begin classics—'

She broke off as the study door opened and Lord Mortenhoe emerged, her brother on his heels.

'Miss Winslow, Miss Elizabeth. How was your walk?'

'Very pleasant, thank you, my lord.' What was Charlie about? He appeared to have positively propelled his guest into the hallway and now was making no effort to either call Bunting or show him out himself. Lord Mortenhoe was regarding her and she felt her colour rising; no doubt she was unbecomingly windswept from the excursion. 'If you will excuse me…'

'I've invited Mortenhoe to dinner tomorrow night,' Charlie said abruptly.

'Oh! I mean…how delightful.' Charlie must be out of his mind! Aunt and Uncle Thredgold and Cousin Hugh were no sort of company to entertain an earl. Leaving aside Uncle Thredgold's tendency to talk of nothing but his experiments in cattle breeding, Aunt's deafness and Hugh's almost perpetual fit of the sullens, the table would be unbalanced with too many men, and the menu, unless some drastic alterations were made, would be decidedly uninspiring, having been chosen with the Thredgolds' bland preferences in mind.

'I am sure it will be.' The earl was accepting his gloves and hat from Bunting. 'Until tomorrow evening, Miss Winslow.'

Charlie escaped back into his study before the front door had closed on Lord Mortenhoe, leaving his sisters regarding each other speculatively in the hall.

'It is too bad of Charlie,' Marina declared, pulling off her gloves. 'Now who can we possibly ask at this late notice? For, fond as we are of the Thredgolds, I really do not think Lord Mortenhoe will be much entertained by them.'

'They are dead bores,' Lizzie retorted. 'Thank goodness they have taken rooms and are not staying with us as they did last year.'

'They are *family*,' Marina said repressively, leading the way into the drawing room before Lizzie made any more unfortunate remarks in front of the servants. 'It behoves us to be hospitable, and besides, it gives Mama much pleasure to be with Aunt.' She cast off her bonnet and sat on the sofa, not troubling to remove her pelisse. 'Now, who would not be offended by a late invitation? We need another lady and another couple at the very least to leaven the mix.'

'I could come,' Lizzie offered hopefully, then subsided at

a look from her sister. 'How about Mr and Mrs Philpott? They never stand on ceremony.'

Certainly their next-door neighbours were a sensible suggestion and, as they had just that morning returned from a visit to an ailing parent, such short notice could be explained away. 'And I will ask Priscilla Hinton,' Marina said with a flash of inspiration. 'Her husband is out of town and we are good enough friends for me to explain the situation.'

'Mrs Hinton is very pretty.'

'Well, yes. What of it?'

'You do not want Lord Mortenhoe to flirt with her, and he is sure to.'

'I am sure the earl will do no such thing, and, even if he should, Priscilla is more than capable of dealing with it,' Marina retorted, flustered. 'Now, I must go and speak with Cook about the menu. I do wish Charlie would think things through sometimes.'

'He is very good looking.' Lizzie, the picture of innocence, was twirling the strings of her bonnet.

'Charlie?'

'No, silly, Lord Mortenhoe. I think he looks nice.'

'And I think he looked angry,' Marina said thoughtfully, recalling the flash of green in his eyes as they parted in the hall and the controlled tension in his long frame. 'I do hope Charlie is not up to something.'

Marina gazed distractedly around the drawing room and prayed she would never have to live through another evening that threatened so much social embarrassment.

Mrs Hinton, the sprightly wife of a diplomat and an old friend of Marina's, was giving an excellent impression of fascination with Uncle Thredgold's lecture on the finer points of Devon Red cattle, Mrs Philpott was doing her best to communicate with Mrs Thredgold, who stubbornly refused to use her ear trumpet in company, and Lady Winslow was discussing the benefits of the Harrogate waters with Mr Philpott while anxiously watching her nephew Hugh.

With a sinking heart Marina saw the young man had abandoned his usual sullen slouch, adopting instead a brooding silence that he doubtless believed to be Byronic. From under thick brows he stared moodily at Mrs Hinton, who fortunately appeared unaware of his attention.

Charlie meanwhile was quite impervious to any awkwardness or lack of social sparkle. 'What is Cook intending for dinner?' he enquired with a glance at the mantel clock. 'I'm devilish hungry.'

'A loin of pork, lobster with a white wine sauce, Milanese escalopes, a timbale—' Marina broke off the recital of the dishes she had persuaded Cook were the bare minimum to lay before an earl and regarded her brother with a frown. 'Why are you looking at me like that, Charlie?'

'Just thinking you look dashed pretty this evening. Why have you got that cap thing on, though?'

'Because I am a twenty-six-year-old spinster and it is appropriate evening wear.'

'Wish you'd take it off.'

'Certainly not! Really, Charlie, since when have you taken the slightest interest in what I wear?'

'Um…' He looked uncomfortable. 'Ah, there's the knocker, must be Mortenhoe.'

Oh, good! What dreadful *timing,* Marina thought, flinching as Aunt Thredgold raised her voice in the apparent belief that Mrs Philpott was as deaf as she. '…disgusting behaviour! I said to the Vicar…'

'Need sturdy hocks if they're to be the slightest use at stud…' That was Uncle Thredgold, well away now.

'…unfortunate smell of rotten eggs, of course,' Mr Philpott remarked just as Lord Mortenhoe entered the room.

Marina fixed a smile of welcome on her lips and wondered if it were possible that his lordship had missed any of this sophisticated conversation. His eyes met hers and he bowed gravely. There was just the hint of a twitch at the corner of his mouth as he straightened up and turned to his host. No, of course not, he had heard every word. At least he showed no sign of considering himself above his company; her apprehension ebbed a little.

'Lord Mortenhoe.' Mama sounded her usual placid self as she shook hands, blissfully impervious to the fact that one of the leading lights of society was facing an evening of the deepest boredom at her table. 'May I introduce you to my sister Mrs Thredgold, her husband…'

She moved around the room, making the presentations, finishing with her daughter. Justin smiled. 'But I already have the pleasure of Miss Winslow's acquaintance. How are Master Giles and his hound?'

Lady Winslow drifted away, apparently content that her guest of honour's entertainment was in safe hands. 'In what can only be described as rude health, my lord, although Hector is in disgrace and has been confined to the stables for treeing Mrs Philpott's cat in the Square and then growling at the gardener when he tried to rescue it.'

'Deplorable,' Lord Mortenhoe agreed. He was regarding her in a way that made her feel as though they were alone in the room—a most disconcerting sensation. Marina decided she had been living rather too quiet a life recently if the arrival of one *ton*nish gentleman for dinner was enough to put her out of countenance. It was a seductively pleasant experience, though, to be looked at in quite that manner.

'Mrs Philpott has been very forgiving about it, although

the gardener had to be placated with a gratuity. Do you still keep a pet dog, Mrs Hinton?' She turned slightly to include her friend in the conversation and Hugh, who had been edging closer with his habitual gaucheness, lounged away again.

'No, not since little Tottie died just after Christmas.' Mrs Hinton, a slender honey blonde, looked up through her lashes at Lord Mortenhoe. 'Doubtless you find me foolishly senti-mental, my lord, but I could not bear to replace her.'

'Not at all,' he said sympathetically. 'I lost my favourite hound last year and it was months before I could consider looking for a new pup. What do you think, Winslow? Are we both too sentimental?'

Once drawn into the discussion, Charlie was soon agreeing that the loss of a favourite pet was a dashed miserable business. Marina could not quite work out how it happened, but suddenly she was talking to Lord Mortenhoe again and Charlie was bearing Mrs Hinton away to see his aunt, who just happened to have a litter of pug puppies to dispose of.

It was too bad of Charlie, removing the most personable of their guests from Lord Mortenhoe's vicinity! She now had to find him someone else congenial to talk to; she had been counting on her friend's vivacious conversation and sophis-ticated charm to distract him from the Thredgolds' oddities. What might he have in common with the Philpotts?

'Have you ever taken the waters at Harrogate, my lord?' She steered him gently in the direction of their neighbours. 'Mr and Mrs Philpott have just returned from there.'

'No, I never have. Did you find it a pleasant experience, Mrs Philpott?' There, now, that was better. Mrs Philpott was a conversable, well-bred woman with an easy style. She and Lord Mortenhoe were soon engaged in a discussion of the waters and whether the accommodations in the spa town might suit an aged aunt of his lordship who suffered greatly from gout and who was bored with Bath and Cheltenham. Mr Philpott joined in with a recommendation for a local livery company and Marina was just thinking she could safely slip away and have a second look at the place settings when her mother appeared, her sister at her side.

'Araminta dear, Mr and Mrs Philpott are just explaining the benefits of the Harrogate waters to his lordship. I am sure you would find them most energising. What do you think, Mrs Philpott?'

Once again Marina found herself on the outside of the group with Lord Mortenhoe at her side. 'I am sorry,' she murmured as they moved away slightly. 'My aunt's deafness makes her a little unaware of the fact other people are engaged in conversation. I do hope you had heard enough to be able to advise your relative.'

'Quite enough, I thank you.' He regarded her with mock-seriousness as she glanced across the room to her uncle. 'Would you think me very rude if I did not engage your uncle in conversation on the subject of cattle breeding? I must confess to being terrified of the beasts and he is sure to despise me.'

That surprised a gurgle of amusement from her. The earl was proving to have a quiet sense of humour, which threatened to overturn her poise. 'My lord! I really cannot believe such a thing, although I have to confess that my uncle is somewhat single-minded in his enthusiasm.'

'And what are your enthusiasms, Miss Winslow?' He stopped, leaning one hand negligently on a sideboard, and effectively foiling her efforts to guide him across the room. This was mystifying. Much as she might enjoy his undivided attention, surely the last thing he wanted was the company of the old maid of the family?

'Mine? Why, I hardly know how to answer you, my lord—' She broke off, perplexed at the question. 'I have many interests, of course; Mama allows me to run the household and I oversee Giles's education. Then there is Lizzie to accompany about town, and my sewing. And my friends, of course, although they are all married now and have young families.'

'But no enthusiasms?' he persisted.

'Ladies do not on the whole have enthusiasms, my lord! Oh, perhaps for good causes, although to really throw oneself into that I always feel one needs to be older and better endowed with wealth than I am. Or perhaps I am just using that as an excuse.' She smiled ruefully. '*Gentlemen* may have enthusiasms—for politics or sport, for example.'

Lord Mortenhoe's eyes were on her face and something in them, some gentleness, made her feel suddenly sorry for herself, which was ridiculous. For someone who had singularly failed to oblige her family by attracting even one eligible offer in the course of three expensive Seasons she was most fortunate in her lot.

'What are your enthusiasms, Hugh?' she asked her cousin, aware that he had once more strayed into their orbit, and grateful for the distraction. Another moment and she was going to succumb to the sympathy in those hazel eyes and start explaining just how fortunate she was.

The youth shrugged with his habitual lack of grace. 'Haven't any.'

'Not sport?' his lordship enquired. 'Horses, perhaps?'

A trace of animation crossed the sullen features. 'No point, but, if I could, racehorses—'

'Surely not gambling, Hugh?' As soon as she had spoken Marina could have bitten her tongue, for the shuttered expression descended again.

'Or bloodlines and breeding?' Lord Mortenhoe suggested.

'Oh, yes, breeding. To be able to produce such beauty and strength is above everything. I read all the stud books, follow form—but Papa will not hear of it. Says I know nothing about it and I would do better to study his work with cattle. Cattle!'

'If he has built up a flourishing line, I can understand he might be disappointed if you do not intend to maintain it,' Mortenhoe said thoughtfully. 'But horse breeding could run alongside cattle breeding, do you not think?'

Stunned by being asked his opinion, Hugh merely gaped. 'Er…yes.'

'Would you like to visit my stud at Newmarket? I will ask your father after dinner. If you would be interested, that is.'

'Oh, yes! Thank you, my lord. Your stud! I'll speak to him now, try to persuade him.'

'That was kind of you. I do not think I have ever heard Hugh utter so many words at one time before.' Marina watched her cousin talking animatedly to his surprised parent.

'He is lonely, I think. Possibly he has no one to share his interest. And here he is rather out of his depth. You are the only young person present and you have to talk to the visitors, not to family.'

'Now you are being ridiculous, my lord,' Marina chided. 'Hugh is seventeen, I am…considerably older.'

'Of course, I should have realised you were on the shady side of thirty.'

'Certainly not—!' She broke off, choking back a laugh at her own instinctive indignation. 'You are teasing me, my lord.'

'Only a little—after all, you have just done your best to convince me you live the life of a sober spinster.'

'I do not!' Natural honesty caught up with her tongue and she added, 'Well, perhaps, but that, after all, is what I am.'

'And do sober spinsters go driving with gentlemen?'

Was that an invitation? Surely not. 'I see no reason why not, my lord, should they be asked.'

'Good. We will discuss the where and when of that later. If I am not mistaken your uncle is coming over.'

He does *intend to invite me to drive with him! But why?* Flustered, Marina managed to smile at her uncle, who had Hugh in tow.

'My son tells me you have invited him to visit your stud, my lord.' Mr Thredgold was, as usual, abrupt.

'Yes, sir, unless you should dislike it. He seems to have inherited your interest in animal breeding, doubtless as a result of observing your renowned expertise at close hand.'

A faintly smug expression came over Mr Thredgold's face at the compliment. 'Horses, though—how is that going to contribute to the Thredgold herd?'

'Diversification, sir.' Marina watched with something approaching awe as Lord Mortenhoe played on the older man's obsession. 'Think, in twenty years' time they will speak of the Thredgold herd and stud with equal admiration—and of you as its founding genius.'

Now that was both kind and clever, Marina decided, seeing how struck her uncle was by this thought. She turned her own approving gaze on his lordship, wondering why he should trouble with an unknown youth. She found he was watching her and experienced a sudden fancy that perhaps he had done it to please her. But why should he? It must be because he was bored by this party and seeking diversion.

'Dinner is served, my lady.' As Bunting held the door Lady Winslow appeared at Lord Mortenhoe's side. Charlie was already offering his arm to Mrs Hinton and the other guests sorted themselves out, leaving Marina to bring up the rear with Cousin Hugh.

She had arranged the place cards earlier, positioning

herself between Mr Philpott and Hugh, but as she neared the table she realised that the two remaining places were between Lord Mortenhoe and Mrs Philpott.

'Bunting, the place cards have become muddled,' she hissed.

'No, Miss Marina, Lord Winslow moved them earlier,' the butler assured her.

It was too late to make a change now. Putting a good face on it, she took her place, trusting that Mrs Philpott would not feel slighted by being next to young Hugh. At least their neighbour was happily occupied in conversation with Charlie at the head of the table. She began to talk to Hugh about his plans for the summer, leaving Lord Mortenhoe to her mother. It would no doubt be a relief to him: the poor man must be thoroughly tired of her company by now.

Far from experiencing any *ennui,* Justin was pleased with how the evening was going. Lady Winslow and her son had managed to throw him together with Marina with considerable aplomb and she appeared quite ignorant of any ulterior motive to his presence. Her clear, unselfconscious gaze was a pleasure to meet, even while he experienced an uneasy pang of conscience about deceiving her. How he was going to propose marriage without breaking his agreement with Winslow and yet at the same time salve his own conscience was a puzzle.

Lady Winslow was pleasant, vague and, he suspected, a lady of little energy. Certainly she appeared to rely heavily on her elder daughter and he soon realised that it was to Marina that Bunting looked for direction during the service of dinner. Another count in her favour if she was as competent a housekeeper as she appeared. Knightshaye would be a far bigger household than this, of course, but he did not think she would be daunted by it.

It would be neglected now, he knew that, mentally bracing himself for finding the immaculate, warm home of his memory dusty and unloved. Winslow had said something about continuing his father's arrangements for its upkeep, but that was not the same as it being lived in by a family. What would his mother have felt if she knew she would be succeeded by the daughter of the very man who had ruined their lives and left her a widow?

He hoped that he would have had her blessing in recovering Knightshaye, even in such a manner, but he had to force a lightness into his voice as he replied to a question from that man's wife. And yet, although he doubted she knew it, Lady Winslow was another victim of her husband's arrogance and cold-blooded selfishness.

She was certainly in her son's confidence over his scheme for Marina. Her expression as it rested on Justin was benevolent and satisfied. *As well it might be*, he thought with a flash of resentment. Without arrogance he knew quite well he was a considerable matrimonial prize for the daughter of a baron; there had been enough encounters with match-making mamas to convince him of his worth.

But not such a big a prize as all that, he reminded himself grimly as he passed a dish of minted peas to his hostess. Not such a prize as would hold a woman once she had seen she could land an even more prestigious catch. It was as well for his pride that no engagement had been announced, although, from what Winslow had said, it seemed rumours had got around about his relationship with Serena Henslow, now the Marchioness of Andover.

'And have you any family in town?' Lady Winslow was asking, making a good show of not knowing his family history inside out.

'No, ma'am, none in town and few at all except for some distant cousins in Scotland and a great-uncle in Cornwall.'

'How sad,' she said sympathetically. 'All the more reason for settling down soon and starting your nursery.' Her vague smile settled on her daughter and lingered just as Marina turned her head to look at them.

Chapter Three

What are they staring at me for? Marina glanced down, convinced that her bodice must be gaping or that she had spilled butter sauce on the silk. A rapid glance assured her that everything was as it should be. But now Mama was regarding her with a fond smile and Lord Mortenhoe was positively…no, not blushing, he was far too assured for that. But his colour was certainly up and that spark of controlled anger was back in his eyes.

There was a stir as the footmen brought in the next course and Marina turned her attention to what they were doing. By the time she had nodded approval to Bunting and turned back again, her mother was conversing with Mr Philpott, and Lord Mortenhoe was patiently waiting to offer her a dish of asparagus.

'Thank you.' She took some spears, then, without allowing herself to consider too carefully what she was saying, asked, 'Did something in the conversation just now anger you, my lord?'

'Did I appear angry? I beg your pardon, Miss Winslow.' His eyes were a calm hazel now and the flash of green was gone.

'No, not angry,' she corrected herself, struggling to find the right words. 'You had your…dangerous look. Your eyes turn green then—did you know?'

One dark brow rose slowly and Marina felt colour staining her cheeks. 'Forgive me, my lord, that was an impertinent observation.'

'Not at all, merely perceptive. I apologise if I appeared *dangerous*. Lady Winslow had made a perfectly innocent remark that happened to touch a nerve, that was all. My momentary irritation was with myself for my own weakness.'

'What…?' Marina shut her mouth with a snap. She had been within a whisker of asking what the sensitive subject was. *Whatever has come over me?* she thought frantically. It was this man, that was the trouble. She looked at him and felt an immediate affiliation, a sense that she could tell him anything, ask anything, rely on him.

'What did she say? That was what you were about to ask me, was it not?' He ignored Marina's flustered murmur of denial. 'Lady Winslow referred to the fact that I am unmarried and implied that perhaps I should be seeking to remedy that.'

'Ah.' He did not seem annoyed now, but she could quite understand that he might well be. How on earth to turn the subject?

'She is quite right, of course,' he said calmly, slicing through an asparagus spear.

'Oh.' Marina gave herself a little shake; she really could not sit here uttering monosyllables like a dummy. If his lordship wished to confide in her, then so be it. 'Perhaps there is a lady with whom you have an understanding?'

She watched his profile and saw the black lashes sweep down, momentarily hiding the betraying eyes. When he looked at her, the hazel gaze was clear and friendly. 'I believe I am far from understanding women, let alone reaching an understanding with one.'

He had turned her question very neatly and she experienced a sense of relief that she could step on to safer ground. 'We are not so difficult to fathom, my lord.'

'You smile, Miss Winslow, you are obviously mocking me.'

It was he who was mocking her, she was certain. 'No, I would not dream of it. Everyone is different, of course, but I think that all women would want to feel wanted, needed, to have a loving family and to know that they are useful in whatever way they can be.'

'That is very laudable, ma'am, but I cannot help but feel we are back to ladies not admitting to enthusiasms! What about rank and status, riches and luxury? Do ladies not covet those?'

Marina felt that she should piously point out that covetousness was a sin, but the crinkle of humour at the corner of his eyes made the unspoken thought seem prissy. 'To have enough money to indulge in little luxuries is very pleasant, of course.'

'And rank and status?'

'Those would bring great responsibility,' she said thoughtfully, 'but I can see that they might have a certain allure.' He smiled and she laughed back at him. 'But you are teasing me again, my lord; I can tell.'

'Why should I do that?' Justin's voice dropped, became warmer. 'You speak as though you are immune to such temptations and I see no reason why you should be.' She opened her mouth to protest, but he carried on remorselessly. 'You are about to remind me of your advanced age and that is, if you will forgive me saying so, a nonsense. Now, Miss Winslow, may I tempt you?'

'T…tempt me?' *What with, for goodness' sake?*

'These almond fritters look almost irresistible to me.'

'They are,' Marina agreed, seizing the opening with gratitude. 'They are quite the best of Cook's specialities and I defy anyone to refuse another once they have sampled one.'

The meal proceeded harmlessly, much to Marina's relief, with conversation about the difficulty of finding a really reliable cook, the latest balloon ascension and if the weather could be expected to continue so fine.

Eventually Lady Winslow rose, gathered the attention of the other ladies with a glance and made her way out of the dining room. Marina followed meekly at the back, unsure whether she was glad or sorry the meal was over.

Conversation in the drawing room was animated, for it seemed that Mrs Thredgold had heard the most fascinating intelligence about the Brighton Pavilion, now supposedly reaching completion after years of building work, and was anxious to share it with the other ladies. As she was too deaf to hear their replies and raised her own voice almost to a shout, a number of cross-conversations were soon in process, allowing Marina to muse on her conversation with Lord Mortenhoe in peace.

If she had not known better, she would have thought he had been flirting with her. *Perhaps he was*, she thought, a little frown line appearing between her brows. Men did not flirt with Marina any more, a circumstance she accepted without rancour. Men flirted with young, pretty girls and even when she had first come out she had known herself not to be pretty. And they expected girls to giggle and flirt back, to make sheep's eyes over the edge of their fans and gaze at them as though they were wonderful.

Marina had rapidly discovered that she was really very bad at flirtation and that nothing would persuade her to gaze with wide-eyed admiration at some callow youth simply because he was male, had a title and a respectable degree of wealth—she felt rather an instinct to laugh at them. She also discovered that sensible, poorly dowered young ladies with a

satirical twinkle in their eye eventually found themselves
seated firmly on the shelf.

'May I sit here, Miss Winslow?' The men had entered the
room without her noticing.

'Yes, of course, my lord.' *Please go and talk to Mrs Hinton,
my lord. Mrs Hinton is pretty and amusing and will flirt very
elegantly with you.*

But Lord Mortenhoe appeared oblivious to the fact that her
friend had left a carefully judged space on the sofa next to her
and sat down beside Marina, settling back and regarding the
drawing room with every appearance of approbation.

'This is a very charming room, if I may say so.'

'Why, thank you, my lord.' Marina could not help but feel
flattered. The room had cost her much work and careful budgeting, but she did feel that it had turned out well and showed
no sign of having been created on a shoestring.

'And may I presume to deduce from that modest look that
you are the creative hand behind it? I suspect that Lady
Winslow relies very much upon you.'

'Mama does let me run things more or less as I will, my
lord. I find it interesting to manage the household.'

'Then perhaps I might ask you for some advice—can you
recommend a good agency for domestic staff? I will be
engaging a complete household for a rural estate shortly and
it is not something with which I have much experience.'

'My goodness! A complete household? I would have to
think about that, for there are several agencies that I could recommend and I think that it would be prudent to approach more
than one. You have acquired a new shooting lodge, I imagine?'

Now, what have I said to amuse him? Lord Mortenhoe's
lips quirked in a wry smile. He really did have the most expressive mouth. *I wonder what it would be like to be kissed...*

'No, not a shooting lodge, a mansion of, if I recall correctly, twenty bedrooms.'

'My goodness, that *is* large.' Marina wrenched her eyes and her unruly imagination away from Lord Mortenhoe's mouth. 'Then you will most definitely need more than one agency. There are no staff there at present?'

'I am not sure, I must ask your brother, but I imagine only a skeleton staff, and he will doubtless wish to retain them and move them to one of his other establishments.'

'My brother? You mean *Charlie* is selling you a house?' Marina's brow furrowed, then cleared. 'Then he must be selling Knightshaye. I had no idea it was not entailed like everything else.'

'It used to be in my family. Your father acquired it, I am retrieving it.' Marina shivered. Lord Mortenhoe's voice was pleasant and unemotional, yet she felt a sudden *frisson* of danger as though a blade had been drawn hissing from its sheath.

'That is good for all of us, I am sure,' she commented, more for something to say than anything else.

'Indeed? Do you dislike it so?'

'I have never been there—in fact, I do not believe Charlie has either. No, I meant it is good that you have been able to get it back and that Charlie has realised money on it.' His profile looked somewhat forbidding, so, in an effort at lightness, she added, 'I shall have to tease a new pair of dining-room curtains out of my brother on the strength of the sale.'

'I should imagine you could tease rather more than that out of him should you try, Miss Winslow. Your brother strikes a hard bargain. But the deal has not yet been concluded.'

Was that resentment in his voice? No, not that, more a wry admiration. Perhaps that was why she had sensed so much tension on his first visit—Charlie had set too high a price and

they were still negotiating. But the thought of what realising
the value of a large mansion would do for the shaky family
fortunes was thrilling—just so long as Charlie did not
promptly gamble it away. *Why on earth have Charlie and
Mama not mentioned it?*

'Have you ever been there?'

'It was my home until three weeks after my eighth birth-
day.'

'Then it must have a most sentimental attachment for you,'
she said warmly. 'I am so glad you are regaining it. Is it as
you remember it? I always find that going back to places I
knew as a child is most disconcerting—they either seem
bigger or much smaller than I recall.'

'I have never been back.' He seemed to hesitate, then
added, 'I swore as we drove away that I would never return
until I owned it again.'

'What a very determined little boy you must have been.'
She smiled at the thought of the childish resolution.

Justin turned to look at her and she almost drew back at
the look in his eyes. There was the ghost of pain there,
overlaid by an iron-hard will. 'And now I am a very determined man,' he remarked evenly. Then, with a smile that
transformed his face, 'But I do not want to bore you with
business, Miss Winslow. Might I hope to find you at home
tomorrow afternoon if I called to take you driving in the
park?'

'So soon?' His eyebrows rose in sharp interrogation and
Marina had the fleeting thought that she had said something
to surprise him. 'I mean, I may not have assembled all the
details of the agencies you will need by then.'

'But that is not why I invited you to drive with me.' His smile
was producing the most extraordinary sensations, as though
her skin was suddenly too hot, or someone had drawn a piece

of velvet across it. Once again she had the illusion that they were alone in the room. *I really must stop looking at his mouth.*

'It is not?' *Can he be flirting with me?* Surely not, not with Priscilla Hinton, lovely, sophisticated and very willing to engage in such an activity, only an arm's reach away. No, he was simply being kind to the sister of the man with whom he was doing business.

'No. I only had the desire to drive in pleasant company. Has anyone ever told you that you are a most soothing companion, Miss Winslow?'

'Soothing? Why, no.' And why, even if she did possess this quality, would a fashionable gentleman wish to seek it out? Marina was mystified. 'I think you are teasing me again, my lord.' Soothing, now she came to think about it, sounded somewhat staid.

'I have said the wrong thing; perhaps a young lady does not wish to hear she is soothing. Possibly I should have said lovely, charming…'

A gurgling laugh escaped Marina's lips. 'Now I *know* you are talking fustian! Here is the tea tray. Please excuse me, Lord Mortenhoe, Mama will wish me to pour.'

'Might I assist you?' He was on his feet before she could answer.

'Oh…thank you.' Marina poured tea and handed him two cups. 'For you and for Mrs Hinton. Do you take milk or lemon?'

'Lemon, thank you.' In the face of two tea cups almost thrust into his hands Lord Mortenhoe carried them across to Priscilla Hinton and, as Marina hoped, was invited with a pretty smile to sit beside her.

Marina dispensed the rest of the tea and came to rest next to Mr Philpott, with whom it was possible to carry on the most comfortable conversation without the slightest discomfiture. Mr Philpott, a serious but kindly man, neither flirted nor teased but spoke in measured tones on dull and unexceptional subjects of interest that allowed one to survey the room and ensure that the company was all provided with refreshment and suitably entertained.

Mama, to Marina's surprise, was regarding her with a less than approving expression. When she had her daughter's attention, she swivelled her eyes to focus on Mrs Hinton's sofa and produced a frown.

Marina responded with the slightest of shrugs. She was more than happy to see their two most distinguished guests amusing themselves, although, now she was watching them, it did seem rather fast of Priscilla to be popping a morsel of her almond cake between Lord Mortenhoe's lips. There was nothing he could be expected to do about that, of course, other than accept it with good grace.

He seemed to sense her gaze upon him and turned his head to meet her eyes, holding them with his own as he slowly licked a crumb of cake from his lower lip. Marina felt herself drawn in as though she had risen to her feet and taken a step towards him. Her skin was hot again with that strange velvety sensation and she broke eye contact with a shiver of alarm.

She sipped her tea, marvelling at her own lack of propriety in reacting so. *But no one has ever flirted with me before, not like this. I do not know what to do.*

No, that was not strictly true. Gauche young men had attempted to flirt with her when she was equally gauche and just out, but, with neither liking nor aptitude for it, she soon found herself eclipsed by more confident, assured and beautiful young ladies such as her friend Priscilla Wilde, now Mrs Hinton. The trouble was, she realised, that either she had not liked the young gentlemen enough to suspend her natural reticence or she found the posturing and play-acting funny, but could find no one with whom safely to share the joke.

But Lord Mortenhoe did seem to be a man who would know immediately what the joke was, and was also someone who could make flirtation rather stimulating. Probably it was the fact that he was older than those callow youths and simply more experienced.

Just how experienced? Marina wondered, watching him over the rim of her tea cup while listening with every appearance of attention to Mr Philpott speaking about the health of the King. Had Charlie introduced her to a rake? The thought made her smile; in the safety of her own home a rake seemed more interesting than alarming. The gentleman in question looked up as she did so and answered the smile with one of his own, a fleeting look of warmth and communication.

Bunting entered, a footman with fresh hot water on his heels. Goodness! Was that the time? It only seemed moments since she had poured the first cups. Marina glanced round hastily, half-expecting to see her guests looking reproachfully into empty teacups. But no one appeared to have noticed her abstraction. With a murmured excuse to Mr Philpott she rose and refreshed the teapot, then began to circulate around the room, checking to see who would like another cup.

This time, much to her surprise, her cousin got to his feet and helped ferry the drinks to and from the tea table. 'Why, thank you, Hugh.' Marina tried not to sound too surprised at his thoughtfulness.

'Thank *you*, Cousin Marina,' he responded as they stood together at the table. 'Papa has been thinking about what Lord Mortenhoe said, and says that he wonders he never thought of horse breeding himself. And he says he will send me to Ireland, to a friend of his with a stud out there so I can buy my first horses with his guidance.' Hugh's normally sullen countenance was transformed by a broad grin he appeared quite unable to control and Marina's heart warmed to him. 'My own horses—think of it!'

'Do not thank me—it is all due to Lord Mortenhoe's suggestion. Why do you not tell him yourself? Here, take the cups for him and Mrs Hinton.' The youth hastened over to the seated couple, his grin replaced with a frown of concentration as he attempted not to spill the tea. As he approached, Priscilla Hinton got to her feet, waving Lord Mortenhoe back into his seat and, taking her cup from Hugh, strolled over to join Marina.

'My dear! I had no idea, you sly thing.'

'What do you mean?' Marina checked that the other guests were comfortable and steered Priscilla to a distant corner. 'Don't be provoking, Pris.' Despite being as dissimilar in most things as they could be, the two young women had been fast friends for years, ever since they had shared a piano teacher and dancing lessons.

Priscilla was an elegant blonde with fine blue eyes, an open and spontaneous manner and a love of frivolity, luxury and fun. Marina could never get her to take anything seriously other than the acquisition of a rich husband, a duty Pris took with the utmost earnestness as being the passport to all the things she enjoyed most.

By great good luck she found a man who was not only rich but who adored her and whose chosen profession of diplomacy gave his young wife the perfect showcase for her charm, looks and love of entertaining.

Now she turned her aquamarine gaze on Marina and said reproachfully, 'It is you who is being provoking, Mar! Here I am, your oldest friend, and you keep the most incredible news from me.'

'What news? I cannot think of a thing that has happened

since we went shopping last week that you would be remotely interested in.'

'Lord Mortenhoe, of course! You attach an eligible suitor and do not breathe a word. Honestly, Mar, I feel positively hurt.'

'Suitor?' Marina regarded her friend with alarm. 'He is no such thing, Pris, we only met yesterday. He is doing business with Charlie, buying some property.' She took a deep breath— it was suddenly very important to disabuse Priscilla of this ridiculous misunderstanding. 'I assure you, Lord Mortenhoe has no more interest in me than I have in him. In fact—'

She broke off at a sharp jab in the ribs from Mrs Hinton. 'He is coming over.'

His lordship was indeed coming towards them. Marina found herself looking at him through her friend's eyes: a powerful, assured, very masculine gentleman with looks that turned foolish female heads. And it seemed she was no more rational than the rest of them, for her heart was beating very strangely and she could feel the colour rising in her cheeks.

'Ladies.' He came to a halt just in front of them. 'I must bid you goodnight. Mrs Hinton, it was a pleasure to meet you. Miss Winslow, I hope two o'clock will be a convenient time for me to call for our drive?'

'Yes, perfectly convenient, my lord.' It came out sounding squeaky, but at least it was a coherent sentence.

'Then, until two tomorrow. Thank you for a delightful dinner party.' He bowed slightly, turned and strolled over to take his farewell of Lady Winslow, his elegant figure tracked across the room by two pairs of eyes, one blue, the other grey.

'Well?' Priscilla demanded. 'What did I say? And you still maintain he has no interest in you?'

Chapter Four

'Yes,' Marina said firmly. 'He is merely being courteous because he and Charlie are negotiating some business and he will doubtless be in and out of the house for a while. That is all.'

'Mar, there are times I utterly despair of you!' Priscilla looked set to continue, but the clock struck the hour and she jumped to her feet with an exclamation of annoyance. 'Look at the time—and I promised darling Henry I would be home before he got back tonight, poor hard-working lamb that he is.' She looked down at Marina, biting her lip. 'There is nothing for it, you need taking in hand, this is an emergency. I will cancel all my appointments and will be with you by ten tomorrow morning. Now, whatever you do, get a good night's sleep, dearest.'

She bent, kissed Marina's cheek and began to walk away, turning after a few steps to stare at her friend's hair. 'I wonder if I can get Monsieur Lamerre at such short notice?' It appeared to be a rhetorical question, for she hastened off to her hostess and in a few moments was gone, along with the Philpotts.

Marina stared rather blankly after her, long after the door

had closed, unconscious of the bustle surrounding the Thredgolds making their way off to their lodgings.

'Miss Marina?' It was Bunting, checking for any last orders or comments on the evening.

'Thank you, Bunting, everything was delightful. Please thank the staff and especially Mrs Leeming. That was an excellent dinner, and at such short notice.'

Marina made her way over to where her mother and Charlie were chatting by the fireside, Charlie nursing a bumper of brandy between his palms.

'I think I will go to bed now, Mama.' Her parent smiled at her and nodded. Marina bit her lip, then added, 'Lord Mortenhoe has invited me to drive with him tomorrow afternoon.'

'That is nice, dear,' Lady Winslow remarked comfortably. 'Goodnight, my love.'

'Goodnight, Mama. Goodnight, Charlie.'

Marina had reached her bedroom before anything about that exchange struck her as odd, but, as she sat in front of her dressing table while her maid removed the pins and bushed out her hair, she frowned at her reflection.

Why was Mama so unconcerned that she was going driving with a gentleman who was virtually unknown to her? Surely she should be in as much of a tizzy as Pris was? Had she known already that Lord Mortenhoe was going to ask her?

Then common sense took over her jumbled thoughts. It was Pris who was acting oddly by being so excited about it. Mama and Charlie put exactly the same construction upon the matter as she herself had—it was a polite invitation to the sister of a man with whom he was doing business and nothing more need be read into it.

This was so obviously the case, Marina decided as she tied her nightcap ribbons, that it was ridiculous that she had considered anything else even for a moment. After all, she was twenty-six years of age, the virtually dowerless daughter of a baron, of no beauty and with no talent other than for house-keeping. Justin Ransome, Earl of Mortenhoe, must be one of the most eligible bachelors in London.

If he was a bachelor. That had not occurred to Marina, but a moment's thought assured her it must be so. Mama would not countenance her driving about town with a married man.

Satisfied that she had the matter aright now, she climbed into bed and blew out her candle. A good night's sleep, then she must fit in time to make a list of the most suitable domestic agencies to recommend to him before Pris descended upon her.

Half an hour later, a wide-awake Miss Winslow slipped out of bed, pulled on her robe and padded downstairs to the library to consult the *Peerage*.

In the master bedchamber of a distinguished town house a few minutes drive away, the peer in question lay back against his pillows and examined his conscience.

His first reaction when Charles Winslow had stipulated his outrageous condition had been to reject it out of hand. He had then, Justin acknowledged to himself, capitulated with very little struggle—and therein lay the rub. Why had he given in to what his instinct told him was wrong?

He wanted Knightshaye. Regaining it had been his single purpose for twenty years, during eleven of which he had been in the position to work single-mindedly to amass sufficient funds to do so. Most of the family income had been tied up in the great house and estate, and what he had inherited from his father had been but a fraction of his former fortune. Which in itself was a puzzle—surely even as dedicated a gambler as Charlie Winslow could not have worked his way through the rents or the income of the Home Farm? On the other hand, there was nothing to have stopped him selling off parcels of farmland locally.

Justin pushed this new worry to the back of his mind and resumed the even less pleasant exercise of examining his motives. Was he really so obsessed that he would have married *anyone* to obtain Knightshaye? *No.* His long, lean frame jerked as he hauled himself upright in rejection of the thought. He had his name to consider. But it was more than that. To marry a woman for whom he could not feel liking and respect was to create a hollow sham, as cruel to her as it was repugnant to him.

But he was uncomfortably aware that he had agreed to court Marina Winslow, knowing nothing about her other than that she had beautiful eyes, a sense of humour, considerable grace and made him feel calm. That was not enough. He should have become better acquainted with her before agreeing to Winslow's condition.

Restless now, Justin swung his legs off the bed and began to pace, still in his shirtsleeves and evening knee breeches. At least now he knew his first impressions of Marina were borne out by closer contact; on longer acquaintance he believed he could come to like her very well. Was that enough to be fair to her?

Moodily, Justin regarded himself in the cheval glass in the corner. Brought up almost exclusively by a trio of old friends of his grandfather, he had never been encouraged to think too highly of his natural attributes, only to value what hard work and the application of his intelligence won him.

He supposed he cut a well-enough figure. His tailor and valet both appeared satisfied and ladies less strictly brought up than Miss Winslow were not reticent in admiring his height, length of leg, breadth of shoulder and ability to avoid standing on their toes on the dance floor. The fortune his hard work had brought him was more silently valued.

Moving closer, he narrowed his eyes at his reflection. Black hair that would never conform to a fashionable crop, even if he could be persuaded to try one. A nose that contrasted disappointingly with the aloof features of the classical bust standing on a column next to the mirror—but then the model for that had presumably never got himself into a fist fight with the blacksmith's son at the age of eleven. A mouth that he considered too wide and had had to learn to keep absolutely in repose when playing cards because, as his last mistress was fond of saying, 'It is *so* expressive, darling,' and those dark-fringed hazel eyes that would change colour so betrayingly with his emotions.

Your dangerous expression. Justin grinned at himself. Marina Winslow could speak her mind when she wanted to. In fact, he had a suspicion that behind that well-bred reticence she harboured all sorts of thoughts and opinions and that it would be interesting to explore them.

So… He prowled back to the bed and resumed his supine position on it. *So*, he liked Miss Winslow and she appeared to have the intelligence and strength of mind to suit him. *So*, he reasoned further, he was not being hypocritical in courting her. *But*, and here was the rub, what did she want and what did she make of him, given that she had no inkling of his intentions?

'She can always refuse me.' Justin considered his own words. Was that likely? He had a shrewd idea of the pressures that would be put on a young lady by her family if an offer to marry an earl came along, years after they had given her up as an old maid. 'So…I had better make sure she does not want to refuse me.' And do it without lying and pretending a love he did not feel.

What was it she had said any woman wanted?

'I think that all women would want to feel wanted, needed,

to have a loving family and to know that they are useful in whatever way they can be.' And what else? *'To have enough money to indulge in little luxuries is very pleasant, of course.'*

And he had asked about rank and status and her response had been that they would bring great responsibility and yet have a certain allure.

She was not then averse to the wealth, the title and the position he could give her. He could certainly make her feel needed, hopefully give her the family she desired. Could he make her feel wanted? Justin was certain she had no intention of referring to physical wants—her clear grey gaze had been innocent and perfectly serious.

It was an important consideration. Justin had no intention of maintaining a mistress once married, whether he was in love with his wife or no, and it would be hard to be leg shackled to a woman for whom one felt little desire. And just at the moment the only way of describing what he felt for Marina Winslow was friendship. That in itself was a novelty. Brought up in a series of masculine households, carefully introduced both to the *haut ton* and the world of expensive pleasures for sale, women had simply never entered his orbit as friends.

At least he felt that he could now look his conscience in the eye, if only after a somewhat shaky start, but he felt no further forward in how, honourably, to advance his courtship of Marina after tomorrow's promised drive in the park.

Restless again, he got up, threw on a robe and ran downstairs to the study. Pulling out a portfolio of suggestions from his agent for property acquisitions in the newly expanding area of St Mary-le-bone, he began to study them with close attention. Having enough money to buy back Knightshaye was one thing, to restore it and support a wife meant he could not rest on his laurels.

* * *

Back in Cavendish Square his proposed bride was also sitting poring over documents, although in Marina's case it was a pile of her household account books and notes which she was scanning in an effort to recall which domestic agencies had been most effective in providing the Winslow household with staff.

Having satisfied herself by careful study of the *Peerage* that Lord Mortenhoe was indeed a single man, she had then taken herself to task for even thinking it important to check. Ten minutes later she had been alarmed to find herself still sitting at Charlie's desk, her chin cupped in one hand, brooding on the puzzle of why he seemed so interested in her company.

By then she was too awake to make bed seem at all attractive, so, despite the clock chiming one o'clock, she took herself off to the morning room, which served the ladies of the house as their private sitting room, and found her notebooks.

Half-an-hour's work produced a respectable selection of agencies. Marina took another sheet of paper and began to draft a list of what servants might be thought necessary for a house the size of Knightshaye. That Lord Mortenhoe might think it presumptuous of her to do such a thing did occur to her, but her perusal of the *Peerage* had shown neither mother, sisters nor sisters-in-law to perform such a service, so she decided to keep it aside and produce it if further conversation showed a need for it.

The night watchman crying the hour outside jerked her out of her thoughts. Two o'clock. Yawning, Marina folded the papers, picked up her chamber stick and made her way upstairs, reflecting sleepily that it was satisfying to do something that, hopefully, would be a service to a friend. That she was thinking of Justin Ransome in those terms did not even occur to her as strange.

* * *

Priscilla swept into the Cavendish Street house at ten on the dot, her maid at her heels clutching two hat boxes and a portmanteau. She took one look at Marina, who had been conning her accounts in the morning room, and let out a faint shriek of horror.

'What have you been doing? You have bags under your eyes and you are positively sallow.'

'Good morning, Priscilla. You are looking delightful as always.' Marina refused to rise to the bait.

'Do you think so?' Priscilla eyed herself in the mirror as she untied her bonnet strings. 'Well, this is a prodigiously pretty hat. Susan, run upstairs and find Miss Marina's woman and show her what we have brought.' She sat down in a ruffle of skirts and peered at Marina more closely. 'A brisk walk around the Square will bring your colour back, but you look as if you hardly slept last night. Do you have any cucumber in the house? Because, if not, you must send out for one—it is the only thing for your eyes.'

'I expect we have.' Marina pushed her books to one side. 'But there is really no need to fuss, Pris, I am only going for a carriage ride.'

'With one of the most eligible men in London! I despair. And what is worse, I could not persuade Monsieur Lemerre to cancel his appointment with the Duchess of Porton, so we will have to manage your hair as best we can.'

'I have done my hair for the day,' Marina said firmly. 'I mean it, Pris—I am not going to get into a tizzy about a simple invitation from a friend of Charlie's.'

'Don't you want to marry and not remain a spinster all your days?' her friend demanded in exasperated tones.

'Yes. But I also wish I had the talent to play the piano, blue eyes and the opportunity to visit the East and none of those things are going to come to pass either, so I am certainly neither going to repine, nor weave ridiculous fantasies about earls.'

Priscilla leapt to her feet and marched towards the door. 'I have given up my morning, I have brought you my newest hat to wear and you are not the slightest bit grateful. Well, you can wither into an old maid, Marina Winslow, just don't blame your friends!'

'Pris, don't be cross, I know you want to help, but do face it, I am not going to attract an eligible earl whatever I do.'

Mrs Hinton swirled round and looked at her. Marina winced inwardly. However affectionate the look was, it was shot through with a pity that Priscilla was always careful not to express. But Marina recognised it and it hurt, just as sharply as her mother's less-well disguised disappointment that she had failed to 'take' or Lizzie's occasional tactless remark.

'But do you not want to enjoy his company, flirt a trifle, enjoy a little envy from others by being seen to be driving with him?'

'No, of course not. I enjoy his company and I would like him for a friend, I think. And going driving would be a treat. Naturally I would not dream of embarrassing him by appearing poorly turned out, but I would hate to have him think I was angling for him.' Marina could feel herself going quite hot at the thought.

'A friend?' Her huff completely forgotten, Priscilla sat down again and looked at Marina with astonishment. 'You mean like Dr Johnson and Mrs Thrale? I do not know of anyone else who is *friends* with a man.'

'But are you not friends with Mr Hinton?'

'Husbands are completely different,' Priscilla pronounced airily. 'So, if you do not wish to be obvious, we must simply be subtle.' This was rather an alien approach for her, but she was obviously prepared to throw herself into the attempt.

'But the first thing is a walk, then the cucumber and a lie down, or he will think you have been awake all night thinking about him.'

It would never have occurred to Marina that one could spend an entire morning getting ready for a simple carriage ride. Priscilla even monitored what she had for luncheon with care. 'You must eat something or your tummy will rumble and that would be fatal, but not too much because of tight lacing.'

'I do not want my stays laced tight,' Marina protested, helpless as, between them, two maidservants, carried away with enthusiasm, and Priscilla, happily directing, removed her morning dress and pulled on her stay laces. Her bosom swelled to an alarming extent over the top of her chemise. 'My walking dress will not fit.'

'That old thing!' Priscilla threw the lid off a bandbox. 'I have brought my new walking dress with a braided Russian bodice.'

'Now that certainly will never fit,' Marina stated confidently, but with an envious glance at the rich green cloth and intricate braid work.

In reply Priscilla gave a last heave on the stay laces. 'Yes, it will.' And it did, provided one was prepared not to breathe. Marina blinked in astonishment at the effect. She had what she considered a reasonable figure, but now she appeared to have a tiny waist and a quite stunning bosom, fortunately modestly covered.

'It is all in the cut and the corsetry,' Priscilla remarked complacently.

'But I cannot breathe!'

'Why do you need to? You aren't walking anywhere. Sit back, smile prettily, flutter your eyelashes—which reminds me, lamp black—and greet every one of his observations as if it was brilliant. One hardly needs to breathe to do that.'

At last the excited maids were dismissed and Marina was

permitted to descend to the drawing room and await his lord-ship's arrival. 'He is bound to bring a high-perch phaeton,' Priscilla remarked. 'Or possibly a curricle, but I think the phaeton would be more likely for the park. And naturally he will be driving his famous Welsh bays, or perhaps the matched blacks. I asked Henry last night and he says Lord Mortenhoe is famous for his horses and for having made most of his fortune himself by being a clever investor, because there was a scandal when his father died and he was left very poorly off.'

Unable to sit comfortably, Marina fidgeted about the room, trying to suppress a secret smile whenever she caught a glimpse of her own reflection in the glass over the mantelshelf. It was lowering to consider how frippery fashions could turn one's head, but it was a delightful novelty to have an expensive outfit on and to know one's beautifully curled locks were topped off by a bonnet in the very first stare of fashion. It was also exciting to imagine being driven behind a team of high-stepping horses in a dashing equipage.

When the door-knocker thudded she started towards the door, only to be pulled back by her friend. 'Not so eager, dearest.'

Priscilla waited, one ear almost on the door panels, then threw the door open and sauntered out, saying over her shoulder, 'Well, I must be going as you cannot accompany me to the library. My lord!' The start of surprise was a masterpiece. 'How charming to see you again. Marina has just reminded me that you are going driving, so I will go and say good afternoon to Lady Winslow.' She fluttered off up the stairs, leaving Marina torn between admiration and exasperation.

'My lord.' She stepped forward and shook hands, surprised at how glad she was to see him again.

'Miss Winslow, how very punctual you are.' His smile

touched something inside her, something that warmed and expanded into a flutter of happiness. 'Shall we go?'

At her nod, he took her arm and guided her to the door, which Bunting threw open with some *élan*. Marina stepped forward, eager for her first glimpse of the fabulous carriage and team.

At the kerb a groom was holding the head of a neatish grey cob, which, although of a pleasing conformation, was clearly of mature years and showing not the slightest sign of exciting high spirits. It stood between the shafts of a plain gig with blue wheels, its top folded down.

Nothing could have been further from her imaginings of making a stylish appearance in Hyde Park.

Chapter Five

J ustin watched Marina's face covertly as she stood on the step beside him. Yes, she was disappointed, although one had to be studying her closely to register that flicker of expression before her innate good manners took over.

'What a pretty gig.' She said it with a smile that seemed entirely genuine.

'Thank you,' he replied gravely, taking her arm and guiding her towards the cob who was being held by a liveried groom. 'And this is Smoke, who is an old fellow and somewhat on his dignity, although he can be persuaded to trot out like a young one if he is in the mood.'

Instead of asking him why he was intending to take her driving in an ordinary gig behind an elderly horse, Marina stroked Smoke's nose with confidence. 'Hello, you are a handsome fellow, are you not?' She was rewarded with a slobbery kiss on her leather gloves, but she wiped them on his mane with a lack of fuss that Justin approved.

'You think you will feel confident behind him, then?' He handed her up into the gig and gathered the reins. 'Thank you, Thomas, you may return home.' The man touched his hat and strode off as Justin clicked his tongue at the cob and they rolled sedately down the road.

'Why, yes. Did you think I would be a nervous passenger?' Marina swivelled on the seat to look at him. 'I assure you I am not, although I have not driven in an open carriage very often. Mama uses a closed carriage and Charlie prefers to ride.' He had also, Justin knew, recently sold his driving horses, presumably to meet some of his debts.

'Not at all, it was just that I thought you might care to learn to drive, and a single horse is much easier to begin with.' He waited with some apprehension for her response. It had seemed, at two in the morning, an excellent idea and one that would allow him an excuse for repeated, informal, excursions in her company. Now he was not so sure; if Marina had wanted to drive with him in order to be seen in fashionable places behind a showy team, she was not going to look kindly on his suggestion.

He risked a glance at her face and realised that her silence was due to delighted surprise and not disapproval. 'Truly? I would so enjoy it!' Then the animation vanished and she added politely, 'But I cannot accept, it would be such an imposition on your time.'

Justin, far from being a selfish man, was still not often in the position of offering treats and that eager flash in her eyes touched him more than he could have expected. It also threw the rest of her daily routine into sharp relief for him. *Good grief, I'd go mad in her shoes—confined to household duties, fetching and carrying, expected to behave like an old maid.* Not that she was looking like any old maid he had ever seen, not in that hat. And how could he have overlooked that voluptuous figure?

'It would give me much pleasure,' he responded, biting down a peremptory demand that she kick over the traces and just enjoy herself for once. 'It would interest me to teach you and you would be doing me a favour.'

'I would?'

He glanced at her again, trusting Smoke to plod stolidly through the traffic of Swallow Street. There was a decidedly sceptical glint in her eye.

'I am much involved with business lately. Somehow many of my former recreations pall. To drive quietly with you, to teach you to enjoy the sport, would be a delightful distraction.'

Silence. Had he mishandled it?

'What made you think I would care to learn?' She sounded genuinely interested.

'You have the air of confidence that is necessary, but you also have patience and sensitivity. And I thought perhaps you would enjoy a small adventure.' Now she was blushing rosily. Deliciously.

'In the face of such compliments I shall have to try hard to acquit myself.' It was acceptance of his suggestion and, relieved, he turned his attention back to his driving. They were almost upon Piccadilly. 'Where are we going?'

'I thought Green Park, if you would not dislike it. Far less fashionable than Hyde Park, of course…'

'Good.' It was said with heartfelt relief. 'If I am to make an exhibition of myself, I would far rather it was before an audience of nursemaids, dairy maids and elderly scholars than the fashionable crowd.'

'You will not make an exhibition of yourself,' he remarked somewhat absently, concentrating on turning right on the busy street past Burlington House.

'You are very confident, my lord!'

'*I* am teaching you,' he responded, unaware of how arrogant that sounded until a gurgle of laughter escaped her. 'Hmm, that was a somewhat dogmatic remark, was it not? I can see I must rely on you to take me down a peg or two when necessary, Marina.'

The use of her first name was a calculated risk and he was prepared for the sharp intake of breath beside him, pretending not to notice as he negotiated the park entrance.

'My lord…'

'Justin. It will be much easier to teach you if I do not have to include "Miss Winslow" in every sentence. And if you wish to berate me for bullying you, or being too demanding, then "Justin" will be so much easier.'

'Will you bully me?' she enquired demurely with that underlying thread of laughter that so attracted him.

'Most certainly. We have just established that I am dogmatic and over-confident, have we not?' He surveyed the greensward in front of them and guided Smoke towards a long track, away from the park's resident herd of milk cows. 'Does anyone shorten your name? Marina suits you when you are on your dignity and being gracious, but it is a somewhat *stately* name.'

'The family always call me Marina. Priscilla—Mrs Hinton—calls me Mar, but that is just a childhood name.'

'Mari. I will call you Mari.' The thought of a pet name for her, something no one else used, was a pleasing idea. She was blushing again.

'Very well, Justin. I do not know what Mama would say.'

'I promise to address you with the strictest propriety within earshot of Lady Winslow.' He registered the touch of pleasure her hesitant use of his name gave him and made himself concentrate on the lesson. It was like gentling an unbroken horse—he had no intention of alarming her by taking anything too fast. Yet.

Marina attempted to sort through her jumbled emotions and discovered that, underneath the shyness and the fear of making a fool of herself in front of a accomplished whip, she was quite simply happy.

Justin pulled up and handed her the reins. 'Here you are. One horse and a plain snaffle bit, so only two reins, which you hold like so…no, thumb here. We will leave the whip for a later date.'

'Oh. Good,' Marina said fervently, already feeling that her hands were rather too full of things and nervously aware that she could feel Smoke mouthing the bit.

'Just keep contact with his mouth. Perfect, now shake the reins slightly and click your tongue. You can say "walk on" if you like.'

One grey ear swivelled back and Marina laughed. 'He is listening. Walk on, Smoke.' If the cob took exception to a rather overenthusiastic shake of the reins, he showed no sign of it, pacing off down the long drive. Marina, hardly daring to take her eyes off the ground in front, exclaimed, 'I am driving!'

'Certainly you are driving. Now, relax your hands and your arms or Smoke will think there is something to worry about.' Beside her Justin turned so that his left arm was behind her and he could take the right rein out of her hand. 'Put your hand over mine and feel how relaxed I keep my fingers. Go on, Mari.'

Tentatively she did as she was told, shaken by the close proximity of his body. *It is no worse than waltzing,* she chided herself, feeling how loose his grasp on the rein was. 'I see.' Justin handed her back the rein, turning to sit straight in the seat again, and she felt a little pang at the loss of the contact.

'What do I do now?'

'Go down this drive to the next bend, then turn right.'

'How?'

'Tighten your fingers on the right rein. I will tell you when.'

And by some miracle it worked. Marina spent a happy hour

guiding the old cob round and round Green Park at a steady walk, glowing with Justin's praises and blissfully unaware that if any of his friends had seen him they would have assumed he was fit only for Bedlam.

At last he pried the reins from her fingers and took them home. Marina sat flexing her shoulders which were surprisingly stiff and asked, 'May I trot tomorrow?'

'Tomorrow?'

'Oh, I am sorry, I spoke without thinking, it is too much to expect you to let me drive two days running.' How mortifying, to have presumed on Justin's good nature in such a way. He was a busy man, he had told her so, and he was only doing this for some whim of kindness.

'Not at all, you may certainly trot tomorrow; I thought you might have been bored.' His questioning glance was so open that she smiled back without constraint.

'I am enjoying it so much. The driving and your company. You see, I never had a male friend before. I suppose it is one of the benefits of being out of the Marriage Mart—one does not have to consider those stuffy conventions so much any more.'

'You see me as a friend?' She tried to fathom any meaning behind the question. 'Why?'

'Because I trust you and it is easy to talk to you.' The gig drew up outside the house and Marina hopped down before Justin could assist her. 'Would you care to come in and take tea? I can ask a footman to come and hold Smoke.'

The door opened before he answered her and Charlie emerged, setting his fashionable hat at a rakish angle on his head. 'Good God, Mortenhoe, what are you doing in that rig?'

'Teaching me to drive, Charlie. Is that not kind of Lord Mortenhoe?'

'Dashed good of him. Look, old chap, there was something

I wanted to discuss if you have a moment, only I'm on my way to the club.'

'Step up, I'll drive you. Thank you, Miss Winslow, I will take up your kind offer on another occasion. The same time tomorrow?'

Marina agreed and stood watching with glee as her brother climbed reluctantly into the unfashionable vehicle and was driven off.

Justin regarded Winslow's efforts to pull his hat low enough to render himself unrecognisable. 'I will drop you off in a minute if you like. What did you want to say to me?'

'Only to ask how it was going with my sister. The driving's a dashed good idea, I must say.'

'I thought so, and Miss Winslow seems to enjoy it. The only trouble is, I am not sure it will achieve much.'

'Why not? Alone together, lots of opportunities to hold hands, not a chaperon in sight. Damn it, man, if you can't make love to her under those circumstances, I don't know what it would take.'

'Miss Winslow considers me to be a friend. I am sure she thinks of me in no other light. If I start to flirt with her now, she is going to take me for a complete coxcomb.' And Marina's good opinion of him was something, Justin realised, that he valued.

'Hell!' Charlie lapsed into thought. 'Leave it to me, I'll see what Mama advises. Look, can you drop me off here, I can see some chaps I know coming.'

With a grin Justin pulled up to let Winslow escape before he was spotted and drove home, wondering what hare-brained ploy Charlie was going to come up with.

Marina recounted the tale of her first driving lesson at dinner, much to Lizzie's wide-eyed interest. 'Has he wonderful horses? A whole team? Did you canter?'

'No, Lizzie, one steady cob and I walked around Green Park.' Marina regarded her sister tolerantly. 'You would have been bored to tears.'

'I'm sure I would! When *I* come out I will be driven every-where in the greatest style by all my beaux, you wait and see.'

'If you cannot speak in a more modest and becoming manner, young lady, you will not be joining us for dinner again,' her mother interjected frowning. 'I had thought you old enough, but now I wonder if I was wrong. You may go to your room directly after dessert.'

When a sulky Elizabeth had trailed off to her room, Lady Winslow swept Marina into the drawing room and patted the sofa beside her. 'I am glad of the opportunity to talk to you alone, dear. Now, you know Charlie is selling Knightshaye to Lord Mortenhoe? Well, the dear boy has a clever scheme to put the money in trust for Giles's education, Lizzie's come-out and my comfortable retirement to the Dower House. He has spoken to me very openly about his rather regrettable tendency to gamble and has hit upon this way of keeping the money safe for all of us. Now, is that not good news?'

It was, but there was an unpleasant hollowness in Marina's stomach. 'And what are his plans for me, Mama?'

'He thought you would be living with me at the Dower House.' The hollowness turned into an icy hole. 'But I thought of something much better.'

With a rush of relief Marina stammered, 'I can stay here and keep house for Charlie?'

'Goodness, no, child! What are you thinking of? You are far too young to be keeping house for a bachelor brother in *London* of all places, and we could never afford a chaperon for you. No, I will have Lizzie's companionship for a year or two until her come-out, so you would be much better employed with Aunt Maria.'

'Great-aunt Maria in Bath? But she never goes out.'

'Exactly. Poor creature, stuck in a gloomy house with only that cantankerous creature Cousin Phillipa for company and a pack of smelly lapdogs—you will do her good. Read to her, go for walks when she ventures out in her chair, generally make yourself useful.' Lady Winslow smiled benignly at her elder daughter. 'I know how you like to feel useful, Marina dear.'

It was a prison sentence, the punishment for the crime of failing to marry, meted out by those she loved in the cheerful belief that it was all for the best. Marina bit down the angry words that rose in her throat, the pleas to have this decision reconsidered. After all, what else was she fit for at twenty-six? Her family was too well bred, too respectable, for her to escape into the only genteel occupation that she might espouse—that of governess.

There was one hope. 'But do you not need me to teach Giles?'

'I think he is too old now for female tuition, dear. He is becoming a little wild. The Vicar is taking one or two other local boys of good family for tuition and Giles will do well with him, I am sure.'

'When? When are we leaving London?' How much longer did she have to walk freely with her maid, to visit Priscilla, to shop, to explore the lending libraries? How much longer to enjoy the company of her new friend and to learn to drive, a skill that would become immediately useless in Bath?

'I think in about six weeks, if Charlie's negotiations with Lord Mortenhoe are successful.'

Somehow Marina managed a tranquil face for the rest of the evening and through the next, interminable, morning. Neither her brother nor mother commented on the dark circles under her eyes, although Lizzie, with typical tactlessness, announced that she looked positively haggard and wondered loudly what could have kept her from sleeping. Without Priscilla's attentions and finery—for her friend was engaged for the day with relatives of her husband—Marina felt that her appearance for her next driving lesson left something to be desired, although at least she could now breathe without Pris's severe tight lacing.

Or she could if it were not for the lump of leaden misery that seemed lodged under her diaphragm.

Justin was prompt again, and her spirits could not help but be lightened simply by his company and the stimulation of their progress through the crowded streets. Marina made conversation and flattered herself that her self-control was equal to the occasion.

Then Justin put the reins in her hands just inside the park gate and pointed to a grove of trees. 'Just walk over there, get used to the reins again.' He was silent as they approached it, other than to say, 'Circle around to the back.' When they reached the little clearing the trees enclosed, deserted of all walkers, he took the reins back, tied them round the whip stand and clasped both her hands in his.

'What is wrong, Mari?' She shook her head. 'No, do not try and tell me nothing is wrong, I can see it in your eyes. Who has hurt you? As your friend, I must either call him out or at least land him a punch on the jaw.'

It was said humorously, but the gentle expression in his eyes and the warmth of his hands clasping hers was almost too much for her self-possession. 'You cannot.' She struggled to find a humorous tone to match his. 'It was only something Mama told me and you most certainly must not punch her.'

'Tell me.'

Why can he not pretend everything is well? Marina realised that she was within an inch of blurting it all out and bit her lip hard. She looked at Justin and forced a smile as she shook her head. His eyes were hard and green and she realised he was angry.

'Is it because of me?'

'The driving lessons? Oh, no, Mama and Charlie seem quite sanguine about those, they hardly asked me about them.' For some reason that did not seem to quench the angry colour.

'Then what? Tell me, Mari, it matters to me.'

Shaken, she stammered, 'When Charlie has the money from the sale of Knightshaye he will set up a trust for Mama and Giles and Lizzie.'

'And you will live with Lady Winslow and Miss Elizabeth?'

'I wanted to stay here and keep house for Charlie, but Mama says that is quite ineligible. So then I thought I would be living at the Dower House with her, but she thinks she would not need me...that I would be of more use with Great-aunt Maria in Bath.'

'And do I deduce that will be no treat?'

Marina nodded. 'She is very reclusive and lives with Cousin Phillipa, who is rather cross, and many lapdogs. Mama thinks I can read to her.'

'And how long will this last?'

'Until she dies, I suppose. And then Cousin Phillipa will need me, I expect.'

'Oh, Mari, poor love, that sounds hellish.'

'Please stop being sympathetic, you will make me cry.' She sniffed resolutely. 'I can manage if I do not feel sorry for myself.' Before she could protest, Marina found herself enfolded in Justin's arms and held against his chest.

It felt wonderful. Strong, safe and remarkably comfortable. Marina snuggled closer into Justin's shirt front and let out a sigh of relief as though she had escaped from a pursuing beast and had found sanctuary. His arms were around her quite tightly, but she had no instinct to struggle. One-handed he appeared to have removed her bonnet and was stroking her hair soothingly while he murmured something unintelligible into it.

Then the feeling of overwhelming peace began to change subtly into something unsettling, something that made her pulse quicken and the heat come into her face. She was aware of his warmth and the scent of him: clean, somehow spicy and definitely male. His heart was beating under her cheek and the soft linen seemed suddenly as sensuous as skin against her own flesh. She realised that her hands had slipped around his body under his coat, her palms were braced against hard muscle and that she was touching a man in a way utterly different from the hugs she exchanged with her brothers.

Slowly she disentangled herself and sat up on the seat of the gig, looking at Justin for reassurance and meeting green eyes that were anything but angry.

Chapter Six

Justin looked into the wide, troubled grey eyes and cursed inwardly. Cursed the Winslows for distressing Mari so much, cursed himself for the urge that filled him to take her in his arms again and kiss that soft mouth with its parted lips. No need to wonder now whether she was capable of passion—he could read it, all unawakened in that innocent gaze and the trembling of her body as he had held it against his.

Her mother had set out for her the fate that awaited the surplus, unwed daughter, confident it would propel her into his arms when he proposed to her. She had not realised, he imagined, just how much she would hurt Marina and just how rapidly she would find herself in that embrace.

And now was most definitely not the moment to make a proposal. She would imagine he was doing it out of pity and he had no desire that she accept him out of desperation. A lifetime was rather too long for regrets.

'I am not going to cry.' She said it with a determination that tugged at his heart, sitting upright on the seat and jamming her bonnet on her head with scant regard for her curls.

'Are you not? You may, if you like. I have a large and clean handkerchief somewhere.'

That produced a choke of amusement and a quizzical look. It seemed the moment of physical awareness had passed. 'Really? Charlie hated it if Lizzie or I cried when we were younger. Lizzie still does when she cannot get her own way and Charlie positively runs out of the room. Mama says that all men are the same.'

Justin grinned and picked up the reins. Smoke swivelled an ear back and then dropped his head again when no command to move came. 'I had always assumed that it would be an excellent opportunity to flirt—beautiful young lady weeps daintily into a lace-edged handkerchief, I make soothing noises…'

This time Marina laughed out loud. 'I suspect there are very few young ladies who can produce just one or two dainty tears. I certainly cannot. I end up with red eyes and a red nose—no wonder Charlie runs away.'

'You are very brave to reveal these horrid details.' Justin shook the reins and Smoke woke up and began to walk round the edge of the grove.

'Why not? You are my friend and will not be so unkind as to tease me about it.'

'No, I would not tease you.' He hesitated, uncertain as to how much he dare hint. 'Do not be too cast down by what your mother said; things may change, other opportunities may open up.'

'You are kind to try to cheer me up, but I will do better to resign myself, I think.' She gave a little shiver and he fought back the urge to put his arm around her again. 'But I cannot spoil this drive. May I take the reins—and will you let me trot today?'

Days passed and nothing more was said about Great-aunt Maria and the Bath scheme for her future. Marina let herself hope that perhaps the old lady had rejected the idea, or that Mama had thought better of it, but then, after two weeks, Charlie mentioned it over Sunday luncheon and the hope withered.

Resolutely Marina pushed the thought to the back of her mind, feeling like a prisoner who has a few weeks of freedom before being sent to their cell. It would be wicked to spoil these last days of liberty anticipating what was to come.

She saw Justin almost every day for a driving lesson and she could now take the paths of Green Park at a spanking trot, turning corners with confidence and even passing through narrow openings without having to close her eyes in anticipation of the crash.

Occasionally he dined with them in Cavendish Square, but Marina found herself resenting the formality this imposed on their conversation. The strange feelings of confusion and awareness she had felt when he had held her that day had turned into something different, an ache when she thought about him, an excitement when she saw him, a warm glow of happiness when they were together. It was certainly very different, being friends with a gentleman.

On a Tuesday towards the end of the month, Justin apologised for not being able to take her driving the next afternoon. 'I am sorry, but I promised to try out a hunter a friend wishes to sell and the only time we could arrange it is tomorrow afternoon.'

'Of course, you must do just as you wish,' Marina protested. 'It is so good of you to let me drive so often.'

'Not at all. Would you care to drive in Hyde Park the day after?'

'Yes, please—if you think I would not disgrace you.' She turned a teasing smile on him. 'Are you sure your credit will stand you being seen as a passenger in a gig being driven by a mere female?'

'It certainly will not,' Justin replied so seriously that for a moment she thought he was in earnest. 'Which is why I thought you might like to drive a phaeton.'

'Truly? A high-perch phaeton and your bays?'

'No! A low-perch and a pair of very steady roans. But still smart enough for you to cut a dash if you wish to let your friends know where you will be at three o'clock.'

Marina laughed. 'I would not dare—imagine how embarrassing if I made a mull of it.'

She was looking forward to the treat too much to repine over her lost drive on Wednesday, so at breakfast suggested that she take Giles and Lizzie for a walk in Hyde Park. Even Mama was kind enough to lend them the carriage—'Providing that dog does not get mud on the seats, mind!'

They therefore disembarked at the Chesterfield Gate in some style, Lizzie and Marina unfurling new parasols to greet the sunshine and Hector trotting obediently at the end of his best scarlet lead. Even Giles was managing to present a tidy appearance and Marina felt quite proud of her little party.

They progressed slowly along the footpath towards the Serpentine and Marina was so far lulled into a false sense of security that she succumbed to Giles's pleas to let Hector off the lead to chase a stick. There were no horses in the vicinity, so this seemed safe enough, and boy and dog romped harmlessly in the wake of the sisters.

When they approached the carriage drive that edged the Serpentine, Marina called to Giles to catch Hector, and, despite sticking out his lower lip mutinously, he did as he was told, holding on to the stick with his other hand.

'Don't you dare throw that in the water,' Lizzie admonished her brother, with the inevitable result that he marched off in a sulk, towing Hector behind him, and stood as close to the edge as he dared, one shoulder turned to his sisters.

'Really, Lizzie, that was certain to put his hackles up, and he was behaving so well too!'

Lizzie merely sniffed, then turned to look out over the water. 'Are those ducks, do you think?'

Marina followed her gaze. A dead branch had been carried by the gentle current to rest at the dam end of the lake and now stuck up out of the water, its gaunt branches providing a perch for a number of waterfowl. 'I have not the slightest idea. Perhaps they are coot. Or moorhens?'

With an attempt to woo Giles out of his sulks, she called to him. 'Giles, you know about these things—are those ducks?'

He came at the run to look, Hector bounding at the end of his lead, barking. The accident happened so quickly that Marina had only a hazy idea of what came first: Hector's barking disturbing the birds, the birds rising in panic, exciting Hector, or Giles tripping on a tussock as he ran and letting go of the lead.

Then the big dog was into the water, managing to both swim and bark at the same time and, with an explosion of wings and frantic quacking, the whole roost flew away. 'Oh, no, he will be soaked! Giles, you will have to walk him home now.'

But Hector was not returning to shore; instead, he seemed fixed where he was, struggling frantically and churning the water into brown waves. 'He's stuck, his lead is in the branches!' Giles, sobbing, made a dash for the water's edge, only to be caught by Lizzie, who wrapped her arms around him tightly.

'You know you cannot swim, Giles!'

'But he'll drown!' Giles twisted and turned in his sister's grasp while Marina looked round desperately, hoping for a park attendant or a boat. All there was to be seen was a crowd of interested onlookers, carefully keeping a safe distance from the water and any involvement in this unseemly rumpus, and a rider approaching at a canter on a big bay hunter.

The man reined in for a moment, assessing the scene, then stripped off his coat, tossed it and his hat to a pair of male pedestrians and rode the horse straight into the water.

'Marina, it is Lord Mortenhoe!' Lizzie let go of her brother in her surprise, but Giles had stopped struggling, his eyes fixed on the horse, which was now belly-deep in the lake.

Marina too could not take her eyes off the scene, torn between a vast relief that Justin was there and taking control of the situation and mortification that he was having to do so. The water was well up his boots now, but he had reached the snag of dead wood and she watched, heart in her mouth, as he leaned down and tried to free the frantically struggling dog.

Hector was resisting all attempts to rescue him. Marina saw a fleeting grimace of resignation cross Justin's face. He threw a leg over the pommel and slid off into the water and the horse plunged for the shore, to be caught by a helpful gentleman. Marina realised her hands were pressed to her mouth in horror as Justin half-walked, half-swam, the water up to his shoulders, and finally seized Hector's lead. After a confused moment the dog broke free and splashed to the bank, bounding out to cover Giles and a shrieking Lizzie with muddy water as he shook and gambolled.

But Marina could only stare as Justin began to walk out of the lake, soaked from head to foot, his shirt plastered to his body, his buckskin breeches saturated. He was mid-thigh in the water when she realised that the expression on his face was not anger, or embarrassment at the growing crowd who were gathering, but a sort of rueful amusement at his own predicament.

She began to smile, then, as he waded towards her, to

laugh. It was too ridiculous, here in one of the most fashionable parks in London, to be standing with a muddy small boy, an even muddier dog and a completely soaked peer of the realm who, if she was not mistaken, had pond weed in his hair.

The laughter grew and bubbled until she was sobbing with it, her hands pressed to her mouth in an effort to keep it back, her sides aching. Beside her Lizzie, obviously in a misery of embarrassment, was tugging at her sleeve. 'Marina, stop it, people are looking!'

Justin trudged on until he reached the edge of the lake right in front of her. 'Good afternoon, Miss Winslow.' He was grinning and the laughter died as her heart did a neat flip in her chest. His shirt was plastered to his body, revealing the broad shoulders and flat stomach his formal clothes only hinted at. His buckskins clung like a second skin to well-muscled thighs. He ran one hand through his wet hair and his green eyes challenged her with questions she did not understand.

'I am so…sorry,' she managed to stammer.

'My dear Miss Winslow, I am quite certain that none of this is your doing.' He splashed the last few feet and stood in front of her. The crowd, her brother and sister, the looming bulk of the wet horse, all vanished from her consciousness.

Marina swallowed. 'I mean…for laughing at you.'

'I would have thought you lacking in humour if you had not. I imagine I present one of the oddest sights seen here since Lord Hitherleigh took the notion of painting his barouche sky blue.' He seemed to see something in her face, for he stopped teasing her and smiled. 'It is nothing, I promise you.'

'But your shirt and your boots are ruined.'

'And my breeches, which you are too well bred to mention, are going to be the despair of my valet, I know. But how would Giles have felt if Hector had drowned? Clothes can be replaced, dogs like that cannot.'

'Thank goodness,' she retorted shakily. It wasn't just the shock of the whole incident, or her own appalling behaviour that was making her feel so strange, but what it was she did not know.

'And I had decided to buy the horse, so returning him somewhat damp is not going to cause any problems,' Justin continued. 'But how are you going to get home?'

'We have the carriage—and Giles will have to walk Hector back.' She made herself meet his eyes, still green with fun and the stimulus of the ridiculous little adventure. 'My lord—I must tell you—you have pond weed in your hair.' A little gasp of returning amusement almost escaped her.

'Then perhaps you would be good enough to remove it, Miss Winslow,' the earl requested, standing patiently while she pulled off one glove and began to pick weed from his bowed head. Ridiculously she felt the urge to run her hand through the wet hair, to feel the shape of his skull under her fingers. 'Thank you.' He hesitated and said with a smile, 'I think I shall call tomorrow morning—perhaps you will ask your brother if he could spare me a few moments.'

'Of course. May I say on what account?' Marina tossed away the weed and carefully pulled on her glove, wondering if by some miracle the growing crowd of onlookers held no one of either her, or Lord Mortenhoe's, acquaintance, and somehow not much minding.

'Perhaps you could tell him I am ready to conclude our business. Until tomorrow then.' He half-turned away, then looked back. 'And, please, do not look so remorseful over your laughter—you look so very lovely when you laugh.'

Marina stood staring after him as he retrieved his hat and coat and mounted the horse with a word of thanks to the gentleman holding it. She was still staring when Lizzie tugged her arm.

'Marina! Come *on*, please. Are you all right?'

'Yes, of course.' She did not move. *No, I feel as though I have a fever.*

'Then come along, people are staring.'

Let them stare. I really do not care. All I care about is knowing why I feel like this. She looked around at Lizzie, flushed and furious, one hand still grasping Giles's collar. 'Do let him go, Lizzie. Giles, is Hector's lead secure this time?'

'Yes, Marina. I'm sorry.'

'So you should be,' Lizzie scolded. 'Thank goodness for Lord Mortenhoe. I must say, he was *wonderful*, do you not think so, Marina? It was most unkind of you to laugh at him so—I thought you liked him.'

'I do, and he did not mind me laughing, he was laughing himself.' She walked as though in a dream—outwardly normal, she was sure, for Lizzie made no comment. Inside her mind was a confusion of images. Justin's kindness in teaching her to drive; his frankness and honesty when they talked; the feel of his body, strong and protective when he had comforted her in the park; the look of that body—so masculine, so elemental—as he strode out of the lake. And the endearing lack of pride, which let him laugh at his own appearance in the middle of a fashionable crowd.

I love him. It was so obvious, so utterly right, that Marina wondered at herself for not having realised it before. *But why should I have? No one has ever made me feel like this before.*

The shock of the realisation took her almost to the park gate and the waiting carriage before her feet seemed to touch ground again. *He is finishing his business with Charlie, and when that happens I will have to go and live with Great-aunt in Bath and I will never see him again.*

She must have made a sound, for Lizzie turned to her, her face concerned. 'Marina? Don't be upset, I am sure there was no one there who knew us.' She bit her lip. 'I am sorry I was so cross. Would you like me to walk back with Giles?'

'No, I am not upset.' Marina fixed a smile on her face and made herself concentrate on the here and now. The sooner she learned to do that, the better. 'I am sure John can go with Giles. And you were only worried about him, I know.' The footman got down from the box at the sight of the returning Winslows. 'Here we are, John—and more than a little muddy, I am afraid. Please will you walk back with Master Giles? I am sure Lady Winslow would not want the dog in the carriage.'

Giles turned a worried face up to her. 'I am sorry I let Hector go, Marina. Do you have to tell Mama and Charlie?'

'I will not, but I think it would be a good idea if you did, do you not agree?' She waited until he nodded reluctantly. 'After all, it is only right that they are able to thank Lord Mortenhoe. Now, off you go with John and be a good boy.'

She climbed into the carriage and sank back with a sigh.

'I know,' Lizzie sympathised with what she assumed was the source of the sigh. 'I love my brothers dearly—who could not?—but Giles is such a harum-scarum and Charlie so wild and expensive. I am resolved, when I come out, to find myself a husband of very even temperament and many virtues.'

Amused, despite her roiling thoughts, Marina smiled at her sister. 'I thought you were insisting upon wealth and good looks.'

'Those too, of course. What a pity Lord Mortenhoe is too old for me.'

'I do not think,' Marina said sadly, 'that Lord Mortenhoe is destined for the sister of a baron.'

Chapter Seven

Giles duly made his confession and the tale was greeted with laughter by Lord Winslow and horror, followed by gratification, by his mama.

'Lord Mortenhoe rescued Hector? How very noble of him! What a true gentleman he is. Marina, I do hope you expressed your thanks in a suitable manner.'

Marina caught her sister's eye and admitted that Lord Mortenhoe had made light of the matter and had brushed aside her thanks. 'Charlie, he said he would call tomorrow morning in the hope of finding you at home and concluding his business with you.'

She was unprepared for the smile that her mother and brother exchanged; the price agreed for Knightshaye must be truly excellent, which was such good news for Giles and Lizzie's futures.

'Had you any plans for tomorrow morning, Marina?'

'Why, yes, Mama, I intended to go out with Priscilla and her cousin Miss Truebody. Miss Truebody is up from Hampshire and Priscilla is intent upon showing her all the best shops.'

'Oh, dear. I did so hope you would be at home. I am expecting several callers and you know how I like you to be here to help me entertain.'

Marina nearly protested, then bit her lip. She must become accustomed to subduing her own preferences to another's. 'Of course, Mama. I will write a note for Priscilla. Who are you expecting?'

'Well…no one *precisely*, only I think…well, definitely Lady Salmon. I am sure.'

That seemed an extremely vague arrangement on which to ask her to cancel her own plans, but Marina swallowed her resentment and got up. 'I will write to Priscilla now.'

'Thank you, dear. I cannot help but think that Mrs Hinton—charming girl that she is—might be a little *fast*.'

So perhaps that was it—a desire to detach her from Pris's influence rather than any need for her company. Marina resolved to accompany her friend and her cousin the day after, come what may. Somehow she was feeling the need for frivolity, diversion, something—anything—to stop her thinking about Justin Ransome. And somehow she had to face him tomorrow afternoon, go driving with him, concentrate because he was trusting her with a pair—and all very much under the public gaze.

The next morning Lady Winslow swept into Marina's room before breakfast, just as her maid was laying out her morning dress on the bed. 'Not that one—so plain, I always think. Where is the jonquil muslin with the moss-green ribbons Miss Winslow bought last month?'

'I am saving it for best, Mama.' Marina put down her hairbrush and regarded her mother with some surprise. 'I thought it was possibly only Lady Salmon who was calling.'

'Well…yes. But I have thought lately that you are not doing yourself justice, Marina dear. The jonquil gown, I think, and your pearls would look charmingly with it.'

'Very well, Mama.' And perhaps Justin would arrive early—or perhaps she could be a little late in changing for their drive… She caught herself fantasising and felt a stab of self-disgust. *What are you doing? Wanting to dress up to attract him? You'll be tightening your stay laces and rouging your cheeks again like an arrant flirt. He is happy enough to be your friend, but what he* wants *is a young lady of title and fortune, not an old maid.*

'Did you sleep well, dear? You look a little peaked.' Lady Winslow peered at her closely.

'I slept indifferently, Mama.' That was an understatement, but Marina did not think it possible to explain that she had lain awake, indulging in hopeless fantasies of Justin, realising he was madly in love with her and sweeping her off to Knightshaye, only to fall asleep at last and to toss and turn all night in the grip of dreams of such disturbing sensuality that it made her blush to recall them.

'A little powder might be excused, I believe.' Lady Winslow considered her elder daughter again. 'And some lip salve.'

Lip salve? Normally that would be enough to call down Mama's condemnation on the wearer as fast beyond redemption. Marina shrugged and found both a pot of rice powder and a tiny jar of lip salve and applied both cautiously. They certainly made her appear less wan.

After breakfast the two ladies settled themselves in the drawing room; Marina with the household accounts, which she hoped would prove sufficiently engrossing that she would not daydream, and Lady Winslow, a notable embroideress, with her latest project of seat cushions for the dining room.

The stroke of ten brought a knock at the door and both looked up expectantly, but the voice in the hall greeting

Bunting was male. Even through the thickness of the heavy door panels Marina recognised the timbre of Justin's voice and her pulse missed a beat. 'Can you match me this shade of rose with something just a touch darker, dear?' Lady Winslow asked, holding out a skein of silk, and Marina put down the pen that she was holding suspended over the page and went to search in her mother's sewing box.

As he was shown into the study, Justin regarded Charles Winslow's cheerful countenance with a degree of caution. He was ready to believe that Winslow loved his sister and thought he was doing the best for her, but he could wish the baron exhibited a bit more imagination and sensitivity.

He imagined the scruples he would feel if he were concocting an arranged marriage for a sister of his. Unless he was much mistaken, Winslow had made no enquiries into his financial position, his private life or anything else, taking for granted that an apparently solvent earl must be a good match. And how did he know that the son of a man ruined by Winslow's own father might not harbour a grudge that he would visit on his new wife?

'Good morning!' Charlie bounced to his feet and waved Justin into the chair opposite his. 'You've decided to pop the question, then?'

Justin regarded his host, his face impassive whilst his mind still whirled. He had intended having one more try at persuading Winslow to let him buy the house at a higher price and without the condition of marriage attached, for he could think of no way to tell Marina the truth and at the same time keep his word to her brother to reveal nothing of the plot.

And yet… He remembered all too clearly her bitter unhappiness at the life that was mapped out for her. And he remembered too her humour, her kindness, her enthusiasm for driving with him and her generous assumption of friendship and trust. And then there was the glimmer of sensual awakening he saw in her eyes and the way that stirred his blood. It might not be a love match, but he could convince himself that marriage to Miss Winslow might be very pleasant. But would it be fair to her?

'I will ask Marina if she will do me the honour of marrying me, yes. But I cannot like the deception you are insisting upon. How will she feel if she ever finds out?'

'Why should she?' Charlie looked shrewdly at him. 'And you do not dislike the prospect? I mean, you like her well enough?'

'I like her too well to deceive her.' Justin got to his feet and shifted restlessly around the room. 'I am not going to pretend to her that this is a love match.'

'Good God, Mama hasn't brought her up to expect that sort of thing. Marina knew it was her duty to marry well, which is why she felt it so when after three Seasons she was still unattached. Very dutiful, my sister.'

Justin fancied it was more a sense of rejection and chagrin that Marina would have felt rather than any sense of duty undone, but he thought it useless to say so. Fond though he was of his sister, Charlie Winslow was not the most sensitive of men.

'If she rejects me today, you will accept I have done what I can to attach her, even though it is not yet two months, as we agreed?'

'It is one month—and, yes, if she rejects you today I am going to hold you to another month to attempt to change her mind.' Charlie looked unusually mulish and determined.

'I do not feel comfortable harassing her.'

'You cannot call taking her driving every day, eating your dinner here now and again and generally being pleasant to her harassment! Anyway, she'll say *yes*, never you fear. The girl's no fool, got a damn sight more sense than I have.' Charlie got to his feet. 'I'll just give Mama the nod, make sure you've a clear field.'

He left Justin standing there, a prey of uncharacteristic indecision. What did he hope for? He knew his one chance of a love match had gone, had been a delusion from the beginning. He liked Marina Winslow very much indeed—but was he doing the right thing?

'Coast's clear.' The man who might well become his brother-in-law held the study door open. 'Come on—or do you want a stiff brandy first?'

Marina put down her pen in exasperation. Mama was the limit! She had kept her at home on what was obviously a paper-thin excuse, just to reduce Priscilla's influence, and now she had vanished because Charlie wanted something. At any minute Lady Salmon was going to call and Marina would have to entertain her single-handed.

The look she shot towards the door as it opened was far from conciliatory, but her ill temper vanished like a soap bubble when she saw who it was.

'Justin! Do come in. I am afraid Mama has just slipped out for a moment.'

'And I am afraid I have grievously displeased you! The look on your face just now could only be described as forbidding.'

'Not at all, I did not realise who it was. Please, come in and I promise not to scowl at you. Would you care for some refreshment?' Her pulse seemed to be executing the most ridiculous rhythms. It was an effort to smile at him normally and neither look away nor stare outrageously.

'Nothing, thank you.' He took the seat she gestured to and regarded her with concern. 'Why were you looking so fierce?'

'Oh, merely the sulks. I was asked to cancel a shopping trip in order to help Mama entertain some callers she expects later and I confess to taking it in poor part.'

'I cannot believe you ever sulk, Mari.' His smile went straight to some nerve at the base of her spine, which sent a warm glow through her. She bit her lip in an effort not to beam at him in a quite ludicrous manner.

'But we have only known each other a few weeks, Justin, and you have obviously not seen me at my worst!' She was pleased with the rallying tone she achieved. 'And have you concluded your business with Charlie? Or should I not ask?'

'No, it is not finished.' He spoke slowly, his face suddenly serious. 'Not completely. Mari, I have to confess that was only an excuse to call this morning. There was something I wished very much to ask you.'

'You do not need an excuse to ask me anything. Is it something about Knightshaye that I can help with?'

'No. Not directly, Mari.' He got to his feet abruptly, seized a footstool and planted it at her side, sitting on it and taking her hand in his. Her already erratic pulse jumped so much she was sure he must feel it. She looked down at his bent head, fighting the urge to run her hand over the thick, dark hair, wondering how it would feel against her palm, recalling the sleek wetness of it yesterday.

'What is it, Justin?'

'You know I am very fond of you? That I admire you greatly for your charm and your honesty and your intelligence?'

'I…why, thank you. You have been kind enough to be my friend, and kinder still to say such things of me.'

He looked up at that, his eyes green and intent on her face. 'I am not being kind, I am being truthful. And I find great pleasure in your grace and elegance, your lovely face—'

'Oh, no, now you are bamming me! I have no pretensions

to anything but the most ordinary looks. You should not tease me so, and I wonder that you do so.' Marina could not decide how she felt at this sudden praise. It was almost as though Justin was about to say 'but…' and crush her with some piece of information. Perhaps he could no longer take her driving.

'I do not tease you, I respect you too much for that. Mari, neither of us is straight from the schoolroom, we have both had a chance to look around, to find that the perfect person for us is not simply going to present themselves.'

So that was it. He had found a lady he loved, was going to propose and wanted to confide in her, his friend, first reassuring her that he admired her in many ways. Only she was not, of course, the one.

'You are about to make a proposal of marriage to someone? I am honoured that you wish to confide in me, Justin. Believe me, I will respect your secret until it is common knowledge.' She was proud of how steady and warm her voice was, while inside a small voice jeered at her. *You fall in love with him one day and the next he is off to some other woman's arms. See how foolish your girlish fantasies were.*

'Yes, I am trying to make a proposal and I very much fear I am making a complete mull of it.'

Trying? Making? Surely he did not mean…?

'Mari. You have my deepest affection and respect—will you do me the honour of being my wife?'

'Me?' It came out as an undignified squeak and she tried again. 'Me? But, Justin, why on earth would you want to marry me?' Now, if this was one of her dreams from yesterday, he should protest his undying love—but she was awake, this was real and he had said nothing about love whatsoever.

'Because it is time I was married and because I think you would make me an excellent wife.' He got up from his cramped position on the footstool and stepped back to lean on the mantelshelf, as though giving her the room to think. 'I promise I would do my best to make you a good husband, Mari.'

'But…' She realised her thoughts were all over the place and paused, biting her lip and staring down at her clasped hands. Looking at Justin made it all seem far too simple, and simple it was not. 'I am the daughter of a mere baron: you are an earl. I have no marriage portion. I am twenty-six years old, and, however kind you are about me, I am far from being an accredited beauty. Society is full of younger, better-looking, more richly dowered ladies.'

'But none I like so well.' He paused, allowing her to digest this. 'Would you dislike it so very much? Without flattering myself, I believe I would be accounted more entertaining than Great-aunt Maria in Bath.'

'That is very true,' she retorted with feeling. 'But then almost anything would be, and to agree to marriage simply to escape from the prospect of tedium seems highly unprincipled.'

'I do not think it was the prospect of tedium that so upset you when you told me about it. I think it was the thought of wasting your life, of seeing your horizons closing in until they were confined to one stuffy house in a spa town when you have the capacity to manage a great household, to be mistress of a great estate.'

'You understand me so well, although I think you flatter me in your opinion of my capacities.' She could not bear to look at him now; it was so hard to do the right thing and to continue to deny him.

'Would you not like to be mistress of Knightshaye? To see your children grow up there?' That brought her head up sharply and she stared at him, the colour mantling her cheeks. *Children. Justin's children…*

'I had not thought of children.' Had given up thinking of them was nearer to the truth.

'I had,' he said with a grin. 'I had thought three, perhaps—although I am open to discussion on the subject. It is a charming place to grow up, but naturally I would retain the town house. Please do not think that I would be the sort of husband who would expect his wife to shut herself away in the country for nine months of the year out of the Season.'

'I am sure you would be an excellent husband,' Marina confessed, fighting desperately with her conscience, which was telling her that it would be outrageous to accept this proposal and that the earl was quite obviously brain-fevered to be contemplating such an alliance.

'And I am convinced you would make an excellent wife, so it appears we are agreed.' Justin came and took both her hands in his, bringing her gently to her feet. 'Say *yes*, Mari.'

The room seemed to be moving around her; she felt dizzy and hot. Marina fought for calm and control. 'Justin, you very honestly make no pretence of love, make no protestations—no…' she freed one hand and placed her fingers over his lips as he opened his mouth '…no, I value your honesty and respect it. But you must tell me, on your honour, is there anyone else who has a claim to your affections?'

The wide hazel gaze was steady on hers. 'On my honour, Mari, I love no other woman, and I have no…liaisons that might cause you grief to know of. I cannot deny that there have been women in my life and I have been no monk, but if you marry me you can be assured of a husband who will be utterly faithful to you in body and mind.'

There was nothing, it seemed, to stop her saying 'yes'. Nothing except the fact that she was in love with him and could not tell him of it. It would embarrass him and he would pity her and that she could not bear. But he genuinely seemed fond of her, or why should the notion to marry her even enter his head? It seemed he must truly want this union. Want her.

'Mari, will you marry me?' he asked again.

She took a deep breath, so deep it made her light headed, and in the moment of dizziness said, 'Yes. Yes, I will marry you, Justin.'

'Thank you. You have made me a very happy man.' She looked up at him, trying to read his feelings in his face, struggling to comprehend that Justin Ransome, Earl of Mortenhoe, wanted to marry her. He bent his head and his lips met hers, very gently.

It was the first time a man had kissed her full on the mouth and Marina found the sudden rush of sensations overwhelming. There was the intimacy of the contact, the warmth of his closeness, the scent of him and then, as his hands came up to her shoulders and he pulled her closer to him, the extraordinary effect the simple meeting of lips was having on her body.

She needed to press herself against him—which, of course, was quite outrageous and had to be resisted; she needed to twine her arms around his neck and pull his head down even closer—so she gripped his coat lapels instead, and wantonly, quite of its own accord, her mouth wanted to open under his. Shockingly Justin seemed to sense this and increased the pressure, subtly nibbling at her lower lip.

Quite how long he had held her, and for how much longer he would have made that shattering kiss last, Marina had no idea. The door opened and let in the sound of her mother speaking loudly to Charlie in the hall. Justin released her and was admiring the portrait of her grandfather over the fireplace by the time Lady Winslow bustled in with a somewhat exaggerated start of surprise at seeing him there.

'My lord! I do beg your pardon for not being here to receive you. I trust Marina has been entertaining you.'

'More than adequately, ma'am.' There was a spark of somewhat cynical amusement in Justin's eyes and Marina cringed inwardly at her mother's obvious stratagems. She must have guessed, or, at least, have been hoping. 'I am honoured to be able to tell you that Miss Winslow has consented to be my wife.'

'Dearest child!' Her mother seized Marina and pressed her to her bosom 'You have made me so happy.' She released her abruptly and went to embrace Justin, kissing him soundly on both cheeks with a cry of, 'I shall be the mother to you that you have so long lacked!'

Marina could only admire Justin's calm acceptance of these raptures. Part of her mind could quite rationally observe her mother and her affianced husband, could realise that Charlie must have known why Justin was there and had called their mother away. She could appreciate how delighted they must be with this alliance and she could feel pleasure that, at long last, she had done the expected thing and made not just a suitable match, but a splendid one beyond their wildest hopes.

But beneath that calm acceptance, the satisfaction of no longer being the disappointment of the family, her mind seemed to flutter like a bird against a window pane: panicking, disorientated, trapped. Had she really agreed to marry a man who did not love her? A man who held high rank, would soon be master of a great estate again and who would expect a wife equally able to support their tenants and organise a society banquet? *I will never be accepted, I will never be able to hide from him how I feel,* she thought. *Is it too late? Can I say it was all a mistake? But I love him so much…*

Then Charlie was in the room, shaking Justin's hand, slapping him on the back, calling for Bunting to fetch the champagne and send for Miss Elizabeth and Master Giles. *It* is *too late*, Marina thought with an almost fatalistic sense of surrender. *And you are glad*, her conscience nagged at her. *You want him too much to give him up, however much you think this is wrong.*

Chapter Eight

'Alone at last.' Justin stretched out long legs and regarded his new countess with pleasure as the carriage rolled away from the church. 'We should make the best of it while we can.' He saw Mari's eyes widen and abandoned his intention to sit next to her and steal kisses all the short way back to Cavendish Square. As their brief engagement had gone on she had seemed more and more reticent, had seemed to retreat into herself further and further. He had expected the opposite; indeed, on those occasions when he had ventured a restrained kiss, or simply taken her hand, he had felt a quiver of response that emboldened him to believe all would be well.

And yet… It was as though Mari too was hiding a secret, just as he pushed to the back of his mind the fact of his arrangement with Winslow. He salved his conscience with the knowledge that he had made her no false declarations and that, given his promise to her brother, was the best he could do.

Had she sensed something? Perhaps it was simply that her mother had been clumsy in talking to her about married life and she was nervous. He could not recall ever having approached an amorous encounter with such a pressing sense of obligation—but then, virgins were unknown territory and hardly one where a gentleman of scruple could practise.

His lips must have quirked at his irreverent musings, for Mari smiled at him. 'A penny for your thoughts.'

'They were most improper,' he admitted, enjoying the charming blush that stained her cheeks.

'Tell me.'

Justin felt his eyebrows rise. His new bride had succeeded in surprising him and he found himself almost lost for words. 'Certainly not—at least not until tonight.'

That made her blush again, but there was a mischievous twinkle in her eyes which reassured him that, whatever else was the matter, it was not that she was frightened of him.

'I have not been able to tell you yet—I think you look beautiful. You took my breath away as you came down the aisle, and I am not sure I have regained it yet.'

'Thank you.' He should have known she would not bridle or protest, but take his compliment as he had meant it, sincerely. The cream silk and lace of her gown, the intricacy of her veil, the chaste sheen of the pearls at her ears and throat, all served to flatter her elegant, understated looks. The colour that had come and gone in her cheeks, leaving her one moment pale, the next delicately flushed, fascinated him. The twinkle returned to her eyes. 'I think you look very nice too.'

'That is a good start to married life,' he conceded gravely. 'What else can we agree upon? I felt the ceremony went well.'

'Yes.' She nodded emphatically. 'But not everyone approves, you know—I could see their faces.'

Justin felt a surge of protective anger. 'That is ridiculous. Who is there with any right to approve or disapprove?'

'Your friends might well feel you could have done better

for yourself—and numerous young ladies are doubtless nursing envy in their bosoms,' she added, as though to lighten the comment, although her expression remained grave.

'I think I have done excellently well in my choice, and it is news to me if I have left a litter of broken hearts behind me.' He watched the glimmer of humour come back and added, 'Do you mind very much that we are going straight down to Knightshaye today, even though the staff only left London this morning?'

'Not at all. I think they will all be excellent at their work, and, even if everything is not perfect immediately, I do not mind that if you do not. Although why on earth Charlie could not finalise things with you before today I cannot imagine.'

Justin could only be thankful she could not. He certainly had no wish to explain to her that her brother had stubbornly insisted on retaining the keys up to the very wedding morning, despite his protestations that *of course* he trusted Justin to go through with the agreement.

'Legal problems,' Justin improvised. 'Your late father left various conditions that have proved onerous to resolve.'

Marina's forehead wrinkled into a frown. 'How very odd of him.' Justin shrugged, making light of it and conscious of relief that his wife appeared to know nothing at all of their families' history. 'Oh, look—' she glanced out of the window and began to straighten her veil '—we are here.'

Half an hour later, descending the staircase with her veil removed and her hair tidied, Marina realised that she was smiling with pure happiness. The doubts had gone, the stresses and worries of the preparations had vanished, Justin seemed content and in no mood to regret his proposal and she had burned her bridges. There was no going back now, and suddenly that was no longer a terrifying thought.

Her new husband was waiting for her at the foot of the stairs and they went to take up their positions to greet the guests arriving for the wedding breakfast. Lady Winslow had bemoaned their decision to leave immediately afterwards for Hertfordshire and even Charlie had made various quite pressing suggestions for honeymoon trips. But Marina knew how anxious Justin was to see his old home again; although she would have preferred to spend the night in London first, she wholeheartedly agreed with his suggestion.

The arrivals passed in a blur before her, many of them old friends and acquaintances, others she knew by sight and then there were some new faces. There were the three elderly gentlemen who had served so faithfully as Justin's guardians, all frail now, but touchingly pleased to kiss the bride and congratulate 'their boy' on his choice. There was even the recently wed Marquis of Andover with, fragile on his arm, his extremely beautiful marchioness. Marina recognised the exquisite blonde as one of the disapproving faces in the congregation.

She managed to virtually ignore Marina, instead kissing Justin on the cheek with a cry of 'Justin, darling, how very *sudden* of you!' before vanishing into the throng that was filling the downstairs reception rooms. It would be a tight fit, despite Mama throwing open all the double doors, Marina thought, attempting to distract herself from the marchioness's snub.

Then they were going in to eat and Marina found herself seated next to Justin in the centre of the long board, all eyes upon her. The meal passed somehow. She supposed she must have eaten what was put in front of her, smiled and responded appropriately to the toasts and compliments, but all she was fully aware of was Justin's presence at her side, of the way he found every excuse to brush her hand with his, touch her arm, murmur in her ear. Her heart began to race and a strange, quivering sense of anticipation possessed her.

Pris's face swam into focus. Mari saw the encouraging smile directed at her and smiled back. The day before she had shut herself up in her friend's bedchamber and demanded to know exactly what it was her mama was skirting round in her hasty, embarrassed references to *married life* and *the, er…night*. Pris, with her usual lack of inhibition, had cheerfully enlightened her, ending up by saying, 'It is a trifle *odd* and just a *leetle* bit painful the first time, but one soon becomes accustomed and really, although a lady is not supposed to admit this, it is quite delightful when one knows what one is about.'

'But I feel so strange inside,' she had confessed. 'All sort of churned up and tense.'

'Desire,' Priscilla had diagnosed immediately. 'And I am not the slightest bit surprised, Lord Mortenhoe is a particularly attractive man. You *are* going to have fun,' she had added wickedly.

Then the meal was over, the last toasts drunk. Justin had calculated that they could spend a further hour circulating amongst their guests and making their farewells before they must leave and she let him take her arm to begin to do just that, only to find herself steered neatly through a door and into Charlie's deserted study.

'Justin?' she managed to begin before his arms came round her, his mouth claimed hers and she found herself deep in her first married kiss. Gone was the polite reticence with which he had held her and lightly kissed her before. Now she was moulded against his body, arched against his arm, her head thrown back in total abandonment as his mouth plundered hers.

Her lips parted under his, her gasp as his tongue invaded and flicked against hers was lost until he began to trail kisses down her throat, across the swell of her bosom. Then she was gasping again with desire, the need to be closer to him, to tangle her hands in his hair, to press herself against a lean, hard body that—even with her inexperience—she realised was thoroughly aroused.

He wants me, he desires me. The words were a cry of triumph in her mind and she almost sobbed in protest as he raised his head and loosened his hold.

'I have been wanting to do that for six weeks,' he said huskily. 'Wanting to be sure you would respond to me as you just have. I am beginning to wish I had not settled on travelling this afternoon—shall we go back to the town house instead?'

'It is tempting.' Marina could scarcely believe she was having this conversation, feeling like this. 'But…'

'But, we have a household of servants waiting for us, I know,' he agreed ruefully. 'I had better go and find where my old guardians have got to, prise them away from whichever ladies they are flirting with and pack them off in their carriages before they become overtired. Lord Beechcombe is eighty-seven, not that he'll admit it.'

'I will be out in a moment,' Marina took a startled look at her reflection in the mirror, 'Just as soon as I have pinned up my hair. You have done quite dreadful things to it.'

With an unrepentant chuckle Justin went out and she heard his voice come back from the hall. 'She's in your study, fixing her hair.'

'There you are.' It was Charlie, his voice a little slurred, his face flushed, his grin broad, a glass in his hand.

'Charlie, darling, you are drunk!'

'Only half-seas over—got to drink to my sister's marriage. Ain't I a good brother to you?'

'Yes, you are.' Marina went and gave him a hug. 'This had been a lovely wedding breakfast.'

'Not what I meant.' He staggered a trifle as she let him go and Marina realised he must have been drinking brandy bumpers along with the champagne. 'Ain't I a good brother for finding you such a good husband?' He slumped into a chair and beamed at her owlishly.

'I think Justin found me,' she corrected him fondly. 'Although it was a wonderful chance that you decided to sell him Knightshaye, otherwise we would probably never have met.'

'Brilliant scheme of mine.'

Marina wondered if she ought to call Bunting and ask him for strong coffee, or whatever sovereign remedy for intoxication he swore by. 'I know, Charlie, darling—Mama and Lizzie and Giles will be quite secure now.'

But her brother was not listening to her. 'Brilliant,' he congratulated himself smugly. 'Thousands for the house and a wife into the bargain—or no bargain at all. My best wheeze ever.'

In the silence Marina stared at him. The room was suddenly quiet except for the sound of her swallowing hard against the lump in her throat. 'You mean you made marrying me a condition of Justin buying Knightshaye?'

'Tha's right.' Charlie hiccupped faintly. 'He didn't want to do it, mind, but I insisted. Wanted an earl for my sister, and an earl I got her.'

'I don't believe you,' Marina whispered, her fingers tight on the back of the chair in front of her. But she did. It explained everything: Mama's complaisance at her driving so frequently with Justin, her casual chaperonage, the lack of surprise she and Charlie had shown when he proposed. The very fact of that proposal at all.

'I trusted him.' The only response was a light snore; Charlie was dozing. *I trusted him*. That was the reason that she had agreed to marry Justin, the quality she valued most of all in him, and that was a sham. He had married her simply to get his hands on a house. And she was tied to him now, quite irretrievably. Tied to a man she could not trust, and still in love with him—that was the bitterest thing of all.

There was nothing she could do now, say now—not with a houseful of guests. Marina stared into the mirror, gave her white cheeks a vicious pinch until the colour came back and, leaving her brother snoring gently, stepped out into the hall again.

She edged into the main reception room, looking for Justin, trying to keep her expression pleasant and not to let the thought of the long journey ahead with him dominate her mind, not yet. There he was, talking to Lady Andover.

As Marina watched him, she began to sense something unsettling in their closeness. The other woman could not, it seemed, keep her hands off him. Long white fingers rested on his sleeve, stroking as she stood close, looking up into his face and talking earnestly and Justin's face as he looked down into hers was intent, his expression intimate.

'Dratted creature.' Marina jumped as Pris's voice, lowered into a hissing whisper, came clearly to her, echoing her thoughts uncannily. She glanced round and realised that her friend must be just the other side of the half-open door and talking to someone else.

'She is hardly discreet.' The other whisper was Jane Harbottle, a mutual friend. 'Does Marina know about her?'

'Well, *I* haven't told her, and I do not think it was widely known; after all, it all took place down in Brighton, there was no engagement announced and then, days after she got back to London, there was the announcement of her betrothal to Andover. I only know about it because Mr Harding was down there, waiting upon the Prince Regent. She had been sent to the seaside because of some measles scare in the family.

Goodness knows why Mortenhoe was there out of season—but he fell head over heels, apparently.'

'Much as I dislike her, one can see why,' Jane whispered back. 'I had heard rumours that he was heartbroken.'

'Apparently so. And look at his face now, that tender sort of concern as he looks at her. Why cannot they be more careful, here of all places? I wouldn't have Marina find out about this for the world.'

Marina backed slowly out into the hall again, her eyes fixed on the two figures, so intimately close and self-absorbed on the other side of the room.

Phrases came back to her with utter clarity. Her own words, questioning: *But you must tell me, on your honour, is there anyone else who has a claim to your affections?'*

Justin's open, honest expression as he reassured her was vivid in her mind. *'On my honour, Mari, I love no other woman, and I have no...liaisons that might cause you grief to know of.'*

It seemed there was nothing she could trust in what he had told her. The rock she had thought her marriage was built on was shifting sand.

By an effort of will Marina made herself enter the room again, a smile firmly on her lips. Justin and Lady Andover were exchanging farewells, with nothing to betray the slightest intimacy, unless, with the light of knowledge, one looked at the yearning in her wide blue eyes and the set of his expressive mouth.

Across the room Justin saw her and his expression changed to one of pleasure. *How easily he deceives*, Marina thought bitterly, then caught a glimpse of her own reflection and saw that she could act just as well.

Lady Winslow appeared to urge her upstairs to change, Charlie blinking owlishly at her shoulder. As they passed at the foot of the stairs Marina caught his arm. 'Charlie, about what you said to me in the study—'

'Were you in the study?' He frowned. 'Afraid I dropped off—had a bit too much to drink, if the truth be told.'

So he did not recall what he had confessed to her. Marina let go of his arm and followed her mother upstairs; there was no point interrogating him. At heart she knew he had told her the truth.

Apparently Mama expected a new bride to be pale and silent and made no comment on her abstraction as she supervised her change of gown and the setting of an elegant hat on her curls. Marina smiled at her maid and wished she had insisted on the girl accompanying them in their carriage instead of agreeing with Justin's provision of a second coach for Jenny and his valet.

Their guests seemed to find nothing amiss with her looks and spirits either; indeed, by the time she reached the front step, she had run such a gauntlet of kisses and hugs that her cheeks were as flushed as anyone could hope for.

Pris gave her one last embrace before she got into the carriage. 'Write to me, tell me absolutely everything you dare!'

'Pris…' Marina held her friend close and looked into her eyes. 'Pris, have I done the right thing?' There it was, the flicker of deceit behind the candid blue gaze. Loving deceit, but deceit none the less.

'Of course you have, darling!' Far too vivacious, even for Pris. 'Why, whatever is the matter? Have you heard something?'

'Nothing, pay me no heed. It is just nerves.' With a last kiss Marina let herself be helped into the carriage. The door shut, the wheels began to turn and, as she looked back towards the house, she saw Jane Harbottle at Pris's side, whispering urgently. They both looked at the carriage and she saw her friend shake her head doubtfully. *Oh, Pris, why could you not tell me the truth? Why does everyone think they know what is best for me?'*

'Now we really are alone, Lady Mortenhoe.' Justin was regarding her with a warmth that sent tremors through her, tremors that made sense with the benefit of Pris's frank explanations. Marina felt herself colouring up and dropped her eyes, unwilling to meet his.

She felt so betrayed, such a fool. And yet, despite that, she loved him still—desired him, if she were to be utterly frank with herself. Perhaps, if she gave him the chance, he would be frank with her at last, even this late. She had to try.

'It was such a pleasure to meet so many of your friends today, however briefly.' She fussed a little with shawl and reticule, spreading her things over the squabs on either side of her so that he would have to move them if he tried to sit next to her. She wanted to watch his face. 'I am sure, though, that they were all wondering what you were about, marrying me.'

'Fishing for compliments?' Justin teased, very relaxed. 'They all saw exactly why I married you—your charm, your style, your character, your beauty.'

'I still find it very strange,' she persisted. 'Perhaps it is just the coincidence.'

'What coincidence?' His brows drew together in a shadow of a frown.

'That you should be doing business with Charlie over the house and just happen to find someone you felt would suit you as a wife. I imagine that if someone told you that, as you knocked on our front door that first time, you would have laughed at their fancy.'

Now, that had touched him. She saw the shadow of it in his eyes. It cooled the green, amorous glint back to watchful hazel. 'No,' he said slowly, 'no, I did not imagine I would find a wife at the same time as I regained Knightshaye.'

Marina laughed. It was a touch brittle to be sure, but she kept her eyes wide and innocent on Justin's face, concealing her knowledge, hiding the rising anger. 'If I were to be very romantic, very foolish, I might think that it was destined: that somehow I went with the house, that some fate linked us both when my father won it from yours all those years ago.'

Chapter Nine

⁓⁓⁓

Somehow Justin kept still, kept his face under control. It was as though Mari knew exactly where the soreness in his heart and conscience was and was touching it, rubbing it raw, rousing the pain. She was more right than she knew, for the thread that the Fates had spun to link them went even further back, before the loss of Knightshaye.

Keeping the truth about his courtship of her secret had not become any easier with time. He salved his conscience as best he might by making no protestations of love, telling her only what was strictly true about his feelings and his circumstances. There was another thing he had omitted, of course, but he preferred not to dwell on it himself; besides, his feelings for Serena now were no threat to his marriage.

Mari did not seem to require an answer to her flight of fancy, instead pouncing with unerring aim on his other vulnerable spot.

'How very beautiful the Marchioness of Andover is. I do not think I have ever seen a lovelier face.'

Justin made himself answer indifferently. 'Indeed, I believe she was generally reckoned to be the most beautiful of all the young ladies making their come-out in the past year or so.'

'I am sure she must have gratified her mama greatly by making such an advantageous match. Do you think she married for love?'

He shrugged. Could Serena feel love for anyone other than herself? 'Unlikely, I think. It was very sudden.'

'But why not? Love at first sight, perhaps. Do you know them well, the Andovers?'

'Not for any length of time.' That was true. How long does it take to meet, to lose your heart, to have it broken and to realise, in the clear light of day, that you had fallen for nothing but a perfect face and a needy, selfish mind?

Mari widened her lovely grey eyes at him. 'I just thought she seemed very, oh, I do not know—very *attached* to you. I thought, if she is an old friend, I must make every effort to get to know her better.'

'No.' She seemed taken aback at his curt response. 'I mean, I hardly know her. I think she must be the sort of woman who likes to make an affectation of closeness, of knowing people.' And yet he could not help but feel pity for her, poor little wretch. She thought money and a fine title would buy happiness, and it seemed she was already finding they were hollow.

'Oh, I see.' Was it his imagination or had Mari withdrawn suddenly into herself? It was as though a shutter had come down. No, that was too hard, too abrupt a simile. She had drawn a curtain closed, so gently that, if he had not been watching her intently, he might never have noticed.

'Are you sad at leaving home?' he asked, wondering if that was behind her withdrawal. 'I should not have asked you to make this journey this afternoon, so suddenly to move from London and all that is familiar to you to a house you do not know.'

For a moment he thought his gentleness would upset her

brave assumption of poise, but he had failed to read her mood yet again. Mari blinked, bit her lip and seemed to straighten before his eyes. 'Not at all. I look forward to it. I have never lived in the country and there will be so much to learn—and much to do, which I always enjoy.'

'Of course.' He smiled at her. 'You like to feel needed, I remember.'

Now what the devil had he said? The moisture welled in her eyes and two fat teardrops rolled slowly down her cheeks. Appalled, he reached out to her, but she waved him away sharply, delving into her reticule with her other hand to find her handkerchief. 'How foolish! People told me I would be a mass of sensibility on my wedding day and I thought they were exaggerating. It is nothing, I promise you.'

Disconcerted, Justin sat back in his seat, trying to fathom what was upsetting her. Or perhaps it was as she said, and it was simply that her sensibilities were heightened by the emotions of the day. It was not just Mari's sensibilities either, he realised as a heavy feeling of desire settled low in him. The sudden waft of her fragrance as she gestured, the sight of her slender hand so tightly clothed in the fragile kid, conjured imaginings of her naked body, freed from the tyranny of stays and laces, fragrant under his caress.

Hastily Justin crossed his legs and leant forward to lower the window an inch. 'Do you mind? I think it is a little stuffy.' Despite the passion of her response to him in the study he had no intention of pouncing on her here, in the carriage. It was too important not to frighten her.

He only hoped her mother had not alarmed her with some nonsense about the wedding night. It did happen; he could recall all too clearly a very drunken confidence from a close friend who had spent a nightmare honeymoon with a near-hysterical bride—the result of her fond mama's instructions.

'No, please do. I am sure I have drunk far too much champagne.' Her eyes were dry again, but somehow those expressive silvery depths were no longer easy to read.

There was silence as they sat, each lost in their own preoccupations, then Mari spoke. 'Tell me about Knightshaye. What do you remember? Is it very hard to recall after twenty years?'

'No. Not hard to remember.' But hard to speak of it, to describe something he had spoken of to no one since he was a child, to make his memories real for someone else. Hard not to let go of his feelings, forget the attention and care he needed to focus on her, in the joy of achieving his dream.

'But you do not wish to speak of it. I am sorry, I will not pry—and besides, I will see it myself soon enough.' Her hands were locked tight on her reticule, and he saw that she was fighting her own battle to stay calm by thinking about him and his feelings. How very like Mari.

'It is your home now,' Justin said simply. 'Let me try to conjure it for you.' He closed his eyes and let the memories wash over him as he had never dared to do since he had reached his teens.

'It is an old house, rambling and, many people would say, ill planned. Generations have added to it, knocked parts down, redesigned or simply tinkered. At the heart is a Tudor stone house, but the west front is from the reign of George I. My great-grandfather built a wing for a ballroom and his son knocked one end of it down to build a turret. Goodness knows why, although it was one of my favourite places. How can a small boy be a knight in armour without a turret to defend?

'My father built the stable block, in dressed flint, very fashionable at the time. And there is a moat—all that is left of the medieval house except for the dovecote. My mother kept white doves and they would circle over the rose garden like a snow shower. The area inside the moat is gardens: rose garden, maze, formal parterre, sloping lawns—my mother's pride and joy. Beyond it the park with deer and the beech woods where I would ride my pony, where my father taught me to shoot.

'I have missed the woods. The beech trees are old and tall with smooth trunks, green with lichens. At the feet the golden brown leaves drift deep into every hollow and the woods are full of birds and deer.

'And inside the house, a maze of rooms large and small. I do not think anyone ever threw anything away. It was polished and cared for until the wood glowed. The walls were hung with tapestries, the windows draped with everything from rich brocades to the filmiest of muslins. When I close my eyes now I can smell the beeswax, the wood smoke and the scent of *pot pourri* from the rose garden. And everywhere there is the rustle of fabrics, the creak of old wood, the chiming of clocks, muffled in distant rooms.'

Silence, then Mari said softly, 'Your mother created a beautiful home.'

'They both did. I have never seen a love match like it since. It was their kingdom and I was part of it. And there was always laughter.'

This was the truth, this was real feeling, real emotion. Marina watched Justin's face opposite her, his eyes shut, his expression peaceful. Even the betraying mouth was still, the mobile lips relaxed. He was so handsome, so male, so desirable and, for the first time since her world had fallen about her at the breakfast, he was telling her something she could believe.

She clung to it as if to a lifeline. If she asked a question, would he answer her, or would the fragile thread of honesty snap? 'Why, then? If they loved it so much, why did your father risk it at play?'

His eyes opened, narrowed, focused, dangerously green. 'Because it was the lesser of two evils.'

'Because he was a gamester?'

'He had no love for card play. Like all gentleman he was an adequate player, but that was all.'

'Not like my father, then?' Now she had started, there appeared to be no going back. It seemed this loss of the house, the estate, was not as she had imagined, the careless gesture of a hardened gamester who threw away something his own son held dear in the heat of play.

'No. Not like your father.' That was said with the flatness that showed either deep indifference, or the deepest hate. 'The late Lord Winslow was able to compel my father to game with him, to pledge the possession he held most dear. And, knowing his skill, he must have been assured of winning.' She opened her mouth to ask the only question left and he forestalled her with a shake of his head. 'No, I cannot tell you why. Do not ask.'

Marina shivered, despite the warmth. She had married not just a man with secrets, but into a subtle web of deceit and concealment. 'I wonder, then, that you should choose to marry his daughter.' It was a lie—she knew the reason all too well. Charlie, as ignorant of this history as she, it seemed, had put Justin in the position of having to not only buy back his heritage, his memories, his home, but had shackled him to the daughter of his bitterest enemy in the process.

Was it any wonder he had not told her? Marina gazed out unseeing at the green hills that were beginning to rise against the skyline. She could understand why he had not, even if it still hurt. Could she trust him, forgive him? The question circled in her brain. Caution told her not to relax her guard, let him any further into her heart than he had already lodged. *But you love him*, the wounded, yearning part of her pleaded. *And he loves the marchioness*, the cold, realistic part argued. *Is he going to be honest about that?*

'Mari?'

'What?' She jerked back to full attention to find Justin looking at her steadily. The dangerous light in his eyes had gone.

'You asked me how I could marry you under those circumstances. Do you really believe I could blame you—or Charles, come to that—for your father's actions?'

'Many men would. Most, perhaps.'

'Then I am not like most men. Hate is a difficult emotion to live with, Mari. I have learned not to let the way I feel for a man, dead and beyond my reach, rule my life. I was fortunate: I could look forward to regaining Knightshaye, not back, regretting the past. He is gone, you are here and both innocent and ignorant of this old history. I should not have told you.'

'I asked,' she said steadily. 'All I want is for you to tell me the truth, Justin, and, if you cannot, then to say so.' Oh, but he was good at concealment. Maturity had taught him how to hide the flare of consciousness in those betraying eyes and experience had given him the skills to school the flexible lips. Watching closely, she saw the flicker of his long lashes, the momentary crease at the corner of his mouth, then his face was as open and honest as any woman could wish for in her bridegroom.

I will tell him that I know, she decided, something sharper than anger clearing the morass of emotions that clouded her mind. *Tell him what Charlie said, tell him I know about the marchioness. I cannot go to his bed with that between us. We have to face it, and if it breaks this marriage now, before it is begun, then so be it.*

Marina opened her mouth to speak, but Justin's attention was no longer on her, but instead on the passing farmland. 'We are here. This is Knightshaye land.'

'The Home Farm?'

'No, tenanted land. It looks well enough. Not in brilliant heart, but well enough.'

'I suppose an absentee landlord can never achieve the same results,' Marina observed. Now was not the time for confrontation. She needed all Justin's attention for that. Later.

'No,' he agreed absently. 'But this should be Home Farm land now, surely? I don't recall a copse here.' On either side of the road the trees grew high and spindly, their bases clogged with blackberry and bracken.

'But it isn't a copse, I can see through to some rough grazing behind,' Marina said helpfully. After all this time it was no wonder he was confused.

'Rough grazing! That was prime pasture and these were laid hedges—what the hell is going on?' Justin was turned in his seat now, craning to see out of the window as the scrubby trees gave way to a high wall of pale stone and brick. 'This is the park wall—look at it.'

He hardly needed to draw her attention. The coping stones were missing over several feet of it at a stretch. Sections bulged ominously and scrub and rushes choked what must have been a ditch between road and wall-foot.

Justin, his face set, reached for the pull-string, but before he could tug it the carriage came to a halt and the footman swung down. 'My lord, is this right? Only…' His voice trailed off as Justin threw open the door and jumped into the road without waiting for the steps to be let down.

Marina leaned forward. They had reached a gateway, flanked by two lodges, once picturesque with thatch and split-flint work. Now the windows were broken, a sapling thrust through one roof and the gardens were overgrown and tangled. On a gnarled apple tree hung the withered remains of last year's crop and between the lodges rusting iron gates had been dragged open. It looked like the entrance to a witch's kingdom—dank, frightening, brooding. She shuddered.

'That is it,' Justin said harshly. 'Drive in.' He swung himself back into the carriage, slamming the door before the startled footman could move. The vehicle jerked forward, through the gates and into the park.

On either side of the carriage stretched rank grassland, patched here and there with scrub. Marina stared until a long hiss of indrawn breath drew her back to Justin's face.

He was white, staring intently out of the carriage window. Marina opened her mouth, then shut it without speaking. Whatever was wrong here, asking questions was not going to help.

The sound of the carriage wheels changed and the vehicle swayed as it passed over a bridge. She craned to see the river, but saw only a stretch of stagnant, weed-choked water. The moat. Her wince of distaste turned to one of horror—this was the beautiful park Justin had spoken of with such love in his voice.

The carriage turned and she saw the house across what must once have been gardens, late afternoon sun came out from behind a cloud, bathing the old stone and brick in a cruel wash of light, exposing every dull and cracked pane of glass, every sagging gutter, every leaf of the cloaking ivy.

This was what a childhood memory of beauty and peace and love had become, a neglected wasteland. Marina swallowed hard against the welling tears of pity for the small boy whose dream had been despoiled, desperate hurt for the man who had come home, after so many years of striving—to this.

And then he turned to face her and the pity and hurt turned

chill with fear. Hard, cold green eyes looked at her as they had never looked before, glowing with fiercely controlled rage in the face of a stranger.

'It seems that one cannot underestimate the power of hatred,' was all he said as the footman threw open the carriage door and let down the steps.

She could not let him go without one word, one desperate attempt at apology. Marina reached out and seized Justin's arm. 'I had no idea…Justin, I am so sorry…'

'Of course you had no idea.' His voice was perfectly steady. He might have been discussing some minor domestic mishap with the china. 'You were merely a pawn on this particular chessboard.'

He gave her his hand to climb down and then walked with her towards the front door, its heavy panels peeling, the great knocker rusted.

Marina stumbled and was caught firmly under the elbow by a rock-steady hand. A pawn, he called her—the first reference he had made to the arrangement that had led to their marriage.

What a price he had paid! Goodness knows how much money and a wife he did not love, nor, after this, could possibly want. And in return he had the desecrated shell of all his precious memories.

The door creaked open as they approached it, forced wide with a vicious shove by Hearnshaw, their new butler. A young man for such a big house, his lack of experience showed itself in his expression as he greeted his employers.

'My lord, my lady…we sent word as soon as we realised how bad things were, but—'

'It did not reach us. No matter.' Still that utter calm, that indifferent tone. But the butler was no more deceived than Marina. He stepped back hastily into the house, retreating in the face of the adamantine eyes that raked the hallway.

'Is there a room habitable for her ladyship? And can something be cooked, water heated?'

'Yes, my lord. Those were our priorities. I managed to get a sweep—'

'Good. Show her ladyship what arrangements you have made.' Without another word he walked slowly towards the double doors facing him, pushed them open with both hands and vanished into the gloom within.

Marina stood there, trying to control the tremors running through her body. And she had asked herself how *she* could ever forgive *him!* It was a miracle he had not turned and repudiated her on the steps of this house. Most men would have done so—after all, what was she but the chattel of first her father, then her brother? Their pawn to barter as they wished, their symbol. Her father had done this out of hatred for God knows what past quarrel. Her brother had done it out of desire for money and an indolent desire to avoid effort or confrontation.

Charlie might never had visited Knightshaye, but he must have known well enough what to expect. No wonder he had pressed them to take an extended honeymoon—anything to put off the evil hour of discovery.

Long-practised discipline took over and somehow saved her from sinking, weeping, on to the dirty marble floor.

'You seem to have done very well, Hearnshaw. What about rooms for yourself and the staff? Have you managed to find something comfortable?' It was one's duty to ensure the servants were properly housed and fed. Until her new husband recalled her presence and doubtless sent her back in the coach to her family, she had a household to manage.

'Oh, yes, my lady. Most of the attics leak, but we found a second-floor range of rooms in the back wing that are sound.'

'Very well. You had better show me the kitchens.' Concentrate on one's duty, that was the only way to cope.

Chapter Ten

The murmur of voices behind him and the sound of retreating footsteps did not reach Justin. He stood in the centre of the once-gracious room surrounded by dusty, mouse-bitten furniture, his feet on a water-marked Aubusson rug. His eyes stared at the huge stain in the ceiling marking where rain had poured through, but he did not see that either.

His eyes saw only sparkling crystal, polished furniture, the gracious sheen of silk. The sounds he heard were laughter: the shared amusement of a middle-aged couple, comfortably in love with each other and with life, the happy shrieks of a small boy chasing his dog through the great hall. He blinked and the vision blurred and gave way to reality.

Justin turned where he stood, taking in the room, absorbing the damage as he might have withstood blows from an opponent in the boxing salon, refusing to show either the impact or the pain. If he did not give way to it, if he did not let it show, perhaps it would not become real and he would not rage and weep as the voices from the past clamoured for him to do.

Don't cry, Mother, I'll get it back... What do I need to learn to give me the knowledge to make money? A great deal of money... No, I know you are my guardians, I know I'm only seventeen, but let me talk to the bankers, to the lawyers...I have to learn... I'll buy this...I'll sell that...I'll build here... It's an investment...an investment...money in the bank for Knightshaye.

A wall hanging had slipped from its fastenings, slumping in lush folds across some obstruction that had prevented it reaching the floor.

Justin strode to it, his feelings released in a rush of energy. With an impatient hand he swept the tapestry aside, revealing an ornate mirror. Its glass had been protected for years by the fabric and reflected back to him his own face with deadly clarity.

He stared, appalled at the harsh features. He had seen that face once before: it was his father's face after he had lost Knightshaye. He seemed to have shed weight since he had shaved that morning, a hundred years ago. His jaw was set, his skin pale across tightly covered cheekbones and his eyes, under the straight slash of dark brows, were a vivid, pure, green. His dangerous look, Mari would say.

He spun on his heel away from the image of that viciously angry stranger. Mari. Had she seen that look on his face? She must be terrified. Terrified of what he might say, of what he might do.

She knew her father and brother were responsible for this—how was she to know what vengeance he might choose to wreck on her? Many husbands would not hesitate to take out their displeasure on their wives' soft skin; they were their lords and masters, after all. Thank God she was ignorant of the reason he had courted her and had married her.

He shuddered and, turning his back on the room, went to find her.

* * *

She was speaking quietly to the butler. What was his name? Hearnshaw, that was it. Calmly, confidently, as though nothing untoward had occurred, as though this chaos could be sorted out by a little dusting and the rearrangement of the furniture.

And already the man was reassured, his own authority over the handful of lower staff reasserted.

Mari gave Hearnshaw an encouraging smile and a nod as though to say, *I have every confidence in you.*

Then she looked up and saw him and the colour drained from her cheeks. Yet all she said was, 'I have asked for dinner to be served to you at eight, if that is not too late, my lord?'

'That will be perfectly acceptable,' he responded automatically, before the precise words she had used penetrated,

'A word, my lady. Are the bedchambers ready?'

'Yes, Hearnshaw has told me which ones have been made up, although I am not sure they are the chambers you would wish to occupy in the long term. Shall we go and see?' She paused as he stood aside to allow her to ascend the stairs before him. 'These spermaceti lamps you had sent down are a great boon, my lord.' She glanced back and saw the butler had disappeared. 'I told him to stay with the other staff and to concentrate on your dinner.'

'Why do you keep referring to *my* dinner? Have you no appetite?' he demanded, catching her arm. Mari stopped immediately, just where she was, on the curve of the half-landing. In the face of his question her gaze dropped, the long dark lashes feathering her cheeks.

'I thought you would want to send me back to London, or at least to the nearest inn.' She drew in a deep breath, which seemed to come from her very toes. 'We have been married today, but it does not mean that the situation is irretrievable.

If I do not stay here tonight, you will be able to have the marriage annulled.'

'*What?*' He did not realise that he had raised his voice to her until he saw her flinch; just the merest recoil, the widening of her eyes. She was expecting his anger, his vengeance, and was braced for them. 'I am sorry, I did not mean to shout at you. No, I do not want you to go back to London, or to an inn, or to be anywhere but here, with me.' He put out a hand and touched her arm. Under his palm she quivered. 'Shh, Mari. Come here.'

Gathered into his arms she stiffened, then relaxed so suddenly that for a moment he thought she had swooned. Against his body she felt warm, sweetly feminine, tranquil. Somehow she had regained her calm and with it the ability to calm him. He clung to her, feeling the bitter anger drain away as surely as if she had been a lightning conductor earthing his distress.

Justin made no attempt to kiss her or to caress the supple body pressed so close to his. Instead he buried his face in the fragrant mass of her hair and let peace fill him. 'Sweetheart, you are so good for me,' he murmured at last.

She tipped up her face at that, a smile touching the corner of her mouth. It seemed a little wry to him, but her voice was soft. 'I hope to be. If you will let me.'

Marina let herself be held for a long moment, then stepped back out of Justin's arms. It felt lonely outside his embrace, but she welcomed the feeling, using it to stiffen her resolution. Almost, she had let her guard down, blurted out her feelings for him, let him glimpse her hurt.

'Really, my lord, it would never do to let the servants see us embracing,' she chided in a rallying tone, as she turned to climb to the landing.

'Indeed? You think they might be shocked?' Justin fell in beside her, but did not attempt to take her arm.

'But of course—it is considered most unfashionable for married couples to do more than exchange the most distant of pleasantries in public.'

Her new husband snorted inelegantly. 'Then I shall have to give up all claim to modish behaviour, madam. I have no intention of being a distant husband.'

Oh. Marina shot him a guarded look from under her lashes. She had not intended to lead the conversation down such dangerous pathways, simply to hide her own embarrassment under a light-hearted quip.

'No, the rooms are further down…' she began, but Justin had stopped outside a panelled door and stood, one hand on the handle, as if in thought.

'This is the master suite.' He pushed the door open, staying on the threshold as it swung back to reveal a large chamber with an ancient four-poster bed draped in dark blue silk shot with silver. For a second Marina thought it was untouched, then she saw it was an illusion. The silk was rotten and shredded, the carpet filthy with bird droppings, a window pane broken in, soot stained the hearth, dust was everywhere.

'Your father's chamber?'

'My parents would have none of the fashionable nonsense about separate rooms. This was their chamber.' Justin's tone was light, but, after one glance at his face, Marina averted her gaze, feeling like an intruder. Justin reached inside, pulled the key from the lock and pulling the door to, turned it, slipping the key into his pocket. 'Well, where are we sleeping?'

'Here.' She hurried down the unfamiliar corridor, hesitated, then with more confidence, pushed open a door. 'I thought I might have this one—there are some suitable clothes presses in the dressing room. Then this one…' she opened a connecting door '…this seemed to have a more masculine feel to it.' Justin did not respond. 'Is that all right?'

'My dear, of course.' He hardly gave the room a glance. 'Wherever you like, so long as you are comfortable.'

Marina was saved from nervously reciting her worries about whether the rooms were suitable by the sound of footsteps on the landing and the arrival of Hearnshaw bringing Jenny, her maid, and Shepton, Justin's valet. This was better. She could cope with the servants.

'Here you are, after a safe journey, I hope! I am sure Hearnshaw has been looking after you and has told you which rooms you are to have. We are rather at sixes and sevens just now, but all will soon be to rights again. Shepton, his lordship's chamber is through there. Jenny, please unpack for me and put out the blue silk for this evening. I will come back shortly and see how you get on.'

'You are good with the servants,' Justin remarked as they made their way downstairs again. 'Hearnshaw was on the brink of going to pieces over this mess, but you have steadied him.'

'All I did was to listen and assure him he could manage very well. He is inexperienced. It is only lack of confidence.' Marina peeped into one reception room after another, careful not to wince or exclaim at the state of them.

'And you are confident you can deal with this house and the chaos here?' Justin asked bluntly.

Marina turned, inexplicably irritated by the question. 'As you wish me to stay, then I can and I must deal with it,' she said coolly. 'It is my duty.'

'Not because it was your father who let it come to this—?' Justin began.

'No.' Marina held his gaze haughtily for a moment, then turned away. 'Because I am your wife.'

She thought she heard a murmured *'Ouch'* from behind her, but swept on towards the door to the servants' quarters.

She was hungry, tired, upset, daunted and not a little frightened and, if she gave way for a moment, she was going to burst into tears.

'Are you not coming?' she demanded as she pushed open the green baize barrier. 'You should know what conditions your staff are working in, my lord.'

Justin came and held the edge of the door, high up. It brought him close, trapping her against the edge. For a moment she thought he was displeased with her abrupt tone, then she saw the smile in his eyes. 'Stiffening your backbone, Lady Mortenhoe?'

'Yes,' she admitted, catching her lower lip between her teeth for a moment to control the surge of emotion his sympathy provoked. 'It will all seem better in the morning.'

'Will it?' Justin's tone was rueful. 'Never mind, I am sure we will feel better in ourselves in the morning.'

With Pris's frank explanations ringing in her head, Marina was not at all sure that would be the case, but there was no time to brood upon that now. Here was Cook to be placated over the discovery of jackdaws nesting in her chimneys and a close stove thirty years out of date and filthy with it.

However, the combination of her mistress exclaiming that no one else but Mrs Hodge could be relied upon to overcome these horrors and the intimidating presence of his lordship resulted in her retreating to harass the kitchen maids while assuring her ladyship that the best possible supper would be laid before them not later than half past seven.

'We dine at a fashionable hour for the country,' Justin observed as they made their way to the Chinese sitting room where Hearnshaw anxiously assured them they would find the furniture dusted and a fire lit.

Marina thought she could detect a somewhat warm glint

in Justin's eyes and retreated hastily to a deep wing chair by the fireside. Only that morning she had responded gladly to just such an expression; now she found her empty stomach cramping with nerves at the thought of his caresses.

'Hearnshaw hopes his lordship will not object to dining in what he supposes must be the breakfast room as he could not undertake to have the tables in either of the formal dining rooms polished in time,' she observed chattily. 'I agreed, assuming you would rather have a well-prepared dinner in modest comfort than have everyone's attention diverted to polishing yards of mahogany.' Justin looked suitably approving as he took the chair opposite, so she ventured a question. 'How many dining rooms do you have here?'

'*We,*' he answered with grave emphasis, 'have the Ladies' breakfast room, the large breakfast room, the small dining room and the large dining room. If your ladyship is desirous of holding a banquet, however, the remains of Great-grand-father's ballroom can be converted to seat one hundred. If you wish to set more covers than that, I regret that we will have to resort to a marquee on the lawn.'

'Goodness,' Marina said faintly. 'Might we postpone the banquet for at least a week?'

'I believe so. We will certainly receive many callers—local society is going to be agog to find out what is happening here—but I will be content with only a number of large formal dinners and a rout to begin with.'

Marina, knowing she was being teased, narrowed her eyes at him and refused to rise to the bait. Oh, goodness, Justin looked so attractive, lounging in the red silk chair. She wanted to go and rub the tense lines from his forehead and kiss the corners of his lips until the wry smile turned into one of genuine pleasure. How much affection would he expect from a wife whom he believed did not love him? How much could she show and not betray the love she felt for him, or the hurt at his lack of honesty towards her?

The clock struck six and she jumped to her feet, glad of any excuse to break the silence, which had become strangely tense. 'Look at the time! I must make sure Hearnshaw needs no more direction, then go and change for dinner. I will make sure Shepton has requested hot water for you.'

'Never mind that, I will speak to Hearnshaw,' Justin said roughly, getting to his feet as she rose. 'Go and lie down for an hour.' He broke off and stood looking down at her. 'Mari, I am sorry.'

'Sorry?' Was he going to tell her the truth, had she misjudged him after all?

'Sorry that I have brought you to this and not to the home you deserve.'

'It is a beautiful house,' she said steadily, watching his troubled hazel eyes. 'And you will make it your home again, given time.'

'We will. Our home.' He smiled down at her.

'Yes, Justin, of course. Our home.' Marina paused at the door and glanced back. The smile had gone and her husband was gazing into the flickering fire, the lines grim around his mouth.

Lying down for an hour did not produce the rest Justin obviously wished for her. Marina lay, gazing up at a large water stain on the ceiling, trying to lull herself to sleep by tracing the coastline of an imaginary continent around it. It failed miserably. That morning her only worry about coming to Knightshaye was that she might be tired after the long day and the journey and be unable to please her new husband. Now, far from feeling tired, she felt as if every nerve was stretched and as though she would never feel sleepy again.

She could hear Jenny moving quietly around in the

dressing room unpacking, the only familiar person left in her world, and one she could not confide in. Justin, who had been her friend and ally, was suddenly the stranger that their short acquaintance truly made him.

The man she loved and now could not trust. The man whom she desired, but who desired another woman. The man her family had so grievously wronged. Could she tell him she knew about his bargain with Charlie, or that she knew he had lied to her about the marchioness? No.

Through no fault of her own, the scales had been abruptly balanced between them; it was her duty and obligation to be a good wife to Justin and to repair the devastation that had swept over Knightshaye. And one day, perhaps, the grandchildren of the two men who had hated each other so much would play in the gardens and run, laughing, through these corridors, and some kind of justice would have been done.

Miserably Marina tossed and turned on the big bed. In order to achieve this she was going to have to become as great a dissembler as Justin when every instinct urged her to honesty. 'And to hell with the consequences,' she murmured.

'Did you call, miss…my lady?' Jenny peeped round the door.

'No.' Marina made herself smile. 'I was just thinking aloud.' It would never do. The first lesson of married life, it seemed, was that, far from being a mingling of souls, it was an institution of secrets.

'It is almost seven o'clock, my lady. The hot water will be brought up in a moment.'

'Yes, of course, I will get up. Now, has my blue silk shaken out all right?'

Justin was waiting at the foot of the stairs for her when Marina came down half an hour later.

'My lady.' Justin held out his hand, then stood back to

regard her, head on one side, eyes dangerously green. 'Mmm. I approve of your trousseau, that is a very fine gown.' His lips quirked. 'Now, what have I said to make you blush like a peony? I never mentioned the delightful low cut of the bodice or just how well it shows off your figure.'

'Oh, shh,' she whispered imploringly, suddenly back with her friend and not with her worrying new husband. 'Jenny has been asking me which nightgown I wanted laid out and I was never so mortified. You would not believe what has been packed. Mama must have asked Priscilla to pick them out.'

'I can imagine,' Justin murmured, his voice a low growl. 'I cannot wait to see whether what you choose lives up to my expectations.'

Marina bit her lip, mortified that she had so far forgotten herself, but strangely warmed. Justin might be in love with another woman, but it seemed her husband still found her attractive enough to flirt with outrageously.

She had been looking forward to dinner so much that at first she was just happy to be eating Mrs Hodge's excellent cooking. The wedding breakfast seemed days away, she was so hungry. Now, soothed by green pea and cucumber soup, salmon in pastry removed by fried celery and the prospect of strawberry fritters set on a bed of fairy butter, Marina found her mind steadier and her nerves calmer.

She dabbed the corner of her mouth delicately with her napkin, hoping that she had not been eating like a starving child, and cast an anxious eye at Justin, then a critical one at the servants. Both passed her scrutiny. Justin was doing full justice to the salmon and Hearnshaw seemed to have the footmen efficiently under control.

Marina drew a deep, thankful, breath and met her husband's eyes. They were green, heavy lidded and full of meaning. No one, however innocent a bride, could mistake their message for enjoyment of the salmon or the weariness of a long day.

Suddenly the strawberry fritters lost their appeal.

Chapter Eleven

Justin paced restlessly along the corridor leading off from the hall to the west wing. How long was one supposed to leave a new bride to her *toilette*? Too short a time and she would be flustered, too long and she would be a mass of nerves.

Damn it, *he* was a mass of nerves. It had been worrying enough, simply facing the prospect of initiating his bride into the arts of love, but at least he had every confidence in his own technique. But now they were both shaken by what they had found at Knightshaye and by Mari's realisation that her own family had wreaked this damage.

And Justin was almost as disturbed by her instinctive expectation that he would cast her off and send her packing, back to her family. Surely she trusted him more than that? Should he go to her tonight, or let her rest and recover a little from the shock? No, she would think he was having second thoughts about the marriage, despite his protestations.

He paced back, becoming aware that his finger and thumb were restlessly rubbing over the small crystal lustre in his pocket. He pulled it out and looked at it as it laid in his palm, glinting in the candlelight. Then, abruptly, he strode down the corridor until he came to a pair of ornate doors. They opened on to a cavernous space. The light he held caught glints off the cornices and walls, but sparked banked fire from the heap of glass that stood in front of him.

On its great iron stand one of the candelabra rested where it had for twenty years. The day before his father's return with the news that had shattered their lives for ever, his mother had ordered the ballroom candelabra cleaned. One by one they would be lowered on their ropes to their iron stands and each trebling lustre individually washed.

It was a fascinating sight for an eight-year-old boy. Justin had stood, watching the sweating footmen hauling on the rope, then lowering down safely the great shimmering mass of this, the first. A few minutes before he had climbed into the carriage to leave he had run back, driven by who knows what impulse, to stand before it for a last time. He walked round it, just as he was doing now, Justin realised, pacing slowly. And then, as his mother's voice called for him, full of pain and anxiety, he had leaned forward and taken one lustre from its wire hook. It had stayed with him, moved from pocket to pocket with every change of clothes and now lay in his palm.

The empty hook was plain to see. It seemed to move slightly, waiting for its burden to be returned. Justin reached out, then slowly drew his hand back. No, not yet. Not until his work here was finished. Not until this was truly his home again. He shoved it back into his pocket impatiently and turned on his heel to stride out of the room. Mari would be waiting.

Marina sat bolt upright in bed and fought the instinct to pull the sheets up to her chin. She did not think she had ever worn anything more indecent, certainly not anything another person would see her in. And this was the most modest of the nightgowns that had been carefully folded between tissue and silver paper in the top of her trunk.

The fine lawn was so thin she could see her nipples. When she had been standing up in it, *everything* had been visible. Jenny had appeared to think nothing amiss in a garment her mistress mentally categorised as fit only for a demi-rep and they had had a brisk tussle over just how loose the ribbons would be tied at the neck. Marina's fingers strayed to them now, fighting the instinct to pull them tighter. But what was the point of a modestly high neckline if the entire gown was next to transparent?

She gave the clock a harassed look for the fifth time in as many minutes. Perhaps Justin was not coming. Perhaps he was too upset about the house, perhaps he had thought better of his denial that he wanted her to go. Perhaps... Perhaps Justin was just tired, Marina told herself firmly. Well, that was good, it put off the moment of reckoning until tomorrow.

Coward, she scolded herself. If only she had thought to ask Pris how she should act. Would Justin expect her to touch him? Caress him? How? Where? What if she got it wrong and gave him a disgust of her for being too forward, or too cold?

The thought of having to wait until the next day to resolve these questions was so worrying that Marina could not suppress the gasp of relief as the interconnecting door opened.

'Good evening again, Lady Mortenhoe.' Justin strolled into the room, an exotic stranger in his long dressing gown of heavily brocaded green silk. 'Had you given me up?'

'No...yes...no! I mean, no.' Marina got her voice under control and smiled tightly. 'I thought perhaps you were tired...'

'Mari, a man who was too tired to make love to a woman who looks like you do should be measured for his coffin.' Justin came to the end of the bed, sat down and leaned back against the post. That seemed safely unthreatening. Marina attempted to unclench her fingers from the edge of the sheets. His feet were bare. She risked another glance and saw bare calf, intriguingly hairy. Perhaps he was wearing nothing under that robe. She swallowed, convinced that her thudding heartbeat must be visible.

'Are *you* too tired?' He watched her, his face giving no clue as to what he wanted her to say.

'No…I mean…'

'You mean you wish this night was over and it was tomorrow morning?' Justin suggested, smiling ruefully. 'May I join you?'

Marina nodded, not trusting her voice, and fixed her gaze on a still life on the opposite wall. Even so, the rustle of falling silk and the flash of bare skin were not reassuring. The bed dipped and the covers were pulled up again. This was her husband, the man who was in love with another woman. And, presumably, the man who was going to find her a very poor substitute.

'It is safe to look now.' He was being very patient. She turned to face him and said so. She expected Justin to reply, but instead he simply took her by the shoulders, pulled her towards him and kissed her.

Miraculously it was as it had been that morning—the sudden surge of desire, the need to press herself close to the hard body holding her, the wave of sensations that the heat of his mouth on hers generated.

Only now he was naked—and she might as well have been. His skin was hot under her hands and against her breast and his mouth, shifting, caressing and demanding on hers, was making her whole body react in ways she never imagined. Her nipples peaked and hardened, thrusting against the subtle friction of the fine cotton and she moaned, twisting restlessly as she searched for the mysterious something her body was aching for.

She was on her back now, unaware of having slid down the bed, Justin's weight half on her, the brand of his arousal hot and terrifying against her thigh. Hot and thrilling. She shifted instinctively, bringing herself on to her side to face him, feeling his body lock with hers as it pressed between her thighs.

'Oh, God.' Justin left her mouth and slid lower, his lips restless over the skin of her throat and shoulder, down, over the edge of her nightgown until he found her right nipple through the fragile lawn. Shockingly he began to nibble, to suck, to nip the tight bud with his teeth.

Marina gasped, her body arching up to meet him in wordless demand. 'Hush.' His hand spread, palm down over her belly, pressing her back, keeping her pinned to the bed. Desperate to find release from the building tension that gripped her, she struggled, lifting herself against his restraint, gasping as his mouth moved from one nipple to another, tormenting her into a fever of mindless need.

'Hush,' he murmured again, leaving her aching breasts and arching over her, his legs pressing hers apart. His weight, supported on his elbows, was tangible, exciting, but not the dominating thing she had feared. She could still move, still shift restlessly beneath him as his fingers tightened at the neck of her nightgown.

'Did you decide you liked this nightgown?' he asked suddenly, resting his forehead against hers so they exchanged breaths, his face so close she could not focus on his eyes.

'No…'

'Good.' His hand moved and the gown ripped like paper, leaving Marina skin to skin with Justin. 'Oh, so lovely.' The words were breathed out like a soft prayer as he pushed back on his braced arms to look down on her. 'So lovely. You have skin like rose petals, white rose petals.' His eyes were a deep, pure green as his hand slid down, caressing over the swell of her breasts, the dip of her waist, the soft curve of her belly to the curls that shielded her last secrets.

Marina knew she should feel shyness, should be afraid, but all she could feel was love, excitement, the fire of ranging desire as Justin slid one finger deep into the dark curls, deep where she was shamefully, mysteriously, aching for him to touch her.

Her gasp of shocked delight as he found what he was seeking was smothered against his shoulder as he lowered himself over her, shifting until he was cradled between her thighs. *Oh, yes, oh, yes*, she prayed silently, only half-aware of what she was asking for, begging for.

'Mari, sweetheart.' He pulled back just a little, enough for him to look down into her face, vulnerable and utterly defenceless against his skilled assault. 'Trust me, just trust me.' And he thrust into her.

Trust me. The words penetrated her mind like forked lightning, illuminating that morning's betrayals in a vivid flash. Justin keeping the whole basis of their marriage from her, Justin, gazing down into the eyes of the woman he loved and who had jilted him, his face full of the love he had denied feeling for any woman. Justin violating all the trust she had felt for him.

As he surged within her Marina's mind closed like a trap snapping shut, and her body closed with it, tightening rigid against Justin's thrust, locking as hard as it was capable against his intrusion—and failing.

Marina's shocked cry of pain was stifled against his mouth. Her body, arching in helpless protest, was overwhelmed by his as Justin spasmed within her, an incoherent gasp of release mingling with her anguish as his mouth ravished hers.

She lay still, Justin's body heavy on her, and listened to the sound of his breathing slowing as he gradually recovered himself. She could feel his heart thudding against her breast and his face was buried in the curve of her neck, his lips pressing gently against the skin as though they were the only part of his body he could move.

It seemed she had satisfied her husband. Marina tried to find comfort in that thought while she struggled to come to terms with what had happened to her. Should it have hurt like that? Surely not. Priscilla had warned it would, a little, but that had been more than a little. Even now she had to fight to stop the tears welling in her eyes.

It had not been any fault of Justin's, she was sure, forcing herself to think through the fog of sensual memories that blurred her memory until that sudden, shocking culmination. He had told her to trust him—reassuring, considerate words from a husband to a new bride. How was he to know that she might love him and desire him, but had felt that very trust shatter only hours before?

It would not be so bad next time, she told herself firmly. She had to remember to relax at the crucial moment, that was all. It would be better.

Her husband stirred against her and she struggled to keep all traces of distress from her expression as he rose on his elbows to look down at her. Despite everything, she could not help the wave of love that swept through her as she saw his face, stripped of everything but the most fundamental emotions.

His hair clung to his damp forehead, his eyes were wide, still green. Every line and angle of his face seemed fresh-drawn to her and his lips curved into a tender, sensual smile. 'Sweetheart.' He pushed her own tumbled hair back from her face. 'I am sorry, that must have hurt you. I promise it will be better next time.'

'Priscilla warned me,' she admitted. Justin's eyebrows went up and she added, 'I did not like to ask Mama about… things.'

'Ah.' He seemed reassured, if somewhat disconcerted.

Despite everything, Marina had to suppress a smile. Perhaps men did not realise that women would confide in friends, not just their mamas, about such matters. And Justin had flirted, quite unexceptionally, with Pris, so perhaps he was now embarrassed that they had discussed him in such a way. A flutter of affection touched her at this insight into male thoughts.

'Let me make you more comfortable.' Before she could question what he meant Justin was out of bed and pouring water into the basin on the washstand. He seemed not to have the slightest self-consciousness about being naked, or that she would be watching him in the candlelight.

The male body was beautiful, she realised, studying the elegant triangle his torso made, with broad shoulders tapering down into narrow waist. Long, powerful legs and tight buttocks—she could recall her frantically searching hands finding and cupping around them at one moment, and blushed.

Then he turned, the basin held carefully between both hands, and she blushed harder, dragging her eyes away and fixing them on a loose thread in the hem of the linen sheet as he placed the basin beside the bed.

'Here, let me.' Justin pushed back the sheets and to her shocked dismay began to lave her gently with the washcloth. 'Blood, poor sweetheart,' he murmured, head bent over his task.

Embarrassed, yet touched, Marina lay passive while he dried her, pulling the bedclothes back over her. She expected him to leave, but no, he snuffed the candles, then climbed back into bed beside her, catching her in his arms against his chest and stroking her hair until she relaxed in the unfamiliar embrace.

Drowsily she let her eyelids flutter closed. That had been far worse than she had expected, in the end, yet far better than she had hoped at first. Perhaps, in a few days' time, when he wanted to make love to her again it would all be fine and would hardly hurt at all.

Justin lay and stared up through the darkness with his eyes wide open while Mari drifted into sleep against his side. His wife. He turned his head and kissed her hair, softly, so as not to wake her. That had been a shattering experience; even now his heartbeat did not seem to have returned to normal.

She had seemed so right in his arms, had looked so beautiful, his grey-eyed wife. Who would have thought that under her neat elegance and modest restraint she was hiding a body so sweet, or so responsive? But he had hurt her, he knew he must have, even as he had joined with her in that desperate, unstoppable thrust. He had never dreamed she would be so tight, and his body had reacted predictably, snatching him into a shattering climax almost at once.

Thinking about it, he felt himself harden with desire again, but he had no trouble fighting it. Mari needed to sleep now. But in the morning, early, just as she was drifting up into wakefulness, he would make love to her again. Gently, slowly, focusing entirely on her pleasure, until all memory of that first hurt faded quite away.

Marina woke to the sound of the curtain rings clattering gently as Jenny pulled them back from the window. She lay, eyes closed, willing the night to have been a dream. Without looking she stretched out a tentative hand, but the other side of the bed was empty, only faintly warm with Justin's body heat.

She had woken, perhaps an hour ago, to the gentle drift of his hands on her body and had turned into his arms, still only half-aware, knowing only that his hands and mouth were pleasuring her. His lips teased and tormented her breasts as they had last night, but his hands…oh, his hands had been touching her in such a way that she had begun to writhe against his fingers, shamefully whimpering for him not to stop, never to stop while the pressure built and built inside her until she knew she was going to have to scream or to die.

And then, it seemed, both happened. She heard her own voice crying out, but surely she was dying, spinning into exploding blackness and sensation such as she had never imagined. She came slowly back to reality, to find herself held tightly in Justin's arms, his eyes fixed on her face.

'That's better, sweeting,' he murmured and shifted his weight over her. 'Open for me, Mari.' And it happened again. She could feel her body's reaction, even through the drugging sweetness of what had just happened. As Justin entered her the memory of yesterday's betrayals and last night's pain locked her tight, even as she fought her own body, searched for some way to relax muscles she had hardly known existed.

The pain as it lanced through her was as bad, worse perhaps, for she had experienced it once and was anticipating as well as feeling, and she could not hold back the little cry, hiding her face in his shoulder as he moved above her. He must have mistaken it for a cry of pleasure or arousal, for he found her mouth with his and kissed her with hard passion as he possessed her.

This is my duty, Marina told herself, holding herself passive with a strength of will she had not known she possessed. *He is my husband, I love him, and this is how I will give him the children we both want so much. It is my duty— and I do not know how I will bear it.*

Chapter Twelve

It had not occurred to Marina to wonder how she would feel about facing the world the morning after her wedding night. Now she had trouble sorting through the emotions that seemed to jostle for attention inside her.

Jenny was being so carefully tactful about ignoring the torn nightgown and the used water on the washstand that it almost reduced her mistress to stammering ineptitudes about the weather. Marina took a steadying breath.

'Were you comfortable in your new room?' she asked. 'I am sorry you had to make do like that after a journey. We were all rather taken by surprise by the state of the house.'

'I was fine, miss…I mean, my lady.' Jenny was setting up a folding screen covered in toile de jouy, which effectively shut off the bed from the rest of the room. 'I'll just ring for the hot water for your bath, my lady. Mr Hearnshaw had found me a very nice room, though it's a good thing you thought to have mattresses and linen sent ahead. What's here isn't good for much. I don't know what that smart new house-keeper is going to say when she arrives tomorrow.'

Marina did not know either. She had secured the services

of the dauntingly well-recommended Mrs Faversham in the teeth of stiff competition. But while an earl's country seat was most definitely a step up from her previous post with the recently deceased Lady Blakestone, this decaying house was not at all what the obviously ambitious upper servant had been led to expect.

Marina sipped her hot chocolate while from behind the screen there was the splash of water, the tread of footmen and Jenny's whispered scolding at them not to walk so heavily and not to splash her ladyship's carpet. She had a household who were strangers to one another, a nervous butler in his first place of such seniority, a superior housekeeper who might well turn on her heel and return to London and a number of far more congenial offers—and a husband.

What did Justin want her to do about the state of his house? She did not even know how much housekeeping he would allow her. The question had not arisen, and, used to making do with a very strict budget, Marina had not had any concerns. But now, how did one calculate what would be needed to restore just the straightforward domestic conveniences of Knightshaye? Just how well off was her husband? Was he going to be able to afford to restore this great house, the grounds, the park, the farmland?

With the memory clear in her mind of both her father's and Charlie's explosions of incredulous wrath at the sight of basic household bills, Marina tried to calculate what the minimum she could ask for would be. Given that she had glimpsed but a handful of the rooms, this was enough to keep her mind off other worries until Jenny announced her bath was ready and she slipped out of bed.

'Ouch!' She was stiff and sore and it took considerable will-power not to hobble towards the bath. 'Oh, dear,' she observed brightly at Jenny's look of concern. 'I misjudged the height of the bed and jarred my heel. That is all right, Jenny, I will soap my own back.'

Left alone, Marina lowered herself gingerly into the water, wincing as it stung. She did wish she could talk to Pris about this, but her friend was miles away in London and the thought of even hinting at the problem in writing made her go hot and cold with horror.

It is all my fault, she concluded miserably. Justin was everything that was patient and considerate, and, until the actual moment when he entered her, she could not deny he had given her pleasure far and beyond what she had imagined. But some ungovernable part of her body—or her mind—would simply not forget his deception, would not stop fighting him.

Still, he had made love to her twice in one night—surely he would not feel the need to do so again for days, perhaps even a week? That would give her the chance to think what to do, for the thought of actually telling Justin the truth seemed impossible. Thoughtfully Marina soaped her arms and torso. Was there something she could do that would satisfy him without him having to…to do *that*?

She was still brooding on this highly improper idea when she entered the breakfast room, automatically checking the dishes set out on the buffet. Mrs Hodge seemed to have coped yet again with the kitchen, and the repast would certainly have satisfied Charlie, Marina's only recent guide to masculine breakfast habits.

'Thank you, Hearnshaw, that looks admirable,' she said with a smile while at the back of her mind she tried to recall exactly what things she had done last night that had seemed to most please Justin.

The images conjured up, although confused, were so

deeply intimate that the subject of them entering the room reduced her to blushes. Convinced the footman must have noticed and drawn his own conclusions, she managed to smile and say, 'Good morning, my lord', with tolerable composure. 'Mrs Hodgken has done us proud, despite the fact that I had not thought to discover your preferences.'

Justin was regarding her with a strange expression and she fell silent. *Oh, Lord, he is like Papa and hates chatter at breakfast.* 'Would you prefer coffee or chocolate? Hicks, please fetch a fresh jug of each.'

He was still looking at her. 'It seems admirable, but you look a trifle discommoded, my dear. Is something wrong?'

Hicks the footman had vanished and Hearnshaw was tactfully doing something to the window blinds. 'I was chattering, and I thought perhaps you were like Papa and preferred silence at breakfast. You looked—'

'I hope I looked like a man who was delighted to find his new wife presiding over what appears to be an admirable breakfast table.' The watchful expression turned into a smile. 'I was enjoying the novelty, and, far from wishing for silence at breakfast, I would welcome your conversation.'

Marina helped herself to cold ham and bread and butter and took her place at the foot of the short table. 'I would be glad of the opportunity for a few words later about housekeeping arrangements,' she ventured. How very strange to be sitting opposite someone with whom one had been engaged, only hours before, in the most intimate of activities, and calmly discussing domestic arrangements.

'I thought the new housekeeper arrived tomorrow.' Justin addressed a large sirloin with vigour.

'Yes, she does, but we have not discussed the housekeeping allowance. I had not considered it a problem, but then I did not know what state we would find Knightshaye in. I need to know to what extent you require rooms opening up and putting back into use, for one thing.'

'I want everything back in order, at whatever speed is easily achievable by you and the staff. Set the housekeeping at whatever level you see fit; when Sheffield, my steward, arrives next week he will arrange its regular payment.' Justin regarded her quizzically. 'Am I heaping too much on you, my dear?'

'No, not at all…' Marina glanced across at the butler who was standing unobtrusively by the buffet. 'Please see what has happened to the coffee and chocolate, Hearnshaw.' When they were alone she said stiffly, 'I was not sure what budget you wanted set for the work, and I did not want to exceed it unwittingly and cause some…difficulty. And I would not wish to stray from setting things to rights and housekeeping into some aspect of the restoration that you wish to oversee.'

'Are you asking me whether I can afford the work, Mari?' He did not seem displeased, but she remained tense. In her experience, gentlemen did not react well to questions about financial matters. 'I have been saving since I was seventeen to buy back this house, and, although your brother struck a hard bargain, I believe I can bring the whole estate around, given time. We have no need to skimp on the interior. Now, what have I said to discompose you?'

Marina knew she had changed colour; she could feel the blood draining away from her cheeks and her fingers trembled as she put down the slice of bread and butter. 'Were Charlie's requirements so very onerous? What did you have to agree to, to obtain Knightshaye?' There, now she had asked. Would he persist in the deception?

Justin named a sum that made Marina gasp. 'Truly? So much? But nothing else? I just wondered, as the negotiations seemed to take quite a while.'

Knowing that he was hiding something from her made it

easier to read the withdrawn expression, the way he dropped his lashes over those betraying eyes under the pretext of reaching for the mustard pot. 'I think that was quite enough, don't you?' he said lightly. 'But it was within my upper limit; I could have gone higher if need be.'

And gone higher, paid more, not to have had to marry me, Marina saw with a flash of insight. 'No wonder it all took so much time,' she said, matching his tone.

'Yes, tiresome at first, but it gave me the opportunity to get to know you.' Justin's smile was warm.

It did not warm Marina. She supposed the two men had thought they were being tactful not to put the arrangement to her as a business proposition, but to leave her with the illusion that she was being wooed and courted. Silenced from discussing finances by the return of Hearnshaw and a flustered footman, who had apparently managed to drop both jugs on the way back from the kitchen, Marina reapplied herself to her food.

Charlie and Justin might have told themselves they were exercising tact, but what they were being, she decided, with a growing sense of injustice, was patronising. In fact, it was worse. Marina took a ruthless spoon to a boiled egg she did not really want. Yesterday she had been hurt simply because Justin had not told her why he was proposing to her, had hidden the truth from her when she had trusted him to be open and honest.

Now she felt as though she had been sold, bartered, made part of the price of Knightshaye. Men disposed of their daughters and sisters and wives as they pleased, she knew of course, it was how the world worked. But she had not believed that Justin was a man like that, one who would trick her into marriage, put his desire for his old home over her rights and feelings.

She had been hopelessly naïve to feel betrayed that he should think like that; it must be because she loved him so much. And only this morning she had been lying in bed, mentally chastising herself for being in some way inadequate. Well, if she was, it was *both* their faults, she decided. Being in love with a man did not stop one feeling angry with him, it seemed.

'Has that egg done something to upset you, my dear?' Justin was regarding the mangled object so comically that she could not maintain her anger. She felt her lips twitch in response.

'I am afraid I was thinking of all that dusting. Would you care for some more coffee, Justin?'

'Thank you.' He passed his cup and sat back, looking out of the window over the tangled mess which was the garden. 'How many gardeners do you think we will need?'

'I have no idea, I have no experience of gardens,' Marina confessed. 'A head gardener, two men and a boy?' she hazarded. 'That ought to do for the ornamental gardens, I should think, but we will need more if you wish to open up the vegetable gardens—I assume there are some.'

'Hmm, yes. A big walled garden, a range of glasshouses, which are probably less glass than splinters now—even a melon house.' He raised an eyebrow. 'Now what are you plotting?'

'I was wondering at what point the cost of putting it all into working order and hiring the staff would be offset by the saving on buying in produce,' Marina confessed. 'It hardly seems worth it for just the two of us and the staff we have now.'

'But the more the house becomes habitable, and the more staff we employ and the more guests we entertain, the more we will need. I think I will set Sheffield to worrying about that. And, of course,' he added so smoothly that it took a moment to sink in, 'once we set up our nursery that will add significantly to the number of mouths to feed.'

'Significantly?' Marina enquired faintly.

'All those nursery maids.' He was teasing her in the way he used to just a few weeks ago when all they were to each other were friends and he was the one person she had felt she could tell anything to.

'Indeed, yes.' She adopted a deliberately exaggerated expression of disapproval that won an even broader smile. 'Should I send for some more toast?'

'Thank you, but no. I must get out and ride round the estate, begin to map out the priorities for Sheffield. But there were some things you wished to discuss first, I believe.'

'Yes.' Marina glanced up at him as he pulled back her chair. 'Yes, just so that I too can set my priorities for Mrs Faversham. Thank you, Hearnshaw, please tell Mrs Hodgken I will be down to see her later this morning.'

She followed Justin across the hall and into a book-lined study, producing a notebook and pencil as she sat down opposite the broad, dusty desk. The practical questions were all there, had seemed so straightforward when she had been thinking about them. Now it was considerably more difficult to put what she wanted to say into words. And Justin, lowering himself into the chair behind the desk, his face expressionless, was suddenly formidably distant. Then she saw his fingers, running caressingly over the ends of the chair-arms where the heavy carving had been worn smooth by the hands of the previous occupants, and glimpsed the emotional strain he was hiding so well.

Justin watched his wife settle herself, twitching her skirts into neat obedience, opening her notebook and running one long finger down the page to keep it flat. So elegant, so understated—so damned dutiful. He had been braced for almost any emotion after the revelations of just what they had come home to. Anything other than the calm, considerate, *dutiful* acceptance of whatever his will would be—whether it was banishment, the requirement to restore the house on a strict budget or his right to throw a display of temperament because she was talking over breakfast.

What had she expected marriage to be like? he wondered, then remembered who her father was. It would have been a miracle if the late Lord Winslow had not been a domestic tyrant. And even her brother must set a fine example of demanding, thoughtlessly selfish manhood.

But she had always trusted him before—he just needed to ensure that she extended that trust into their married life, because making Mari happy was becoming more important than he had ever expected it to be.

Justin shifted in the old chair, remembering last night. Had she been happy with their lovemaking? She had seemed so, as far as he could judge, given his lack of experience with well brought-up, innocent virgins. And yet there had been a reserve, a feeling once again that she was hiding something from him, keeping some emotion back. Nerves, embarrassment and inexperience, he told himself. When he made love to her tonight he would take it very slowly, see if he could entice her into overcoming her bashfulness to talk to him.

His body stirred, tightened, at the thought and he spoke more abruptly than he had intended. 'So, you wanted to talk to me about the house?'

Mari started, obviously lost in her own thoughts while she waited patiently for him to gather his. 'Yes. Obviously there are all the normal things one would do to set a house as neglected as this to rights, and when Mr Sheffield arrives I will speak to him about arranging chimney sweeps, mending broken windows, cleaning the outside glass and so forth. But I fear that many items will be damaged beyond repair, especially the textiles.

'Would you wish me to set aside anything that is damaged for your assessment? And would you like me to have the patterns matched as accurately as possible so I can replace things as nearly as they were?'

What did he want? Justin looked around the study, felt his palms curving over the smoothly polished arms of the chair he could recall his father, and before him, his grandfather, sitting in. Their room, their things. Now his. Into his mind came the recollection of an elegantly comfortable drawing room at the Winslows' town house and Mari's quiet pride when he had complimented her on it. He made a decision and knew, as he articulated it, that it was right.

'I do not want to live in a museum. Do as you see fit, buy whatever you need. Keep what you want, dispose of anything else as you judge best. Make this *our* home, Mari.'

She looked up, surprised, and, he realised, pleased. 'Very well, but I will leave the ordering of this room and your bed-chamber and dressing room to you, and simply have them cleaned,' she said, with a confidence that delighted him. He had said the right thing.

Then he recalled one room, the room whose key lay in his pocket, chiming occasionally against the lustre. What to do about his parents' room? He did not know, and worried that it would embarrass Mari to have to deal with so intimate a chamber when he could not decide himself how he felt about it. Better to leave it alone until he could cope with it and not burden her.

'And my parents' room. Please leave that entirely. I will keep the key.' Her head was bent over the notebook, although the busy pencil had stilled. What else? Oh yes, money. 'Have the bills sent to Sheffield. Perhaps you could tell him yourself what weekly, or monthly, amounts you wish to have in cash for the housekeeping. He will also make sure your personal allowance is available to you in whatever way you wish.'

Marina kept her head down under the pretext of making notes she did not need until she had her expression under control. It had been like a slap in the face, coming after the pleasure of finding that Justin trusted her enough to give her a free hand with the house. And then to realise that this was superficial only. He would trust her with the public rooms, but not to have the tact or sensitivity to restore his parents' room. She would not have dreamt of touching anything without his permission—why did he feel he had to lock it against her? Telling her to leave it would have been sufficient.

She felt tears welling hot and treacherous, and swallowed hard, fighting them back until she could look at him dry-eyed. She could even smile. 'Very well, thank you. I can see we are both going to have a busy day ahead of us.' As Justin rose to leave she thought, *I could have been sent to Bath and Great-aunt Maria.* Would such a fate actually be preferable to this marriage?

It was only as she was standing on the front step, waving Justin goodbye as he cantered off, a groom at his side, that it came to her that the threat of Great-aunt Maria had been a sham, that Mama had used it to propel her into Justin's arms. Even as he had comforted her in Green Park he must have guessed that was exactly what it was and yet he had cynically gone along with it and left her in her misery and suspense.

She could trust *nothing* that her instincts told her about her husband, Marina thought as she turned back into the house. The sooner she learned that lesson the better, because it seemed to trust was to be hurt. This marriage was going to survive because she had made her vows to uphold it, to love, honour and obey Justin. And like a fool she had promised herself happiness. Whatever happened, that was the only promise that she was going to see broken.

Chapter Thirteen

The day passed more agreeably than Marina would have predicted when she waved Justin goodbye that morning. With *carte blanche* to do what she wanted with virtually every room in the house, she set the maids to work on completely cleaning the servants' temporary quarters. Then she won Mrs Hodgken's everlasting approval by agreeing to her employing as many local women for the rough cleaning as it took to restore the kitchens, storerooms, pantries and all the rest of her complex kingdom to order.

Hearnshaw and the two footmen were taking their time cleaning the silver and plate while regarding the bustling women around them with lofty male superiority. They rapidly found the smirks wiped off their faces when their mistress ordered them fetch cleaning materials and repair to the study.

'Baize aprons and Undress in the *front* of the house, my lady?' Hearnshaw might be relatively inexperienced, but he knew what was due to the butler of a big house, and appearing on the wrong side of the green baize door in his shirt, sleeve-protectors and voluminous apron was well beneath his dignity.

It was all very well for the footmen tending the grates or washing the inside of windows first thing in the morning, but for any of them, let alone the butler, to be seen *cleaning*? It was not helpful that her ladyship's woman was obviously suppressing giggles at the sight of them.

'We are all going to clean his lordship's study from ceiling to skirtings, and that includes myself—and you too, Jenny,' Marina added, removing the smirk from the abigail's face, much to Hearnshaw's gratification. 'All the books are to be taken out and dusted, but everything is to go back exactly as it was.'

It took the five of them all morning, but eventually the room gleamed with a subdued masculine richness. Spiders had been chased from the strongholds of twenty years, windows scrubbed with brown paper and vinegar, each and every book removed, banged together and carefully replaced on the dusted shelf and the carpets rolled up, dragged outside and beaten vigorously before being laid out and covered in damp tea leaves.

Marina took the desk and chair herself, lifting out the contents of each drawer, dusting without disturbing the order and relining with fresh paper before replacing them. Then she polished until the room filled with the scent of beeswax and lavender and the old leather chair turned from a shabby relic into a mellow, comfortable antique.

As she chased her hot and dusty workers out for their luncheon, Marina stood in the doorway and regarded their achievement. It had been important to give Justin a comfortable room to work in, she had decided, viewing it with satisfaction. And the absence of the curtains, which were being laboriously washed in the kitchen yard, and the carpets, which were having the tea leaves beaten out of them, would not be missed for a few summer evenings.

Something *was* missing, though. Nibbling her lower lip thoughtfully, Marina went to raid the boxes of fine white wax candles they had brought and filled all the candlesticks. No, that wasn't it. Then the warm breeze brought in the scent of grass and flowers through the wide open casements and she followed it out into the overgrown garden, looking around her for the source of the scent. Around the corner of the building she found it: a tangle of roses spilling over some vanished garden building.

The thorns pricked her fingers and caught at her skirts, but Marina was heedless, enchanted by the scent and the wild abandon of the flowers, flung like a voluptuous carpet over the ruin.

Mrs Hodgken returned from a successful excursion to the village with two local women at her heels, delighted at the prospect of unlimited work at the Big House. They were agog at the sight of her ladyship unceremoniously perched on the kitchen table with a pair of scissors in hand, creating flower arrangements out of a pile of roses, wild grasses and the spearing leaves of iris.

Fortunately, unlike Cook at home, whose temperaments were legendary in the Winslow household, Mrs Hodgken seemed able to take curtain washing, flower arrangement and the diversion of one of her girls to polishing pewter ewers in her stride. Nor did she object to providing luncheon as and when the various staff came in for it, cheerfully directing her new women to attack the range while assuring Marina that a light repast in the breakfast room was far more fitting than her sitting down to share bread and cheese at one end of the long pine table.

'A treasure,' Marina observed to Jenny as the two of them carried up the jugs of roses. 'You set yours down in the hall, there and here on this chest, and then run along and find something to eat.'

She had been right, she decided, setting a pewter tankard of deep red roses down on one end of the desk and placing the other, fragrant with pink and white single blooms offset by wands of grass, down on the window seat.

Yes, this was satisfaction, making something beautiful out of chaos for the man she loved. She ran her hand over the smooth surface of the desk with sensual pleasure. Perhaps it would be enough to make her happy, loving Justin, coming to love this house—even if her love was not returned by anything except affection.

Children would return love. The thought caught her unawares and she found her hand had moved instinctively to her flat stomach. She could already be with child: surely that was worth all the pain it took to conceive it?

But more likely she was not. Mama had confided her distress that it was only after two years of marriage that she had presented Lord Winslow with a son and heir. 'And I felt the shame of it greatly, as you may imagine, my dear. However, he was most gratified it was a son, which was a mercy. Imagine how dreadful if you had been born first!'

Shaking off the nightmare thought of failing to do her duty and ending up giving Justin only daughters, Marina went in search of her luncheon. *But I would like daughters,* a rebellious voice whispered in her head. Perhaps Mama would allow her to have Lizzie to stay.

A tour of the servants' quarters, and a preliminary review of what passed for the linen cupboard, produced an alarming shopping list. Before the end of the week she must send off the first of no doubt many orders to Layton and Shears at Bedford House. Adding notes as she walked, Marina went to survey what the maids had done to prepare Mrs Faversham's rooms. The Winslows' housekeeper would be delighted to merit such accommodation—Marina had the gloomy premonition that it would take more than a well-appointed bedchamber and sitting room to persuade her new housekeeper to remain.

Confident that at least her husband could work, and the servants sleep, in comfort, Marina reviewed progress. She gave Shepton command of two footmen and a maid and set him to deal with Justin's bedchamber and dressing room, sure that he would know better than she what his master required to make him comfortable, and concentrated the rest of her forces on the entrance hall and the Chinese sitting room. It could not be long before local society started to call and at least they must be received with some degree of elegance.

By five, although it was not perfect, Marina decided that she and Justin would not be put to the blush by the arrival of the local squirearchy and dismissed the staff for a well-earned rest before dinner.

But she could not rest as Jenny urged her to do, with a sly reference to 'disturbed nights'. When would Justin return? Would he be pleased with what she had done? What sort of day had he had? Abstractedly jotting notes about laundry maids and queries to herself about hiring some specialist sempstresses to work on restoring the textiles, Marina found her eyes wandering more and more to the window overlooking the drive.

When she finally saw the bay horse cantering up to the house, the accompanying grey a length behind, she sprang out of the chair and tugged the bell. 'Harris, send hot water for a bath up to his lordship's room immediately.'

The second footman bowed. 'Mr Shepton ordered it a

minute ago, my lady. I think he was looking out from the up-per-landing window, ma'am.'

'Very good.' Marina was unaware of sounding abstracted as she stood looking out through the glass at the approach-ing riders. It was only the second time she had seen Justin on horseback, and the first time—when he had rescued Hector from the lake—she had been too preoccupied to pay any at-tention to his style.

Now she could see and appreciate the elegance of the way he sat the big bay, riding one-handed, the other hand resting on his thigh. He did not appear to have to think what he was doing, not even when the gelding shied at a wind-blown leaf that crossed its path. By comparison the groom was obviously weary, and nowhere near such a good rider in the first place, Marina thought critically, watching as the two men reined in at the front door.

Justin swung down from his mount and tossed the reins to the groom with a word of thanks. The man touched his whip to his hat and trotted off round to the stables, leaving Justin standing staring down the drive.

He is beautiful, Marina thought, her view of her husband suddenly coloured by the memory of him standing naked in her bedchamber. Now she could imagine the muscled back, the strong thighs, the lean figure beneath the well-cut riding clothes. A feeling, very like that she had experienced as she watched him walking out of the Serpentine, gripped her, only now she knew it for what it was: physical desire.

He pulled off his hat and ran his hand through his hair, then simply stood, eyes fixed on the view down the long drive. His stance signalled something beyond weariness to Marina as she watched. What he had found on his tour of the estate must have depressed him far more than he had expected.

She fought the impulse to run out and hug him, assure him

it would all be well. That would be foolish when she had no idea what he had discovered. But after he had bathed and they had dined, then she would talk to him, draw out what was so concerning him—surely he would confide in her to that extent?

Justin realised he had been standing on his own front step for several minutes, hat, whip and gloves in one hand, the other clenched with tension. *Damn it*, he had expected things to be bad—how could he not have after seeing the fields they had passed as they arrived? But he had not expected to find the Home Farm entirely out of use, the farmhouse where he had expected to lodge his steward in as bad a case as the main house and the tenants neglected and surly.

He couldn't blame them. He would feel surly if he was expected to pay rent to a landlord he never saw, for land that was never improved and cottages that cried out for repair. It answered the question of why Charlie Winslow had not made more money from the estate—he simply could not ask more with any hope of receiving it.

Which meant, Justin thought grimly, that he could not expect the land to start earning its keep until he poured money into it. He realised that his shoulders had sagged and pushed them back, wiping the frown from his face as he did so. It would never do to let Mari realise the extent of the problem with the land. She was obviously already worried about their finances—who wouldn't be, with Charlie Winslow as their brother? Life must have been one financial crisis after another in that household.

If she thought there was a problem, then she would skimp and save on the house, and he wanted her to enjoy restoring Knightshaye, not find it a burden. And it was not as though money was short; he simply resented the necessity to spend it in such a way on the estate when the minimum of attention would have kept the land in reasonable order.

It was hard to remember that hating a dead man was no answer and that blaming his brother-in-law for fecklessness was about as helpful as blaming the north wind for bringing snow.

Taking a deep breath, Justin pushed open the front door and walked in. For a moment he could not work out what was different and he looked around, puzzled. Then he realised— everything shone with cleanliness, polish and care, from the subdued sheen on the marble floor, to the rich dark oak of the panelling and staircase. The windows were sparkling, letting light flood in and candle sconces and metal work gleamed.

He shut his eyes and inhaled: beeswax, lavender, roses. The house was alive again, breathing. He was home. Then the sensation of being watched made him open his eyes and look around. Mari was standing in the doorway, regarding him gravely, her hands folded in front of her as she stood, neat as a pin, already dressed for dinner.

'It is a miracle,' he said simply. 'Thank you.'

She smiled and came out into the hall, the silk of her skirts rustling softly. 'We have not done much yet, just cleaning, but I thought we should be prepared to receive callers soon.'

The way she was dressed recalled him to his own state. 'Am I very late for dinner?'

She caught his meaning at once. 'Oh, no. I changed early—it seemed foolish to change again after I shed my houseworking clothes, so I dressed for the evening.'

'It is a very becoming gown,' he observed, conscious that the sight of her—calm and elegant as she was—was working powerfully on him. He knew now what it was to hold her naked in his arms, to hear her gasp as she shuddered under his caresses—and it seemed that he was a long way from being sated with that pleasure.

'Thank you.' Her smile lit up her face in the way that had first drawn him to her. There was humour there, and some-

thing he realised had been absent since their arrival at Knightshaye—a trusting friendliness. 'Shepton is preparing your
bath. I believe he has been keeping watch from upstairs for
your arrival.'

'I will go straight up.' Justin tossed his gloves, whip and
hat on to the Armada chest and recalled the notebook in his
pocket. 'I'll just put my notes in the study.

The state of the hall had been a pleasant surprise. The
sight, and smell, of his study brought him up short on the
threshold. It glowed in the evening light slanting in through
the undraped windows. Fresh candles, ink in the inkwells,
a great sheaf of grasses and ferns filling the empty fireplace, the desktop clear and waiting for whatever he chose
to spread out on it, the old leather chair gleaming like a
polished conker.

And roses in neat, somehow old-fashioned, arrangements
in masculine pewter pots.

'Mari.'

'Yes?' She was at his elbow, head cocked to one side as
she watched his reaction with just a hint of anxiety in those
deep grey eyes.

'The servants did not do this. This was done with—' he
almost said *love* '—with such care.'

'I did it, and Jenny and Hearnshaw and the footmen. You
should have seen Hearnshaw's face, Justin! All upon his
dignity because I insisted the men appear at the front of the
house in their baize aprons and do *dusting*.'

Justin grinned. He could imagine the scene, and it was all
too obvious who had won that battle of wills. He stepped into
the room and Mari came in too, passing him to retrieve a
fallen rose petal from the desktop.

The wave of affection, shot through with urgent desire, that
swept him as he watched her slender figure bending over the

desk, had him pushing the door closed. The lock clicked as he twisted the key in it.

'Thank you, again. You are working miracles already. You must not overdo it, Mari.'

She looked up at him, amusement warming her face. 'What a poor honey you must think me! Do you expect me to be exhausted by a little housework?'

'No,' he said huskily, taking her in his arms. 'By my love-making.'

She gave an endearing squeak of alarm as his arms came round her. He knew he was hot, and dusty and certainly sweaty, and that he should go upstairs and wash and change and come down to dinner in a civilised manner. But he did not want to be civilised, he wanted to make love to his wife, here and now on this wide desk. He wanted to be very uncivilised indeed.

'This is a most convenient height.'

'For what?' Her eyes were wide as she looked up at him from the circle of his arms. Mari had obviously expected him to kiss her, not discuss furniture.

'For this.' He lifted her easily until she was perched on the edge, then moved in close, nudging her legs apart. 'Mmm.' He nuzzled the soft curve of her neck appreciatively, making her gasp and put up her hands to his shoulders to steady herself.

The soft folds of her sapphire blue dinner dress were deceptive. He had thought them wide enough for what he had in mind, but her petticoats were tight underneath, preventing him getting as close as he wanted.

Impatient now, Justin pushed up skirts and petticoats until they pooled in Mari's lap, leaving her legs exposed in their gartered stockings.

'Justin!' He could tell by the breathless laugh that she was torn between shock and mischief. 'What are you doing?'

'This, my sweet.' He tipped back her head and found her mouth, slanting his lips over hers hard so that she parted for him and his tongue could dart into the heat of her mouth even as his fingers slipped between her round thighs, found the slit in her drawers, slid insinuatingly into the warm, moist tangle of curls.

Mari moaned against the mastering pressure of his mouth but she was not afraid; already he could feel her response to him. She was learning quickly, this wife of his—and teaching her was fascinating. Justin deepened the kiss, making it more demanding, drawing the warm honey-taste of her into his lungs, trapping her head in one hand while the other teased and explored until she was pressing against him in wordless demand.

Oh, she tasted good. With the thought came another idea that had his breath catching in his throat. Would Mari be too shocked, too alarmed? Would he be going too fast? Justin pushed her back gently on to the top of the desk, having the forethought, just in time, to move the inkwells one-handed to the side as he did so.

'Justin? This is your *desk*!' To his amusement she sounded more querulous at him ceasing to kiss her than alarmed as he slid to his knees between her slender legs and leaned forward. *Ah, yes, honey...*

Chapter Fourteen

Confused, disorientated and disappointed that he had stopped kissing her, Marina struggled to raise herself on her elbows, then fell back with a muffled cry of alarm. It turned to one of horrified pleasure as Justin's mouth found her.

'Justin! Stop it!' She struggled to sit up, but the intensity of the sensations his wickedly flickering tongue was producing seemed to have sapped all her strength. He stopped and sat back. She could just see a pair of laughing green eyes regarding her. 'Oh, don't…'

'You told me to stop,' he said innocently.

'Yes…no…oh, please, don't stop.' It was the most outrageous, shameful, ecstatic sensation, one she would never have dreamed possible. Marina's blindly grasping hands found the edge of the table as Justin tipped her over into a mindless spiral of velvet blackness where all she was conscious of was her own gasping sobs and the convulsions racking her body.

She came to herself to find that she was still sprawled in total abandon on the hard desk, her legs dangling and Justin standing between them, his eyes burning with a mixture of desire and tenderness that stifled the incoherent words which came to her lips.

'Oh, sweetheart, to come home to you at the end of a long day…' His fingers were busy with the fastenings of his breeches and Marina's pleasure-saturated brain finally managed to focus on what was about to happen.

No, not here, she thought desperately, not in broad daylight when he could not help but realise the pain she was trying to hide when he took her. Not now, when she was still half-drugged by the pleasures he was teaching her.

'My lord?' The study door handle rattled and Marina gave a startled gasp, scrabbling to sit up, sweep her disordered skirts down to hide her legs. 'My lord, excuse me, but your bathwater is getting cold. Would you wish me to send for some fresh hot water in a little while?'

'*Damn*. No, thank you, Shepton. I will be right up, just as soon as I have put these papers away.'

'Papers, indeed!' Marina knew her voice was emerging as an unbecoming yelp as she scrambled off the desk, swiping frantically at her skirts. 'Justin, that was outrageous, and in broad daylight, and in your study of all places!'

'Mmm.' He caught her and pulled her close to him, indulging himself with a leisurely kiss. He smelt of leather and horse and sweat and under it the soap he used and the elusive scent that was simply male. Her male. Helpless with love and dizzy with outrageously satisfied desire, Marina pressed herself against him, aware of his arousal, aroused herself by it, even though she was frightened of what it meant.

'I think we should make love in every room in the house as it is finished,' he remarked, reluctantly putting her from him and going to unlock the door.

'Even the hall?' Thank goodness her skirts were only slightly creased, Marina patted distractedly at her hair as she followed Justin out of the study, fighting the shaky feeling that she should really go and sit down before her knees gave way.

'It might be tactically difficult, I suppose.' He paused with one foot on the bottom step. 'Three in the morning, perhaps. No, I couldn't face the thought of being interrupted by Hearnshaw with a shotgun convinced we were being burgled. We could give all the servants the afternoon off.'

'They would guess,' she hissed. How could he talk about such things in a normal tone of voice? Anyone could hear.

'What, that I had dismissed them so I could make love to you on the Armada chest? What lurid imaginations our staff must have.' He was chuckling as he vanished round the bend in the stairs, leaving Marina pink, flustered and half-inclined to giggle.

She was feeling so much more comfortable with him now. It was almost like the weeks when she had thought him motivated by nothing but friendship, only now with the added knowledge of each other that their physical intimacy gave. But Justin was still not confiding in her about anything that mattered. If she had not seen his betraying weariness and discouragement before he entered the house, she would suspect nothing was wrong.

Hearnshaw emerged through the green baize door and hesitated when he saw her. 'Might I have a few words, my lady?'

Oh dear. That sounded distinctly like Domestic Trouble to Marina's experienced ears. 'Yes, of course, Hearnshaw. Shall we go into the Chinese room?'

Marina sat down and waited, intrigued that Hearnshaw was developing enough confidence to come and air what she suspected was a grievance.

'I was going to ask, my lady, seeing that Mrs Hodgken has additional help in the kitchen, if I can have at least another under-footman and a boot boy. Seeing that the shortage of maids requires us to leave our duties to carry out dusting,' he added darkly. Hearnshaw was going red about the ears;

whether from embarrassment at making such a request, or annoyance over having been asked to take part in the demeaning dusting, she was not sure.

Marina regarded him calmly, rather pleased that he was asserting himself—butlers had to learn to be a power in the household. 'When Mrs Faversham arrives tomorrow, one of the first things I will be discussing with her is the hiring of more maids; we are definitely under-staffed in that department. That will ensure we do not have to call on your staff so frequently. However, until we begin entertaining, I do not think I can justify two more male staff. Which would be your higher priority—the footman or the boy?'

If Hearnshaw wanted to puff up his own authority, he would choose the under-footman, she thought. If they really did have too many menial tasks, the boot boy was a much more sensible choice. He bit his underlip, his thought processes obvious. Marina hid a smile; soon he would learn to think through his strategy before approaching her.

'The boy, my lady,' he decided.

'Good—a very sensible decision. And if you need to employ extra men from the village for the chimneys and any rough work, please do so on your own authority.'

That sent him away with a barely suppressed expression of glee on his face. Marina decided she must start a proper wages book as soon as possible. In fact, she should do so at once—there were some unused ledgers in the study. But suddenly it was all too much effort. She sat back in the chair instead, surprised that she should feel so weary. The day had not been so very tiring for a young lady used to walking, gardening and assisting around the house. And her back ached.

Grumbling, Marina rubbed it, then realised that disporting herself on the desk top was probably the cause of that. As a result, when the gong rang, she walked into the dining room with a very flushed countenance, wondering how one was ever to preserve one's dignity as a countess when the earl insisted on such wanton romps at all hours of the day.

The earl in question was already in the room, discussing how the wine he had sent on ahead was settling. 'I would appreciate it if your lordship would give me your instruction on the best place to store the port,' Hearnshaw was saying. 'The old racks marked up for it look to be in a damp corner of the cellar.'

'We'll see tomorrow.' Justin beat him to Marina's chair and helped her to sit with a smile that combined a polite greeting with a dangerous hint of wickedness. She felt herself go pinker still.

Marina had decreed service in the Russian style. After soup had been cleared and the main dishes set out, she nodded to Hearnshaw. 'Thank you. We will serve ourselves. I will ring when we require dessert. Will you carve the chicken, my lord?'

'This is all very intimate,' Justin observed, standing to address the roast fowl.

'I thought it silly to have the table covered in dishes and the servants rushing round clearing and setting out removes when there are just the two of us. But if you dislike it, I will tell Hearnshaw to revert to *service à la français*. I feel we should in any case, when we are entertaining; I imagine it is still more accepted in the country.'

'It is an admirable idea.' Justin helped her to the sliced chicken and accepted some of the collops of veal from the dish set before her. 'An excellent dinner, my lady, you may send my compliments to the cook.'

Marina regarded him from under her lashes as they ate, exchanging comfortable small talk about the weather, the varieties of roses she had found in the garden and her decision to employ a boot boy. Justin seemed in a good mood now, but then he was extremely good at hiding his moods and his feelings. She would ask him directly about the estate, she decided.

And if he was frank with her, shared his worries, then she would take heart from that and admit that she knew about the arranged marriage, confess how much it was distressing her. But she could not bring herself to even consider talking to him about his relationship with Serena, the lovely Marchioness of Andover. That betrayal went too deep, cut too savagely at her self-confidence.

'How was your day? In what state did you find things?'

Clear hazel eyes met hers with complete candour as he smiled. 'Neglected, as you might expect, but nothing a little care will not remedy.'

'Did you meet any of the tenants? How is their land?' she persisted.

'Well enough. They have missed having someone taking a direct interest, but that will change now.'

'And the Home Farm?' This was like drawing teeth. What did it take for Justin to confide his worries to her? This was hardly a little thing.

'Sheffield will soon have that licked into shape.' There, the lowered lashes, shielding some emotion he was not going to share with her.

'It is in good heart, then?' she enquired more sharply than she intended and received a very direct look from under raised brows at the tone.

'Not as good as I would have hoped, but it will soon be remedied.'

'I am glad,' Marina said sweetly, hiding her chagrin. Well, if he was not going to confide in her, she would just have to find out for herself. But in her turn, she was most definitely not going to confide her distress, or her intimate problems, to a man who deceived her and shut her out. Even if she did love him.

And she was in no mood to try and winkle anything out of

Justin tonight, that was certain. Her lower back was one dull, miserable ache now. 'Have you finished, my lord? I will ring for dessert.'

It was as she was spooning up a delicious mouthful of Chantilly cream that she realised just why she was feeling so poorly. Marina put down her spoon with a rattle and did some rapid mental arithmetic. How could she have forgotten, especially after she and Mama had done such careful forward planning to ensure that the day Justin wanted for the wedding did not coincide with entirely the wrong time of the month?

It was a day or two early, but unlike Pris, who had once confided that the Greenwich Observatory could be kept on time by the working of her system, Marina often found her courses irregular.

How wonderful—an entire week when she was quite safe from the need to dread Justin coming to her bed! Then her spirits sank—an entire week when she would be deprived of Justin's kisses and those wickedly sensual caresses she was becoming addicted to. And how did she tell him why he must not come to her bed? Oh, goodness, neither Mama or Priscilla had explained how one went about *that*.

At least she had half an hour while Justin lingered over his port before he would join her in the Chinese room. Time to run upstairs and take a little of the cordial that helped the ache, before coming down to preside over the tea tray later.

Justin came to pull back her chair when she announced her intention to leave him to his port and she smiled, struggling with the contradictory emotions that coloured her every contact with him: love, anger, betrayal, admiration, desire, fear.

He went to hold open the door and she unthinkingly pressed her hand into the small of her back as she walked towards him, snatching it away when she saw his eyes sharpen. 'Does your back hurt?' His voice held so much concern that she smiled at him reassuringly.

'Only an ache, it is nothing.'

He glanced round, saw that Harris was busy clearing the buffet, and said firmly, 'I will pass on the port this evening and join you in the Chinese room.'

Flustered, Marina allowed herself to be shepherded into the sitting room and pressed into the upholstered chair by the bay window. Justin came and hunkered down by the side of it, taking her hand in his and looking her straight in the eye.

'Now, do not try to be brave with me, Mari; I must have hurt your back in the study. Of all the stupid things to do, to give way to the urge to make love to you in such a situation, on that hard desk. It was incredibly selfish of me.'

'It was very nice,' Marina ventured, touched by his self-reproach. He was so kind to her—when he had nothing to hide.

'Well, I thought so.' He smiled ruefully. 'But I have obviously caused you to strain a muscle. Now, do you want me to send for the doctor now, or see how you feel in the morning if I carry you up to bed?'

'Oh my goodness, no!' Now what was she going to say? The truth apparently, there was nothing else for it, however embarrassing. She could not allow him to summon the local physician only to have to explain to the poor man that she was suffering from nothing more than the normal female monthly nuisance. 'I haven't hurt my back. It is just that by tomorrow I will have…I mean, my back always aches before I…' He was looking blank, as well he might. 'I am about to start my courses,' she blurted out.

'Ah.' Justin sat back on his heels and grinned. 'How dense of me. That's what comes of being brought up in an all-male household—one forgets that there is a certain rhythm to female existence.'

'But what about all your mistresses?' Marina asked without thinking. 'They must have been unavailable at regular intervals.'

'Well, yes, but one didn't have to live with it, as it were.' Justin got to his feet and went to sprawl elegantly on the upholstered window seat close beside her. 'And what do you mean, *all* of my mistresses?'

'I doubt you got your experience from just one,' Marina countered, rallying now the hideous embarrassment of telling him was past.

'I am flattered you find me experienced.' His grin was positively wicked. 'It is normal for gentlemen to have mistresses. One at a time, naturally.' He must have seen the question in her eyes. 'Unmarried gentlemen, of course.'

'*And* married ones. I know Papa had a mistress, for she was very expensive, which upset Mama almost more than anything about the matter. And Priscilla says she is very glad her husband does not, for it is common in society.'

Justin leant over, took her hand and kissed her fingertips. 'I do not have a mistress, I have not had one for six months and I have no intention of getting another one.' Marina smiled back at him, then felt the expression freeze on her lips as he added, 'I give you my word, Marina.'

On my honour, Mari, I love no other woman. That was what Justin had promised her when he proposed—and that had proven to be a lie. Perhaps he meant to keep to this promise, but Marina had a sinking feeling that, if she did not continue to please him in bed, it was asking a lot of him to remain faithful.

'Now, you must go up to bed and rest. Can you walk? Shall I carry you up? Or should I ring for your woman to help you?' Despite all her doubts, Marina could not help smiling at him. Bless the man, he was doing his best to come to terms with this feminine mystery, even if he did appear to think she was going to be an invalid for a week.

'Justin, I will be fine. I am not ill, it is just a routine happening. A dratted nuisance,' she added candidly, 'but nothing out of the ordinary. I'll go up and take some cordial and then I have some ideas for the garden, which I would like to discuss with you. Unless you have paperwork to be going over? Your notes from today?'

'Nothing that cannot wait until tomorrow.' Justin got up and tugged the bell pull. 'Harris, please send her ladyship's woman to her chamber immediately.' When the footman left he helped her to her feet and stood for a moment looking down at her. 'Do you think you will be happy here, Mari? Are you ready to forgive me yet?'

'Whatever for?' She found her hand was at her throat and forced herself to stay calm. Was he going to confess about the marriage? Or even about Serena?

'For dragging you into the depths of the country and asking you to live in a wreck of a house. Most wives would expect at least a honeymoon first.'

'One of those trips Charlie was so eager to suggest to us?' Marina steadied her breathing. No, there was no danger that she was going to have to deal with any confessions. 'He only wanted to put off the day when you discovered what had been happening here.' She smiled with rueful affection. 'The wretch.'

The idea came to Marina as she was climbing the stairs. If Justin would not tell her about the estate, why, then, she would go and see for herself, show him it did no good to hide things from her. And she had every reason to do so: it was her duty to visit the tenants and see to their welfare.

Tomorrow—no, the new housekeeper was arriving then. The day after tomorrow she would ask one of the grooms to harness a gig and drive her round the tenants' cottages. Justin would just have to learn that keeping everything from his wife was not possible.

Chapter Fifteen

'What an absolutely beautiful house, my lady.' Mrs Faversham gazed down the length of the Long Gallery and sighed happily, apparently oblivious to mouse-eaten rush matting, festoons of cobwebs, hearths stained with fallen soot and mouldering hangings. She had remained silent throughout a tour of the part of the house Marina herself was familiar with—the women had not even ventured into the other areas—and Marina had been conscious of her spirits sinking ever lower the longer the dismal tour went on. This enthusiasm was blessedly unexpected.

'I think so too,' Marina answered, 'but frankly, Mrs Faversham, I was prepared for you to take one look and go straight back to London.' The new housekeeper turned in surprise, so she added, 'I have to tell you that Knightshaye is in far worse a condition than my husband or I expected.'

'But what a challenge, Lady Mortenhoe! This is exactly what I was hoping for, yet never thought to find.' The housekeeper stroked one hand tenderly down a filthy curtain. 'To be able to make a difference to somewhere like this will be such a satisfaction.'

Marina sighed with relief. Not only had she found a house-keeper who was prepared to stay, but one who obviously felt as she did, someone who would be an ally.

'I feel exactly the same,' she confessed. 'Now, if you would care to take some time to settle into your rooms, we can meet after luncheon to discuss our plan of campaign. I have allo-cated Kitty to you as your personal maid until you are in a position to make your own choice, but I feel one of your first decisions will be about the hiring of more staff.'

Marina made her way down to the Chinese room, almost laughing out loud with relief. As she reached the empty hall she executed a reckless twirl out of sheer high spirits, her sensible morning gown flying out around her ankles. Behind her a door opened and she stopped abruptly, staggered, and found herself swept into Justin's embrace.

'Mari, sweet, are you all right? Are you dizzy? I knew you should keep to your room and rest.' Oh, but it was so good to be held against his chest, to feel cared for and cosseted, that she almost succumbed to the temptation to murmur that perhaps she did feel a little unwell, just to experience him catching her up in his arms and carrying her upstairs.

But that would be pure self-indulgence. Marine stiffened her spine and shook her head. 'It was my own silly fault, I was dancing a jig out of delight at our new housekeeper. Justin, she is going to be a *treasure*. She loves the house and is delighted at the challenge of helping to set it to rights. Can you imagine? I had been in despair, convinced she would take one look and demand to return to town immediately!'

'I took one look at her and went and hid,' he confessed. 'She looked so formidable, I was quite cowed at the thought of meeting her and failing to come up to her expectations.'

'I suspect you and I may fail to do that,' Marina agreed, tucking her hand under the crook of his arm in a friendly manner, 'but she is so in love with Knightshaye that I am sure she will overlook our faults. No, do not try and escape back into your study, my lord! You must tell me now which rooms you wish us to deal with next.'

'Your bedchamber and dressing rooms, one of the larger salons and a dining room,' Justin pronounced. 'Now, I must go and concentrate on these estate papers.'

'As a result of your tour yesterday?' Marina asked innocently, hoping her fishing was not obvious.

'No, not particularly.' Justin freed his arm and headed back into the study. 'I must be on top of things before Sheffield arrives, that is all.'

Must you, indeed? Marina thought grimly, more than ever determined to find out the true state of matters for herself. Beside anything else, if things were as bad as his grim weariness she had glimpsed yesterday betokened, then she would have to start budgeting carefully after all.

'And I have a list here of additional staff for you to review, Lady Mortenhoe.' Mrs Faversham drew to the end of an efficient recital of her plan of campaign for the next week, her predictions on the housekeeping budget required and her preliminary opinion of the existing staff.

Marina took the sheets of paper feeling rather breathless. 'This is excellent progress, Mrs Faversham—you appear to have accomplished a great deal in scarce twenty-four hours.'

'There is a great deal to be done, my lady.' That was undoubtedly true and Marina felt rather guilty at leaving the new housekeeper to her own devices on only her second day.

'I will look over this list carefully later,' she promised, folding it and placing it on the little table beside her chair in the Chinese room. She had better form an opinion on the state of the estate and the likely costs of restoring it—not that she

knew the first thing about rural affairs, she admitted to herself—before she made extravagant demands for domestic
staff. 'But I am afraid I must leave you to get on with things
now—I simply cannot delay visiting the tenants any longer.'

'Of course, Lady Mortenhoe.' Mrs Faversham nodded
emphatic approval without disturbing a hair of her rigidly
coifed black hair. Marina wondered how old she was. Thir-
ty-five, perhaps? 'If you are able to supply me with a list of
those who are in need of medical supplies or restorative food,
I will ensure that they are catered for on a regular basis. Are
there many estate homes to visit?'

'I am not sure,' Marina prevaricated, realising that she not
only did not know how many tenants they had, but she did
not have a clue where they lived or the extent of the estate.
And the grooms, as new to the place as she, would not know
either.

One thing she could not do was to go to ask Justin for a
map or directions; she had a strong suspicion that he would
say she should not go out without him and should be at home
resting.

Marina dismissed Mrs Faversham and sat brooding. Justin
was genuinely concerned for her health and well-being, she
had no doubt of that, but she was equally aware that he was
quite intelligent enough to use that concern to hide the true
state of affairs from her. But how long could he hope to keep
that up? A few days at most and then he would have to think
of something else.

She rose at the sound of voices in the hall and moved to
the door. Hearnshaw was speaking. 'I am not certain where
her ladyship is, my lord. Shall I send for her woman?'

'No, I only wanted to let her know that I am driving into
Aylesbury—I forgot to mention it at breakfast.'

'Very good, my lord, I will ensure that her ladyship is

informed immediately. Will your lordship be returning by dinner time?'

'Yes, thank you, Hearnshaw. About six, I should imagine.'

Marina went to step out and bid Justin goodbye, then stopped, her fingers curling around the door handle. He was sure to ask her how she intended to spend her day and she could not bring herself to lie to him. She had been on tenter-hooks all through breakfast, expecting that very question.

Wistfully she watched as he strode across the apron of gravel before the house to where Harris was waiting with the phaeton. She would have liked to go with him, or at least to have kissed him goodbye. 'Justin,' she whispered, flattening one palm against the glass as the carriage turned and vanished over the moat bridge.

Then she realised that, unless he had locked the study behind him, she could now look at estate plans to her heart's content. Marina positively ran across the room, out into the hall and abruptly slowed to a decorous walk as she saw Hearn-shaw still there.

'My lady! I do apologise, I did not realise you were in that room. His lordship has just left for Aylesbury and will not return until six this evening.'

'Oh dear, I missed him.' Marina counterfeited a look of regret. 'Never mind. That will be all for the moment, Hearnshaw.'

He effaced himself with a bow and Marina turned the handle of the study door. It was open. She went in, feeling absurdly guilty, and saw, in the middle of the desk, a neat black notebook, tied with a thin strip of leather to keep it from flapping open in a pocket. *Justin's notebook.* That would tell her all she wanted to know. Marina reached out a hand, then snatched it back. No, she could not snoop and pry into his private notes, that would make her as bad in her deceit as he.

Resolutely turning her back on temptation, Marina

scanned the shelves. At some point she recalled the footmen dusting large rolls which, surely, were plans of the estate. Now, where had they put them?

It took only a few minutes to locate the plans, but rather longer to sketch out a copy that would enable her to direct the groom to the various clusters of tenant homes and to find the Home Farm. Marina tucked it into her reticule and rang for Hearnshaw.

'Please send Jenny to my room and ask one of the grooms to bring the Dennett gig round to the front door in about fifteen minutes. I will be driving around the estate and visiting tenants this morning. I would expect to be back for luncheon around half past one.'

It was tempting to take the reins herself, but Marina hesitated to risk looking less than competent in front of Fulton. And she suspected that Justin would be far from happy that she was driving without his supervision. She smoothed out her sketch map and gazed around her as they crossed the moat into the park. 'Down to the point where the track leads off to the right, Fulton, and follow that. We should find the first group of cottages in a quarter of a mile.'

The state of the park with its thickets of thorn and the high, waving grass, came as no shock, but Marina's first sight of the group of cottages fulfilled her worst apprehensions.

Thatch bulged and sagged, patched all over and held down in several places by roughly tied planks. Fences were rickety, windows and doors cracked and peeling. The cottage gardens were productive enough, filled with rows of vegetables and clumps of cottage flowers that provided a note of cheer, but somehow they did not have that air of prosperity and confidence that Marina had observed when visiting the estates of some of Charlie's friends.

Fulton drew up at the first gate and helped Marina down. A dog barked, then a small child appeared at the door, took one look and ran back inside screaming. *A good start!* she thought, opening the gate after a brief tussle with the twine that closed it.

A woman appeared on the doorstep, rubbing her hands on a coarse sacking apron. She looked tired and distinctly un-welcoming. 'Have you lost your way, ma'am?' she asked, civilly enough.

'No, indeed not. I am Lady Mortenhoe and I have come to meet the estate tenants. I am afraid I do not know your name, Mrs—?'

'Field.' The woman's face did not relax on hearing who she was addressing, although she bobbed what might pass for a curtsy if one was feeling charitable. After a long moment she added, 'Would you care to come in, my lady?'

Marina maintained her determined smile and accepted, finding herself in a dark room that seemed to serve as both kitchen and living room. The child she had seen earlier stared at her wide-eyed from behind a chair.

'Hello, what is your name?'

'That's Harriett, my lady. The other three are out helping their father.'

'Not at school, Mrs Field? Is there a school for the local children?'

The woman looked at her as though she were mad. 'School? What would they be wanting with the likes of that? They're more use working with their father.'

'I am afraid the cottages have been allowed to become very run down.' Marina tried another tack. 'Lord Mortenhoe will be attending to that once his steward arrives next week.'

The woman's face revealed nothing but a faint scepticism. 'That'd be good, my lady. When it happens.' She paused, then added slyly, 'Your ladyship's brother used to own the estate, didn't he?'

Oh, Lord. Marina had not realised the tenants would know of her connection with Knightshaye. No wonder she was receiving such an off-hand reception here. 'Yes, indeed. Lord Mortenhoe, however, will not be an absentee landlord.' That was as far as she was prepared to go in implied criticism of her brother and father. People would learn soon enough that Justin was not going to neglect them, and neither was she.

'Well, I must get on, if I am to get round all the cottages today,' she said with a firm smile. 'Goodbye, Harriett, Mrs Field.'

By the time Marina had visited ten cottages she was feeling weary, not so much for want of her luncheon, which was well overdue, but from the solid wall of hostility she was encountering and the extent of the work that would be needed.

She had brought her own notebook with her and her jottings filled several pages. She glanced up from noting that the last cottage she had called at was occupied by an elderly widower called Ben Harris, who would benefit from receiving regular supplies from the Knightshaye kitchens and some new blankets for his bed, to see that Fulton was drawing up in front of the last cottage and that another gig was already there.

As she got down a man appeared at the door. Tall, dark and somehow elegant, despite a very simple suit of clerical black, he doffed his hat when he saw her. 'Madam.'

'Good day. I am Lady Mortenhoe.' It must be the vicar, although he appeared rather young. Marina found herself smiling into friendly blue eyes.

'And I am Jeremy Coulter, the curate of this parish. May I welcome you to Knightshaye, Lady Mortenhoe?'

'Thank you.' The relief at finding someone prepared to be

pleasant was a bright spot in a difficult morning. 'I am making myself acquainted with our tenants.'

The smile vanished from Mr Coulter's face. 'It was a great relief to hear that Knightshaye would be inhabited again. The neighbourhood has suffered considerably from that lack.'

'Indeed,' Marina agreed coolly. 'My husband is deeply concerned.' And if he was not already, he assuredly would be once she had spoken to him that evening! 'We will be doing everything we can to improve matters for the tenants.'

'So you say, my lady!' A man appeared in the doorway behind the curate. Tall, almost hulking, Marina realised with a shock that he must have been very ill, for the flesh had fallen away, leaving his shabby clothes too large for him, and his face was an unhealthy colour. 'And what will you do for my wife and childer that I can't afford to keep and have had to go and live with my brother and his wife? What will you do for them, eh?'

'Now then, Joe,' Mr Coulter took the man's arm, tried to turn him back into the cottage and was pushed away.

'Don't you "now then" me, Curate!' He lurched forward, waving a calloused finger at Marina. 'It was her father and brother that let this place get in the state it is—what good is she going to do? My land floods, winter after winter, and the water stands, souring the earth so I can't get no crops worth anything off it and the beasts get the rot in their feet. And would they do anything about drainage? Would they hell!'

Fulton moved up beside Marina protectively and the curate took the angry man's arm again, but Marina ignored them. 'I give you my word that your land will be drained,' she said steadily, forcing herself not to wince at the sour breath as he glowered at her. 'What is your name?'

'Joe Elliott. And what good's your word, or his fancy lordship's? It'll all be the same.'

'You will see how good our word is by the end of the month when the drainage work starts, Elliott.' How long would it take to start it? Was this the right time of year? Marina dismissed these worries; if she had to hire the labourers herself, the work was going to get done.

The big man shrugged, still glowering, then was seized by a racking cough. 'I will send medicine for that,' she promised. He shrugged again and turned back into his ramshackle cottage, slamming the door behind him.

'Ma'am, I do apologise.' She turned, frowning, to find the curate watching her anxiously.

'Why should you? No wonder he is angry and bitter.' Marina made a brief note in her book, then thrust it into her reticule. 'I am returning to the house for luncheon, Mr Coulter. Can you join me? I would value your opinion on how best to help these people.'

His young, worried face split into a broad smile that lifted her heart. 'I am entirely at your service, my lady.'

By five that afternoon, with Mr Coulter's help, Marina had lists of all the tenants' names, their families and their pressing needs. Mrs Faversham and Cook had been summoned and had gone their separate ways to make broth and bread, raid Marina's small stock of medicines and sort through piles of rugs and blankets to try to find some that were not too moth eaten and ragged to be washed and mended.

Marina had ink stains on her fingers, her hair was coming down at the back and she and the curate were on first-name terms. How that had happened Marina was not sure, for he seemed a very proper young man. Somehow the afternoon of scribbling and plotting, one each side of Justin's big desk with the estate map spread out on the floor, left them on as good terms as brother and sister.

'But, Jeremy—look, the Widow Hall's is only a few yards from Ben Harris's cottage.' She was on her hands and knees beside the map, pointing. Mr Coulter came and crouched down beside her. 'I could pay her each week to cook for him and do his laundry. She needs the money, and he needs looking after, it would be perfect—'

Marina broke off, looking up as the door opened. Beside her Jeremy Coulter scrambled to his feet. 'Justin! Oh, I am sorry, can't you get in? I'll just move this map.' She stood, pulling the map back as she did so, and her husband came fully into the room.

'Are you going to introduce me, my dear?' He must be tired, his voice sounded flat and somehow chilly.

'Of course, how remiss of me. Jeremy, this is my husband, Lord Mortenhoe. Justin, Mr Coulter is our curate. We have been visiting the tenants and deciding what can best be done to help them.' Enthusiastically she gathered up the sheaf of papers on the desk. 'You see how busy we have been.'

'Exceedingly busy.' Now he sounded dry as well as cold.

'And it is absolutely imperative that work starts as soon as possible draining Joe Elliott's land. His beasts are getting foot rot…' The atmosphere finally penetrated her urgency. Mr Coulter was looking positively uncomfortable and her husband—her husband was a different, forbidding stranger.

'Why, look at the clock,' Marina said brightly. 'I declare it is almost dinner time. Will you not stay and eat with us, Jer…Mr Coulter?'

He was already reaching for his hat. 'That is most kind, Lady Mortenhoe, but I must decline. Thank you for your enthusiastic support—now I have every confidence that want in the parish will be rapidly reduced.' He bowed stiffly to Justin, looking absurdly young. 'Lord Mortenhoe. A pleasure to have met you. I will see myself out…'

The door closed behind him, leaving the study in silence. What on earth was the matter with Justin? Had he had bad news? Had he a headache? Then, meeting the hard blaze of his green eyes, Marina realised. He was furiously angry—with her.

The dressing gong shattered the silence between them.

Chapter Sixteen

The dressing gong shattered the silence between them.
Justin opened the door and stood punctiliously to one side
to let her out.

'Justin…'

He raised one eyebrow and nodded in the direction of the
butler who was returning the hammer to its stand by the brass
gong. 'Good evening, Hearnshaw.'

'Good evening, my lord. Dinner will be served in thirty
minutes if that is acceptable.'

Marina tried to speak again as they went upstairs. 'Justin,
Mr Coulter says—'

'I am sure the opinions of our youthful curate are fascinating. However, if you will excuse me, my dear, I really must
go and change.' He left her standing at her bedchamber door
staring after him, a cold knot forming in the pit of her
stomach. Justin had never, ever, spoken to her like that before.

Biting her lip, she went into her room and stared blankly at
Jenny who was bustling around setting out her evening clothes.

'Oh! See the state of your fingers, my lady! It looks as
though you have been dabbling in the ink pot. Come into the

dressing room and soak them, quickly, and I'll find the pumice stone. Tsk!' Marina followed obediently and stood with her hands in soapy water while Jenny rummaged for the stone. 'Here it is, and the nail brush.'

The ink began to come off, leaving black swirls in the water and making the bubbles burst. Marina stared at it. How could she have handled that so badly, blurting out demands about what must be done before Justin had scarce got his hat off? And she must have looked a complete romp, kneeling on the floor like that. But he seemed so coldly annoyed. Surely it was not just disapproval of her hoydenish behaviour? Perhaps he was tired.

'Let me undo this gown, my lady.' Jenny began to work her way down the buttons while Marina scrubbed unthinkingly at her nails. Perhaps he had had another bad day. Where had he gone? Aylesbury, that was it; the nearest large market town. He must have gone to make sure his banking arrangements were satisfactory and transact some business.

Oh, goodness. If he had been talking to his banker about what he had discovered yesterday and making enquiries about what it would cost to put all to rights, perhaps he had realised that his fortune would not be enough after all. She dried her hands on the towel and let Jenny help her out of her gown, fiddling with the brushes on the dressing table while the maid changed the water in the bowl.

And he had come home to his wife making demands that he spend what must be a significant sum immediately, and in front of a complete stranger. No wonder Justin was annoyed.

Thoroughly anxious now, Marina could only be glad she had not made a snap decision on the new staff Mrs Faversham wanted to employ. What had she gleaned about Justin's financial history? She racked her brains, piecing together snippets of gossip that Pris had dropped, along with Charlie's comments.

The family had been all but ruined when his father lost Knightshaye and Justin himself had rebuilt the fortune. But how much money could one man make in ten years while still maintaining a respectable presence in fashionable London? Marina realised she had no idea.

Anxious, and braced to make an abject apology, Marina went downstairs to find Justin waiting for her in the dining room and Hearnshaw and a footman already in attendance.

'Is Aylesbury a pleasant town?' she enquired as they began on their soup. Once the tureens were removed she could dismiss the servants and be alone with him. The hot liquid settled uneasily in her queasy stomach.

'Well enough. It seems very prosperous and considerably larger than I had remembered. There is a market twice a week.'

'Oh.' She could not think of anything else to ask about Aylesbury and Justin did not seem inclined to add to his brief comments. The footman began to clear and set out the dishes for the main course. 'Thank you, Hearnshaw—'

'Remain, if you please, Hearnshaw.' Justin cut across her. 'I am disinclined to carve this evening.'

Marina swallowed. They could hardly sit there in silence. What would the servants think? 'I took the Dennett gig out this morning,' she ventured bravely. 'With the bay cob.'

'Indeed? Would you care for some peas?'

'It was a very nice day for a drive.'

'I found it so.' Justin's face was perfectly bland, his body seemed relaxed and at ease. But Marina saw how level his brows were, as though he was fighting to keep a frown from appearing. And his eyes were vivid green. 'How did you find the cob?'

'He seemed to go very well for Fulton.'

One of those forbidding eyebrows winged upwards. 'You did not drive yourself?'

'I did not care to. I did not think you would wish me to, in your absence.' Marina chewed a mouthful of lamb that appeared to consist entirely of sawdust.

'How very dutiful. I had no idea you would be so sensitive to my wishes, my dear.' His voice was perfectly pleasant and the hovering servants would have caught no satirical edge to it. Marina found herself flushing painfully.

'I try to be,' she responded, her voice hardly more than a whisper. She just wanted to be alone with him, explain, make him stop behaving like a courteous, distant stranger.

The meal dragged on and Marina gave up all attempt to make small talk. Justin filled the silence with occasional comments about the food, offers to pass her items and a short discussion with Hearnshaw on the number of bottles of Rhenish wine remaining.

At last she was able to put down her spoon to cover the custard cream she had been chasing round her plate and stood up. 'I will leave you to your port, my lord.'

Justin stood as she did, acknowledging her words with a bow, but when he spoke it was to the butler. 'Hearnshaw, bring me that bottle without a label, I have been meaning to try it and see what it is.'

She had been so certain that he would forgo his solitary drink and join her that Marina stopped, staring at her husband until his politely enquiring expression sent her from the room.

It was a full half-hour before he strolled in the Chinese room. Marina had been doggedly going through Mrs Faversham's list of suggestions for improvements and for additional staff and putting crosses against virtually everything. The welfare of the tenants had to come first. As Justin came in she folded the list and set it down on a side table.

'Justin—' She broke off, uncertain how to begin. 'Justin,

I can tell you are annoyed with me. I should never have blurted out what must have seemed like a demand in that manner, not with a visitor present.'

He went over to the window, looked out for a long moment, then came back to take the chair opposite hers, crossing one long leg over the other and folding his hands together. 'Indeed? You imagine that was what annoyed me?'

'Yes. And, obviously, I should not have been sitting on the floor like that. It was unbefitting of my station.'

Justin made himself breathe slowly, suppressing the urge to spring to his feet and thunder that her position on the floor was the very least of it. With an effort that hurt he said mildly, 'It appears not to have occurred to you that I would have wished to know that you were driving about the countryside with a groom who is relatively new to my employ and who is a compete stranger to the area?'

She flushed pinkly, confirming a suspicion that was festering in his breast, but did not answer. 'But of course it did. In fact, you knew I would not approve of the entire expedition, did you not? Or otherwise why did you find it necessary to sneak out?'

Mari's head came up at that and the hurt expression in her eyes gave him a savage satisfaction. 'I did not sneak!'

'You did not tell me at breakfast what you were going to do, and you made yourself very scarce when I was leaving the house. Presumably to avoid questions.' Yes, she looked guilty. 'And then you were able to search the study for the notebook that I so carelessly left behind.'

'I did not touch your notebook,' she said flatly. The grey eyes looking back at him held anger now.

'No? Then how did you know where to go?'

'You disbelieve my word? I looked at the rolls of estate

maps—you had no objection to me dusting them. Perhaps you should make it clear which items I am allowed to clean but not look at.'

'Now you are being foolish.' No, she was managing to make him feel he was acting unjustly. But the roiling anger would not be quenched so easily. The realisation that she had gone out, quite unsuspecting amongst hostile tenants, protected only by an unarmed groom, clutched at his guts, and the knowledge that he had not foreseen it did nothing to make him feel any better.

'Perhaps,' she retorted. 'But keeping this house in order is my responsibility, as is tending to our tenants. It is the duty and the obligation of the lady of the manor.'

'If you had discussed it with me—'

'I tried to, the other night.' Mari got to her feet in an angry swish of silk and took two abrupt steps towards the window. 'I saw you come back from riding around the estate. I saw how tired and depressed you looked, before you came into the house. And I asked you.' She took another sharp step, her low heels clicking on the polished boards. 'I asked about the tenants and their land, about the Home Farm and whether the land was in good heart. And you fobbed me off with platitudes.' Mari swung round, her eyes glittering angrily. 'Things were *well enough*. The estate would soon be—how did you put it?—*licked into shape*. Things might not be as good as you hoped, but it would soon be remedied.'

'I do not expect you to have to worry about the estate,' he began, shaken by her vehemence. 'And I did not want you to be exposed to the hostility of the tenants.'

'Then why did you not tell me that they knew my connection to the previous owners?' she demanded. 'Did you expect me to stay here in ignorance, locked in my dusty ivory tower, polishing it for you while old men and widows are in need of

some simple support and concern? When fathers who should
be raising their families are sick and bitter and have to send
them away because they cannot support them? Why did you
not tell me so I could help and make amends?'

'Because you have nothing to make amends for,' he
retorted. Then he saw that the angry glitter in her eyes was
tears and something inside him stuttered, as though his heart
had stopped for a moment. She was hurt and angry and upset
and it was his fault.

'Mari,' he began gently, reaching out a hand, but she was
not to be mollified.

'And poor Mr Coulter, you were so haughty with him, no
wonder he fled and did not stay to dinner.'

'Oh, yes. Your *Jeremy*.' He sounded jealous, he could hear
it, and, damn it, he *was* jealous. Jealous of the open, involved
expression on her face as she had smiled up at that puppy of
a curate. It seemed a long time since he had seen that confiding expression when he looked at her. Now, since the
wedding, she seemed to be shutting her thoughts and feelings
away from him.

'Oh, for goodness' sake!' Her exasperated exclamation re-
kindled his temper. 'He is the curate, a boy, scarce out of uni-
versity, I imagine. Anyone would think you jealous, Justin,
to hear you.'

Damn it, he *was* jealous, furiously jealous. She was his
wife, he loved her— *Loved her.* Justin stood quite still, absorbing the shock. When had that happened? *How* had it
happened? When had liking and admiration and desire turned
by some mysterious alchemy into love?

'Why should I not be jealous?' he demanded, struggling
to come to terms with this new feeling.

'Because it ill becomes your dignity,' she said, as near a
snap as he had ever heard Mari use. 'We have a marriage of

convenience, do we not? This is not a love match and to carry on as though you had found me in the arms of another man is ridiculous.' She broke off, dashing away her tears with an impatient swipe of her hand. 'Trust is very important to me, Justin. I had hoped to be able to trust you, to make that the foundation of our marriage. If you cannot trust me, then what is there for us?'

No, she did not love him. He had always known that—why did it hurt so much to acknowledge it now? She was angry, quite rightly, because he had not thought about her role and had kept his worries to himself. And she was right, to be jealous of that stripling cleric made him ridiculous.

'I trust you, Mari.' He took her in his arms as he had done on the stairs that first evening. 'I trust you. Whether I can learn to trust young men who find themselves alone with you is another matter.' Unlike the other evening she did not relax into his embrace, but remained standing stiffly within his arms. He breathed in her soft, arousing fragrance and indulged himself by laying his cheek against the caress of her hair.

'Come to bed, sweetheart. Let me kiss away those tears and see if we cannot change our anger into something better.'

Mari stepped back and he released her. 'I am sorry, my lord, but I am unable to accommodate you, if you recall. By Monday, I am sure, I will be able to do my duty—in this respect, if nothing else.'

Marina swept out of the door, meeting Hearnshaw with the tea tray. 'I have a headache. Please have tea sent up to my room.' She fought with her temper all the way up the stairs, only wrestling it into something like submission as she reached her door. She was a countess and a grown woman, for goodness' sake—she should not be stomping around the house like Lizzie in a sulk.

Losing her temper was rare for Marina. She did not have the temperament for drama and shouting. It merely made her feel ill. Besides, spinster daughters rapidly learned that meek compliance with everyone else's wishes was their expected lot in life and experience had taught her that vehement protest rarely achieved anything.

Now she felt queasy and had no sense of triumph over having the last word. She rubbed her aching temples and began to pace about the room. It had been such a strange quarrel. She had been prepared to apologise and see his point of view, and then to try to show Justin that none of this would have occurred if only he had confided in her.

But the things she expected him to be angry about seemed the least of his grievances. And what was that nonsense about poor Jeremy Coulter? How could Justin be jealous of such a young, well-meaning person? Of course, he was a good-looking man, but she was in love with Justin; it was ludicrous to think she might even contemplate dallying with the curate.

But Justin did not know that, of course. Marina stopped pacing and sat down on the bed. Her reflection in the long pier glass stared back at her, the reflection's white face ghostly in the summer evening light.

The quarrel had had all the pointlessness of a lovers' tiff, but without the logical conclusion to it. She recalled Pris, smug as a pampered cat, showing off a new necklace and confiding that it was a peace offering after a particularly energetic row with her husband—and, Marina had gathered from her friend's blushes and giggles, an equally energetic session of lovemaking to make up afterwards.

She should not have rejected Justin the way she had. It was true she could not take him to her bed, but she could have reminded him of that tactfully, with a kiss, a touch. Miserable, she curled up on the bed against the pillows. She wanted him, not to make love to her, but to hold, kiss and caress her. And she wanted it so badly that she ached for him. Now what could she do? To go downstairs to try and make amends would be so dangerous. She was afraid she would simply blurt out how she felt for him, and then he would add pity to the exasperation he doubtless felt at the moment.

It was so much more difficult coping with a husband than it had been managing a relationship with a friend. Why had she not had the foresight to consider that before she had agreed to this marriage? Wistfully, Mari wondered if Justin would come to her room that night to make peace and show he had forgiven her.

A tap on the door had her scooting up against the pillows and assuming a tranquil face as Jenny came in with the tea tray. One's life might be crumbling about one's ears, but appearances in front of the servants must be kept up at all costs.

Downstairs Justin threw himself into a chair and tried to think calmly about what had just happened, what he had discovered. He was in love with his wife, who quite assuredly did not love him. She regarded his lovemaking as a duty ranking somewhere on the scale with ensuring the tenants' welfare, but, he suspected, somewhat lower down.

He was in danger of making a complete fool of himself over her friendship with the curate and he had grievously mishandled not only that but her whole role as his wife.

More for something to do than anything else he poured tea he did not want into a cup and took an unthinking gulp of the hot liquid. *Damn! That hurt.* Irritably he banged the cup down on a little table and the tea splashed over the side on to some folded papers.

Curious, he picked them up and unfolded them, his brow knitting at the sight of the unfamiliar handwriting. Then, as

he read, it made sense. Mrs Faversham was obviously a very
competent woman with a good grasp of priorities and at first
glance he was inclined to agree with everything she had noted.

But another hand, one he recognised, had annotated the list
in pencil. Justin tipped it towards the candlelight and read, his
frown deepening. Somehow he was going to have to convince
Mari to trust him, believe what he said about the estate and
his ability to pay for it. He got to his feet, then dropped back
into the chair. No, not tonight, in the morning when they
were both calmer and there was less risk he would simply
succumb to the urge to seize her in his arms and kiss her until
she told him she loved him too.

And that was less likely than a blue moon.

Chapter Seventeen

Marina woke heavy eyed and with the unwelcome certainty that she had overslept. The soft chime of the mantel clock marking nine o'clock confirmed it. Where on earth had Jenny got to? She rolled over, rubbing her eyes, then gasped as, with a rattle of rings, the curtains at the window were drawn back.

'Jenny! I did not hear you there. What are you about, to let me lie in like this?'

'Merely obeying orders.' The amused, deep voice had her sitting bolt upright, ridiculously clasping the neck of her nightgown. 'I thought you should rest,' her husband continued, appearing at the foot of the bed. 'I will go and get your breakfast.'

Marina stared at the closing door, then jumped out of bed and ran to the dressing room with more haste than dignity. By the time Justin returned, ushering in a maid bearing a laden tray, which she set down on the table in the window, she was back in bed clad in a wrapper, her hair brushed and the worst of the sleep splashed out of her eyes.

Justin pulled up a chair and began to pour hot chocolate. 'Would you like breakfast in bed, or will you join me?'

'I…I will get up, thank you. Justin, this is very…nice, but I have so much to do.'

'And a very capable housekeeper to assist with it.' He passed her the chocolate and began to pour his own coffee. 'A woman of admirable sense. Why do you feel it necessary to veto her suggestions for improvements?' He reached into the breast of his coat and pulled out folded sheets of paper. 'You left them on the table by your chair last night and I am afraid I splashed tea on them.'

'Thank you.' Marina took the sheets and pushed them awkwardly between her cup and the chocolate pot. 'I just thought that what she was suggesting would be expensive and, what with one thing and another…' She trailed to a halt and looked at Justin. He seemed perfectly amiable, although to be sitting there with him, *en négligé* and within arm's length of the bed, was unsettling. 'I was concerned not to be spending too much when the estate obviously requires considerable attention.'

'And I came home looking tired and depressed, avoided discussing it, and you put two and two together and made a serious financial problem?'

'Um, yes.'

'I was concerned not to worry you,' he confessed ruefully, 'and I appear to have ended up doing just that.' Justin broke a sweet roll in half, reached for the butter, then put down his knife without taking any. 'Mari, without wishing to speak disrespectfully of your brother, I realise that living with him may well have given you a tendency to be somewhat anxious about money.'

There was nothing much to say to that other than to nod.

'I have been single-mindedly making my fortune since I was seventeen and my trustees allowed me to become involved with my own affairs. I have a knack for investment, it seems, and a healthy degree of caution about losing money.'

'Knightshaye must have been a strong incentive.' Marina looked around the shabby, gracious, room with affection. 'I can feel the pull of it already, after only a few days.'

'It was, and is, something akin to a passion.' His face lost its animation for a moment; the expression in his eyes seemed somehow clouded. 'Like falling in love: it happens once and is for ever.' Marina stared fixedly at her plate until she could look up with a steady gaze again. If he loved Serena with a tenth of the tenacity he had shown for this house, then nothing would ever match her in his heart.

'Fortunately my guardians were wise men who taught me early that to squirrel away every penny and think of nothing but accumulating wealth would make me a shabbaroon, or, as Lord Beechcombe puts it in his inimitable way, a stick-bum.'

Marina choked back a giggle. It seemed that Justin had not lost his ability to make her laugh, however scandalously he did so, and however low she was feeling. 'And that would never do,' she agreed.

'Quite. So I learned early to put out my money to ensure my comfort and entertainment.' He smiled at her, a gentle smile that almost overset her. 'What I am trying to say, Mari, is that I can afford to do what is needed here, even if it involves draining every field on the entire estate upon your instructions. And I can do that and ensure that you have sufficient servants and the resources to restore this house. I might even run to allowing you a new gown twice a year. Only one hat, though.'

She did not rise to the bait, sending him a slanting look from beneath her lashes. 'May I visit the tenants, then?'

'Yes, provided you never go without one of the grooms and you tell me when you do so.' He reached across the little table and cupped her cheek with one hand. 'Mari, I was angry because I was frightened for you. They will come to understand that the neglect of your family cannot be laid at your door, but it will take time and I would not risk you suffering any insult. And you may order whatever you and Mrs Faversham require.' He put down his coffee cup and stood up. 'I will leave you in peace now. Oh, yes, and feel free to consult with your young curate—only do not blame me if he falls in love with you.'

'Jeremy Coulter?' Marina laughed out loud. 'Justin, that is ridiculous! I thought you were only cross about him because you were cross about the other things. But why should he fall in love with *me*?'

'How could he not?' Justin asked lightly, bending to kiss the tip of her nose.

Marina stared after him, half-convinced he must have had one glass of wine too many. And as for kissing her nose— why, she just did not have the sort of nose that got kissed. Pris did, Lizzie would have. She, sensible Marina, about whom the most flattering things anyone ever said were *elegant* and *has countenance*—no, she did not have a kissable nose. Justin had clearly been at the brandy.

It was the last morning that week that she stayed late in bed, for it seemed that the neighbourhood had decided the Mortenhoes' honeymoon was over. That afternoon, and the next day, Saturday, they began to call in droves. Marina declared to her staff that she would be At Home from three until five every afternoon, which left the mornings for supervising the housework and visiting tenants and the evenings for planning, list making and writing orders, letters and everything else.

It was obvious after only two days that her wardrobe simply would not cope. She had waved aside most of the numerous afternoon gowns her mama had tried to insist upon, convinced there would be no need for them in the country. But local society intended to dress up to call upon the intriguing new couple and Marina knew that to fail to meet their expectations would be seen as a subtle snub to them. As the highest-ranking lady in the district, her style and fashions would be studied with interest and to neglect her appearance would be unthinkable.

'What are you doing?' Justin came into the Chinese room on the seventh evening, their first Sunday at Knightshaye. He poked a long finger at the teetering pile of letters folded ready for his frank, then had to flatten his hand on them to stop them falling over. 'You are working too hard, Mari. Your eyes will be sore and you will be too tired to sleep.'

'Those at the bottom are the last of the bread-and-butter letters for wedding gifts and messages. Then there are orders for linens to Clerk and Debenham's and for furniture for the servants' rooms to Gillow's. That one—' she pointed to the top of the pile '—is to Priscilla, asking her to find me a reliable fabric restorer, and now I am writing to Mama to beg her to order me at least six more afternoon gowns. I am afraid she will say *I told you so*.'

'Six? Am I giving you a large enough quarterly allowance for this sort of wild extravagance?' He perched on the edge of her desk, too dangerously close to her peace of mind and far too large and male to be allowed anywhere near her fragile little desk.

Marina looked up, saw the amusement in his voice echoed in the twinkle in his eyes, and smiled back. 'I will be sure to ask you if it proves not to be the case.' She had finally come to believe that he really could carry the cost of this enterprise, and of supporting a wife, and was hiding nothing from her on that score. 'I have to confess to feeling thoroughly wicked—and enjoying the sensation very much.'

'Mmm?' Justin slid off the desk and went to stand behind her, resting his hands lightly on her shoulders. Marina could feel the heat of him through her back and shoulders, despite the chair. Or perhaps it was just her imagination; she was certainly feeling very breathless. He began to stroke her shoulders, letting his fingertips tangle with the wisps of curl around her hairline. Then his thumbs came together on the nape of her neck, running up and down, tracing the line of her spine exposed by the low cut evening gown.

'Just how wicked are you feeling?' He leaned forward until his breath tickled her ear. Marina shivered deliciously, luxuriating in the sensation of his hands caressing her body. Her breasts felt heavy and far too tight in the scoop of her bodice. Surely he could see their swelling, the tormenting way her nipples were peaking at his touch? 'I am feeling very wicked.' His voice was a low purr in her ear now.

Oh, Heaven help me, I want him so much—and I cannot, I cannot bear it if it is still so painful... Feeling a complete coward, Marina snatched at her one genuine excuse. 'Not tonight, Justin. I am sorry.'

'Ah.' His lips brushed her hot cheeks. 'Tomorrow?'

'Yes, tomorrow.' She shivered. There would be no possible reason why not tomorrow.

'Good. I find I am a very impatient husband, and I always used to pride myself on my patience. You are a bad influence on me, Marina.' To her relief he released her and went to sit by the window, opening the newspaper and folding it to be scanned. 'Are you telling your mama that I am a satisfactory husband?'

'You may read it, of course.' Marina's hand trembled, perilously near to causing a blot as she thought of what she wished to be writing and asking about.

'Do you think I should insist on reading your letters, Mari?' Justin lowered the paper and smiled at her earnest expression. 'I am not so tyrannical. Give my affectionate duty to Lady Winslow, if you would, and of course my regards to Lizzie and Charles.'

'I had a letter from Mama yesterday. Did I tell you?' Marina frowned, recalling the vague hints that still worried her. 'She thinks Charlie is up to something, but she does not know quite what.'

'Well, he can't be spending the Knightshaye money, that has been settled in trust,' Justin remarked, the paper rustling as he turned to the court news. Marina bit her lip, trying to suppress the treacherous anxiety that perhaps Charlie had never got as far as that with the money and that it was still burning a hole in his bank account. 'It has, believe me—I accompanied him to the bank and to the lawyers. I am one of your mother's trustees now, Mari.'

'Oh, thank you, that is a relief.' How kind of Justin to have embroiled himself in the business. 'Charlie would not do anything dishonest, of course, but if he saw what he thought was a sure thing he might not consider the risk.'

'Whatever it is, it is not that, so you must not lose any sleep over it. Perhaps he is in love,' Justin suggested lightly.

'*Charlie?*' Marina laughed out loud. 'I do not think so, he is so wary of responsibility, I am sure the last thing he would be about is thinking of getting married.' She caught the satirical glint in her husband's eye. 'You mean a less respectable liaison? I fear it would have to be, for no father is going to want his daughter marrying someone with Charlie's reputation.'

Worried now, she signed the letter and reached for the box of sealing wafers. 'I do hope it isn't that, I would hate for poor Charlie to be hopelessly in love and for his feelings not to be returned.' But at least her brother would not have to endure the agony of being daily with the one he loved so vainly.

'Indeed,' Justin agreed. 'That is a bitter place to be.' Marina glanced sharply across at him, hardly believing that he would hint so openly at his feelings for Serena. But the close-packed type of the front page of *The Times* defeated her and she turned back to write the direction on the letter home, her heart silently absorbing one more tiny poisoned dart.

Monday began with Marina and Jeremy Coulter, accompanied by Fulton, calling upon old Ben Harris and his neighbour, the Widow Hall. It took some diplomacy to convince him that he would like to have his dinners cooked and his laundry washed by someone he stigmatised as *a scrawny old besom*, but rather less to convince Mrs Hall that a regular wage was more than adequate compensation for putting up with the old man's cantankerous grumblings.

'They will end up married by the end of the year,' Marina prophesied cheerfully as the gig rattled back along the track towards the church. Jeremy was due for a meeting with the churchwardens on the vexed subject of churchyard maintenance.

He grinned. 'If I were a gambling man, I would lay you long odds against it! But you are newly married and wanting to set the whole world to partners to match your own happiness, I am sure.'

'But of course,' Marina said brightly. 'I am sure all newlyweds are the same.' She smiled at him and was disconcerted to be met with a look of doubt.

When they arrived at the gate to the churchyard of St Margaret of Antioch he climbed down, hesitated, then turned again. 'I am a little early for my meeting. Would you care to see some of the monuments in the church, Lady Mortenhoe?'

'Why, yes, thank you.' Marina gathered her skirts and jumped down, steadied by his hand. 'I will only be about fifteen minutes, Fulton.'

'What is it?' she asked as they walked up the path to the porch. 'There is something you wish to say to me, is there not?'

'Yes.' He opened the great church door for her, glancing round the cool interior to make sure they were alone. 'You are perceptive, Lady Mortenhoe.'

'Marina, please, Jeremy,' she corrected, wondering uneasily what he was about to say.

'Thank you. Marina.' He hesitated, biting his lip. 'I venture to speak, not just as a friend but also, in some sort, your spiritual advisor. Forgive me, but are you happy in your marriage?'

Startled, she stared at him, the rebuttal rising instantly to her lips. 'But of course! How can you ask?'

'Because I sense some deep reserve in you.' The dark eyes regarding her were serious. 'I am here to confide in, you know. I may not be very experienced yet, but you may place complete trust in my discretion and desire to assist you in any way possible.'

Marina took a shaky breath. What did he see? Why was he so sure she was troubled? *Only do not blame me if he falls in love with you...* Justin's teasing words came back to haunt her. Was the young curate building on Justin's anger the other evening to find an excuse to become closer to her? Or did he truly sense her distress and was seeking, as any good man of the church would, to help her?

Of course it was ridiculous to think he had fallen for her. Justin's jealousy was affecting her. And her first duty was loyalty to her husband. 'Everything is perfect,' she said firmly.

'I am very happy in my marriage, merely a little concerned about my brother, whose affairs are somewhat tangled at present. Now, where are the family tombs?'

He inclined his head, apparently taking her snub in good part. 'Down here, in the side chapel.' A breath of air seemed to stir the dusty atmosphere and was gone. Marina followed down the aisle and into a chapel full of imposing tombs. A knight in full armour, a lion at his feet and his lady at his side, filled the centre.

'Oh, look.' Marina was enchanted, 'See, her little lap dog to match his lion.'

Justin closed the vestry door, leaned back against it and surveyed the churchyard with unseeing eyes. He had come to visit the family tombs alone, unsure how he would feel on seeing them again after so long. Now, at last, he could arrange for the removal of his parents to this ancient place where they should be lying. Something tickled his hand and he looked down, flicking away the rose petal that clung to his palm. He had felt foolish, gathering the flowers in the overgrown garden, walking down across the park with them overflowing his arms like a wild wedding bouquet.

But when he had filled the urn with water from the churchyard pump and set them in place on the slab marking the entrance to the vault, the feeling was akin to that he had experienced entering the cleaned and garnished hall. Life was coming back to his home, even to the place where the dead rested.

The sound of voices in the nave had made him start, almost guiltily. Mari and the curate, low voiced and earnest. He glimpsed them through the fretwork of the screen and instantly felt guilty. Why had he not asked her to come with him? She was so warm and sympathetic about his feelings for Knightshaye, but he had the uneasy feeling that she might find his desire to open the crypt morbid or would feel uncomfortable at the reminder of his parents' premature deaths and her father's part in them.

What were they talking about? They looked so solemn. Then Mari had shaken her head decisively and begun to walk briskly down the aisle towards him. His half-formed suspicions of the handsome young man in the clerical black returned. Was he flirting with her and she had just rebuffed him?

Then Justin realised that it would look most odd to be found lurking in the chapel when he could not have avoided hearing them come in. Hefting the now empty pail, he slid silently out of the chapel, through the vestry and into the sunshine. If Coulter were flirting with Mari, she seemed more than able to deal with him, and if she were not, he felt confident she would tell him. His wife might not love him, but he had no doubts about either her chastity or her loyalty.

The pail clanked as he grounded it beside the pump and began to walk back through the park. He had agreed to a marriage of convenience. He had made his bed as surely as Mari had, and to repine because he had unexpectedly lost his heart to his wife was fruitless. Fruitless, and damnably painful.

In the side chapel Marina walked slowly round the table tombs, fascinated as Jeremy pointed out tiny details: the buckle of the knight's belt, the looped buttonholes on the lady's kirtle, the curls of his lion and the ornate collar on her little dog. The chapel was a shaded mass of greys and white stone, cool and colourless except for the golden bar of sunlight striking across the altar cloth.

And then she turned the corner of the tomb and there, on the worn flags, was a spilling mass of roses, pink and red and white, an exuberance of life and colour amidst the frozen monuments.

'How lovely!' She stooped and inhaled the fragrance, still warm from the sunlight. As she did so a drop of water rolled down a leaf and splashed, dark on the pale stone.

'Someone must just have brought them,' Jeremy remarked.

Brought them within the last few minutes, Marina realised, as another leaf shed its splash of water. Surely nowhere else close by had this combination of lush old roses, the same that she was gathering daily for the rooms at Knightshaye?

Beneath the urn letters were carved deep into the slab— *RANSOME*—above a coat of arms and a great iron ring recessed into the stone. The family vault. Justin had brought these flowers, set them here only moments before. She recalled the soft breath of air as they had approached the chapel. And he had slipped out when he saw her, rather than share this emotional moment with his wife.

It was understandable, Marina told herself as she smiled and took her leave of Mr Coulter at the door. Why should he wish to visit somewhere so personal, so important, with the daughter of the man who had torn this from him? Understandable, and so deeply hurtful.

Chapter Eighteen

Was Justin coming to her room tonight or not? Marina regarded the connecting door apprehensively. She had a plan, a frightening, embarrassing plan, but she had no notion whether she could carry it through. And yet, under her nerves and her apprehension, her heart was pounding with something else—desire. She loved him; perhaps she had found a way she could show that without her mind and her body fighting her.

No. He was not coming. The clock on the mantel struck ten, echoed by the myriad of clocks throughout the house. She distracted herself by trying to count them and failed. It would be a long task for the footman Hearnshaw had assigned to clock duty to keep them all wound and regulated.

A creaking board jerked her out of her contemplation of clocks and back to the reality of the bedchamber. The door opened as she stared at it and her husband paused on the threshold, his right eyebrow cocked in quizzical enquiry.

'Mari, why are you regarding me as though I had horns and claws?'

'You haven't! I mean, it was nothing to do with you, Justin. Only the board creaks and I was thinking I must have something done about it.' He must think her deranged to be prattling on about floorboards at a time like this.

'How does one stop a floorboard creaking?' Justin asked with every appearance of interest, strolling towards the bed. His dressing gown flapped open as he walked, revealing long, strong legs. Long, strong, *bare* legs.

'You have them lifted and coat the knees—I mean the nails—with candle wax.'

'Ah. I'll get Sheffield to have the carpenter check the boards in all the rooms that have been cleaned.'

'How is Sheffield settling in?' Her mouth was dry. 'Is he comfortable at the Home Farm? I am sending maids over every day until we get it all in order. Mrs Faversham was going to discuss his staffing requirements with him.'

'I am sure he is fine, despite the fact that he is retiring to a lonely bed, unlike his most fortunate employer.' Justin was untying the sash of his dressing gown. Marina realised she was staring and jerked her eyes away. The robe slid to the floor in a slither of silk and Justin flipped back the covers. 'My dear, that is quite the most provocative nightgown I believe I have ever seen.'

His voice was a growl dipped in honey and his weight on the bed next to her angled the mattress so that her hip touched his flank. His skin was hot.

'Oh! I am sorry…'

'I am not. Mind you, I give you fair warning: I will shoot any man who sees you in it.' He took the edge of the bedclothes, which were still lying half over her, and tossed them back so that they hit the floor on the far side of the bed. It did not reduce the temperature one iota. 'This has been a long six days…'

'You forgot the candles.' The room seemed as bright as day.

'Oh, no, I haven't.' Justin's fingers were tangling with the ribbons at her neckline, not with any apparent urgency, but with the leisurely pleasure of someone trailing wool for a kitten. 'I love looking at you, Mari. I love it when you blush, I love it when you drop your lashes like that to try to hide the expression in your eyes, I love it when you make those little sounds—yes, like that—when I touch you.'

She gasped again as his fingertips brushed the line of her collarbone. *Focus on how it feels, do not think...* How hard that was to do. Her mind ran off along its own unhappy path. *He loves all those things about me, but he does not love me. He does not trust me. He will not share his life or his worries or his secrets with me. His secrets.*

'There, that is all the ribbons.' The fine lawn slid back from her shoulders, down to stop on the curve of her breasts, then to fall away as Justin bent his head to brush his lips over the swell. His tongue touched one nipple fleetingly, teasing, then touched again, and again until the hard peak throbbed and Marina found her fingers were tangling in Justin's hair, desperately.

She forced herself to let go and he chuckled softly, moving to torment the other breast. Marina struggled to rise above the flood of sensation and to learn—for if her plan were to succeed she had to discover how to make love to her husband, and quickly.

She looked down at the bent head, registering how the ends of his hair flicked against her skin as he moved, separating that feeling from the heavy ache of her breast, the shocking dart of pleasure as he rubbed her nipple between finger and thumb.

He was easing her nightgown away now, moving to lie over her. Marina put up her hands to his chest and pushed gently, managing to smile through her shyness and nerves. 'No. Justin, I want to…explore you.'

His eyebrow quirked up. 'Indeed?' He did not seem displeased at the request; in fact, Marina realised that the skin below his throat was faintly flushed and his breathing, although steady, somehow seemed heavier. 'And how would you like to conduct this exploration?'

'If you would lie on your back,' she requested earnestly, catching her underlip between her teeth as she thought.

'It seems a very serious matter.' Justin obligingly turned on his back and lay there, hands at his side, regarding her. This had the unnerving effect of displaying the full glory of a well-muscled, thoroughly aroused male body to Marina's nervous scrutiny. 'Do you require a map and compass?'

That made her laugh as she twisted round on her knees at his side. 'I think I will manage with the use of ranging rods and a theodolite,' she countered, bending to kiss his neck. She glanced up, meeting passion-darkened eyes. 'You promise me you will lie still?'

'Yes.' It was reluctant, but he lay back, surrendering to her. Mmm, but his skin tasted good, smelled good. A little bit salty, a little of his cologne but mainly of hot, clean man. Under her lips the big artery throbbed, urgent with life and strength.

She wriggled a little, gasping as her breasts brushed his chest, the tips catching the light scattering of hair. Against her mouth she felt his reaction, the faint shudder as he controlled it.

Slowly, go slowly, she admonished herself, finding the hard ridge of his collarbone with her mouth, following it down to the notch at the base of his throat, circling her tongue there until his head tipped back against the pillow. *He is not laughing now*, a little voice whispered in her head. *In a minute he will be moaning…*

Marina slid down until she was lying against his side. She caught his wrist, pulling his arm up until she could press closer, keeping it trapped in her grip as the pulse thudded wildly under her fingers. *He is so strong, he could twist free in a second, yet he lets me hold him when his body wants nothing more than to master mine.*

With her free hand she stroked down Justin's chest, over the flat muscled plane of the pectorals, following with her lips, nibbling and licking. *His skin is so smooth, and under it the muscle and bone are so hard.* She had never realised before how soft, how fragile, her own body felt against his and yet how safe he made her feel.

Her palm found his nipple and circled over it while her lips caught the other. Just as hers had, his hardened with her attentions, fascinating her so that she nibbled and licked, stroked and teased until at last she wrenched a groan from his throat and he arched his chest up against the flattened hand pressed against it.

Increasingly confident now, Marina slid a little lower, freeing Justin's wrist and using both her hands to trace the hard ridges of muscle across his stomach. How did he keep so fit? There were some faint bruises over his ribs, the old scar of a cut. Boxing and fencing? Perhaps. Riding and driving certainly.

She ran her palms down his sides, raising her head and found he was not watching her. His head was thrown back on the pillows, his eyes closed and both hands were fisted into the under-sheet. A sensation of power filled her. Inexperienced as she was, she could reduce a strong man to this.

As she moved her head, her hair fell across his chest and he shuddered. Marina recalled the tantalising sensation of his hair on her. Carefully she raised her head and allowed just the very tips of the curling locks to brush his chest. His knuckles whitened. Experimentally she took some in her hand and flicked it over one nipple. *That was not a groan, that was a growl, a beast provoked.*

Breathless, uncertain how far she could push him before she reached her ultimate goal, Marina bent and kissed the flat stomach, circling her tongue around Justin's navel. *Interesting—that does not produce the same reaction as teasing his nipple.* She stored the information and slid lower, her hands at his waist now, her breasts brushing against the tangle of coarse hair, the aroused length of him.

'Mari!' He pushed upwards on his elbows, producing an alarming conjunction of breasts and groin. 'Mari, stop. You cannot—'

'You promised me you would lie still.' Now she had gone so far Marina was not to be deterred. 'What is the matter? Have I hurt you?'

'Oh, God!' It sounded like a heartfelt prayer as he fell back again. 'Mari, you are my wife, it isn't fitting—'

'Oh, really?' Indignant now, she glared up the length of the beautiful, hard body, almost oblivious to the sensations as their skin touched. 'And for whom is it fitting, might I ask?'

'It is not the sort of thing a man asks his wife to do.' The words came from between gritted teeth.

'Why not?' She did not wait for his answer, simply bent her head and kissed the solid rod that thrust achingly between her breasts. Softest doeskin over steel, she thought, confused by the torrent of emotion the intimacy of the act released in her and the lightning strike of sheer lust that hit her own loins as her lips caressed him.

Justin's body arched as though in agony. Hazily she recalled the sensations that had lanced through her as he had made love to her with his lips and tongue on the desk that day. Gripping his lean hips hard, she ran her tongue down the straining length of him. *Yes! This gives you pleasure.* She sent the message silently, willing him to hear her thoughts. *And it gives me pleasure. I love you. I love you...* All it would take was a few moments longer, she could tell Justin was near the edge of his ability to hold out against her.

Greatly daring, she parted her lips and took him into her mouth.

There was a confused turmoil of bodies, things happening too fast to follow, and then she was lying on her back, Justin's weight pressing her down on to the bed, his mouth desperate on hers as he thrust into her, crying out as his climax took him over the edge, muffling her own sob of pain.

Justin lay back, staring up through the fading light at the plasterwork of the ceiling. Mari was curled with her back pressed against his side, asleep as she had been virtually from the moment he rolled off her body, his head spinning. He had surfaced through a fog of erotic sensation, intent on taking her in his arms and making love to her for an hour to make up for his lack of self-control. But it seemed her daring had exhausted her and all he could do was hold her gently and stroke her hair while he thought.

Wives just did not do that sort of thing. Did they? Respectable ladies might enjoy being made love to—he was not so unenlightened to expect his wife to lie back like a log while he took his pleasure of her—but to take the lead, to stroke and arouse their husbands, surely that was shocking behaviour?

Justin tried to be shocked and failed. He was aroused, amazed, shaken by the natural sensuality of the woman he had married, but not shocked. He was angry with himself for his lack of control. Damn it, he had almost spent as she caressed him, and that would have shocked her deeply. Where on earth had she learned such a trick? A courtesan's trick.

From you, his conscience told him. She was intelligent enough, and daring enough, to deduce that what gave her pleasure might also give him pleasure and she cared enough to overcome her shyness and modesty to try.

I love you. Mari, I love you. He would tell her. In the

morning he would make love to her until she could think of nothing but him and then he would tell her he loved her. If she did not love him, at least she cared enough to go to any length to pleasure him. Was that enough for a beginning? How would he feel if she turned from him, embarrassed by his feelings?

Against him she shifted, murmuring a little in her sleep as though his restless thoughts disturbed her. Justin made himself lie still, breathing steadily until she quietened, stunned by the wave of tenderness that flooded through him as he held her. His wife. His love. He was going to make this work if he had to wait for years until she returned his feelings.

At some point sleep overcame him. When he woke to the dawn chorus well into its full song, Mari was still curled up as though she had not moved all night. But he had turned so that he curved around her, holding her protectively.

It was a perfect position to kiss the ear that peeped out of the tumbled mass of brown hair obscuring her face. She smelled of warm, sleepy woman, of jasmine and of the muskiness of satisfied sex. Mari stirred a little and he licked instead, provoking a shake of her head as she put up a hand to brush away whatever it was that was tickling.

'Justin?' She twisted round, pushing back the weight of brown silky strands, and his body tightened, remembering their caress as they tumbled across his chest last night.

His feelings must have shown in his face, for she blushed and lowered her lashes. 'What's this?' He reached out and touched under her eyes with the pad of his thumb, following the snail tracks of dried tears which just showed on the fine skin. 'Crying?'

'I think I had a bad dream.' She ducked her head away from his scrutiny.

'Then I must kiss the memory away.' He pressed her chin

up. 'I did nothing but take last night, now I want to give.' Mari's lips trembled under the pressure of his, yielded to his tongue's invasion, but the responsive flicker of her own tongue that he had come to expect did not happen and her hands pressed flat on his shoulders, instead of gripping.

She is shy after her boldness last night. Justin put aside ideas of abandoned passion and concentrated on breaking down her reserve all over again. He kissed, slanting his lips over hers until she began to respond, pushing his hand between their closely pressed bodies to find her nipple and tease it until he could feel her moans under his mouth, then sliding it down to invade the moist curls with a wickedly probing finger until the moans turned to pants and she was twisting, fluid and fragile in his arms.

He shifted his weight over her, forcing his mind to calm and control to prolong the pleasure for her as long as he possibly could. The pressure built in him, hot and hard and almost over-mastering, but he fought it, intent on the woman beneath him who was shuddering with each stroke, her fingers curling into his back, each nail an erotic brand of fire on his shoulders.

Then it was too much to resist. He heard his own shout of release as he arched over her, heard the gasping cry from Mari's lips, and sank into the softness of her.

How long had he lain there? One minute? An hour? Justin realised he was too relaxed to roll off and smiled contentedly into the angle of Mari's neck and shoulder where his head had fallen. If he could just work out how to control his knees and elbows, he could take the weight off her...

'I'm sorry, I'm squashing you.' He managed it at last, levering himself up until he could look down at her. The smile congealed into ice as he saw her face.

Mari had twisted he head aside as far as she was able, but his pinioning body gave her no chance to turn from him and her hands were trapped so she could not wipe away the tears that were coursing unstoppably down her cheeks.

'Mari, darling, what is it?' He scrambled off her, pulling her with him until he could sit up with her cradled against his chest. 'Sweetheart, tell me.' He felt sick with anxiety for her, with shock, with rising anger with whatever had hurt her. All he got were her tightly shut eyes, a sharp shake of her head and a glimpse of absolute misery as she tried to turn her head away.

'Tell me!' He gave her a little shake, desperate now. 'You cannot say nothing after this. Who has hurt you?'

'You have.' Her voice was a whisper. Justin could not believe he had heard her aright.

'What did you say? Dear heart, I cannot hear you.'

'You have.' Mari looked up, her grey eyes leaden with tears and misery. 'You hurt me, Justin.'

Chapter Nineteen

It was said. Marina stared at him, as aghast to have uttered the words as Justin was to have heard them. His face went blank, but his eyes widened and a shiver went through him before he stilled it with an effort of will.

'I hurt you? I hurt you last night and when I thought you were asleep you were crying? I hurt you this morning? Mari…' She could see Justin struggling to keep his voice steady. 'Mari, I know it hurts the first time for a virgin, but surely…?'

'It is not that. It…the first time… It was all right, I was not frightened, only shy. But then you told me to trust you, just before you…you…' she cast around wildly for a way to say it '…entered me and I couldn't. I knew I could not trust you and everything just seemed to lock tight. As though my body was trying to shut you out,' she explained earnestly, trying to find words to make him understand. 'And ever since then it has been the same.'

'But why can you not trust me?' Justin shook his head as though trying to shake off a blow.

'Because you lied to me and I found out,' Marina said bleakly. 'I found out, and everything I thought I knew about you, everything that had convinced me to marry you—that shattered.

'I told myself I would do everything in my power to make you a good wife. It is my duty to lie with you, to give you pleasure in bed. And—' she felt the blush burning '—you gave me pleasure too. It is only when you—'

'When I force myself on you,' he finished for her bitterly. 'What is this lie that causes so much pain?'

Marina tried to push herself free. Talking like this, so close that she could feel the heat of his skin, see the tiny changes in the colour of his eyes as the emotions hit him, was a fresh agony. But Justin's hands stayed tight on her arms.

'You courted me under false pretences. You proposed marriage to me under false pretences. You married me for this house. It was bad enough before I saw it, but afterwards I realised just what hate there must have been between our families, realised what lengths you would go to to secure it. Even tricking the daughter of your enemy into marriage.'

She wanted him to deny it, to give her a reason for Charles's words that would put an entirely different complexion upon it. Anything, anything even half-way plausible, and she would seize on it gratefully. But Justin released her, swung his legs off the bed and strode to the window, utterly ignoring the fact that he was naked.

'How did you find out?' His voice was gritty as he stared out over the ruin of the park.

'Charlie got drunk on our wedding day and told me. He was so pleased with himself, securing an earl for his old maid of a sister. And all that money, of course. You must have been very desperate to take me as well as pay that price. And look what you got for it.'

'I got a beautiful wife and my home back,' Justin said evenly. 'And your fool of a brother made me give my word that I would not tell you of the bargain.'

'And you *agreed*?' Marina knew she was sounding shrill

and fought her voice back under control. Control, dignity, that was all she had to hang on to.

'Yes. It was wrong, but once I had given my word I only had two choices: walk away or go through with it and try to find a way to be honest with you.'

'You did not succeed.' Marina slid off the bed and caught up her *négligé*. She felt slightly better clothed. Nudity did not appear to worry Justin.

'No. I could not find a way to tell you the truth and keep my word. So I resolved to be as honest as I could with you.' He swung round suddenly, his fist thumping into the panelling beside the window. 'I did my best. I never pretended a love I did not feel, I set out to you my circumstances as honestly as I could.'

'I do not believe you.' Marina could hardly believe she had said the words. 'I do not believe you are being honest with me, even now.'

'I give you my word.'

'You give your word very easily when it suits you.' One look at Justin's face was enough to make her take a step back. *I have insulted his honour...but he lied about the marchioness, he has not been truthful with me.*

'I see.' How he was controlling himself she had no idea; it was clear from his face that he wanted to shake her, to shout at her, but all he did was seize the back of a chair and stand there rigid while he stared at her. 'Despite the fact you think I have no honour, you feel it your duty to make me a good wife, do you?'

'Yes.'

'To warm my bed?'

'Yes.'

'Even if it means learning to play the whore in it so I can expend my lust without entering your body?'

'Yes.' She was going to be sick in a moment.

'And you consider it your duty to give me children?'

'Yes.'

'Then you may be comforted by the fact that that is one pain you will not have to endure out of duty. Nothing, Lady Mortenhoe, is going to persuade me to return to your bed and inflict myself upon you again.'

Justin released the chair so abruptly that it rocked. Ignoring the crumpled pile of silk that was his dressing gown, he strode naked to the door, wrenched it open and shut it behind him with a slam that shook the ornaments on the mantelshelf. In the echoing silence that followed, Marina heard the key click in the lock of the connecting door.

'It is so delightful to have Knightshaye occupied again,' Lady Barton beamed at Marina across the tea table. 'I was only saying to Mr Coulter that your arrival is just what local society needs to give it a much-needed lead.'

The curate smiled politely and passed the biscuits to Miss Barton, who was sitting next to her mother.

Marina smiled back serenely, wondering that none of her callers realised that she was seeing and hearing them through a mist of misery. She felt bruised, in her mind and heart, and strangely, in her body, as though Justin had literally beaten her with his hand instead of just his words.

She shifted cautiously, trying not to wince, and made herself concentrate on an exchange between Miss Barton and Mrs Grimsby, the other local matron who had called that afternoon.

'Things have been so dull lately,' Miss Barton pouted, turning from a discussion of the last church social to regard Marina with soulful blue eyes. 'Until you and his lordship arrived, Lady Mortenhoe. Will you be giving a ball soon?'

'Clara!' her mother remonstrated with an apologetic glance at her hostess.

'Not for a while, Miss Barton. The house is in great need of restoration and I am afraid the ballroom is in a very poor state.'

The talk drifted to various local matters until finally the ladies rose to leave. Jeremy rose with them, but instead of following them out remained behind, regarding Marina with concern.

'Lady Mortenhoe…Marina, I could not help but notice you seem a little unwell.' He stood there, tall and young and earnest.

What he would do if I threw myself on his chest and sobbed all over him? Marina wondered wildly. Faint, probably.

'I am feeling rather stiff.' Indeed, she felt she had been moving like an old lady since yesterday morning. Perhaps she *was* going to be ill. 'I think perhaps I have been a trifle too busy.'

'If that is all it is, then you must rest.' He came and stood beside her, his hand resting on her arm in a gesture of support, the dark eyes in his handsome face radiating concern.

Marina looked away, struggling to resist the urge to turn into the strong body so close to hers and just cling to it for comfort.

'Seeking spiritual guidance, my dear?' Justin had come into the room so quietly that neither of them had noticed. Marina knew her own cheeks were betrayingly flushed, but Jeremy simply inclined his head, presumably with the comfort of a good conscience.

'Good afternoon, my lord. I was urging Lady Mortenhoe to rest—she has admitted she is overdoing things.'

'Perhaps she will listen to you, Mr Coulter.' Somehow Justin was standing by the door in a way that made it impossible for Jeremy not to take the hint and leave. 'Lady Mortenhoe has a very strong sense of her duties as a wife and exerts herself in many directions. Going already? Then I will bid you good day.'

He strolled into the room as the door shut behind the curate. 'Will you not sit down, my dear? The perceptive Mr Coulter is correct. You do not look well, you should rest.'

Marina sat down and reached for the tea pot. 'Would you care for a cup of tea, Justin?'

'Thank you.' He took the proffered cup and began to stir it slowly. 'Perhaps I should make it clear: by quitting your bed I do not intend that anyone else should share it. And that includes our well-meaning young curate.'

Marina put down the teapot so suddenly that hot liquid splashed from the spout. She reached for a napkin and began to mop it up before she realised that her vision was hazy with angry tears.

She threw down the stained cloth and made herself meet her husband's eyes. 'Mr Coulter has no such intentions. And if you think so poorly of me, I wonder that you did not send me packing the night we reached this house.'

Justin got to his feet and stood looking down at her. Marina straightened her aching back and met his gaze defiantly. 'I thought I had married quite another woman,' he said softly. 'You must forgive me if I find I have no point of reference to understand you any longer.'

He kept walking after he left the salon, striding along the nearest corridor, through the ballroom, out of the far door into the garden at the cost of a split seam where he had to apply his shoulder to the swollen wood to force it open.

Damn it, she must be able to see the look in that holy young idiot's eyes for what it is. Justin strode on until the scrub along the moat edge brought him to a standstill. *If he isn't in love with her yet, he soon will be.*

And then what? Did he really believe that Mari would deceive him, have affairs? Of course not. She was, for all her sensually passionate nature, chaste.

'Hell.' He reached the wreck of an old gazebo overlooking the now-stagnant long reach of the moat and flung himself down on the remains of the seat, heedless of the effect on his clothes. 'Hell. She doesn't trust me. She doesn't love me. She quite likes me making love to her—up to a point. She thinks I have no honour—but she sees it as her duty to fulfil her marriage vows.'

Justin leaned down and picked up a stone, tossing it at the tangled mass of water lily leaves that choked this stretch of the moat. Another followed, then another. He focussed on hitting the same leaf over and over again until it disintegrated, a tattered mass on the scummy surface.

Just how was it possible for one, supposedly intelligent, man to get it so wrong twice in a row? He thought he had fallen in love with an accredited beauty and found her to be hollow, selfish, grasping and desperately needy. Then he had married for common sense, calm and ruthless practicality— and found himself in love with a woman who apparently despised him.

To be accused of lying—in effect, of having no honour— was so wounding that he seemed to have no defences against the hurt. If a man had said as much he would have challenged him, called him out, risked his life to defend that honour. What could one do with a wife who thought you had none? How did you win the love of a woman who thought you a liar?

It seemed only hours ago that he had lain in her bed, convinced that her daring, arousing, lovemaking proved she was growing to love him. And all it had proved in truth was that she would go to any lengths to avoid his embraces. Unless duty forced her. And Marina would, at all costs, do her duty—that at least he knew of her.

'The post has arrived, my lady.' Hearnshaw brought in the silver salver as Marina was just reaching for a slice of toast. She had to eat or Jeremy would be proved right and she would indeed become ill. Nothing tasted of anything any more, just as every movement seemed an effort, but making herself sick would achieve nothing. Life had to go on. She had her duties. Eventually something would give her some pleasure, would arouse a spark of interest; she had to believe that.

'Thank you, Hearnshaw.' There was quite a pile of correspondence for her, just as much for Justin, although most of his looked depressingly serious and businesslike.

Marina sorted rapidly through her pile, pushing aside all the correspondence that was obviously from tradesmen. A letter from Mama, nothing from Priscilla, but, surprisingly, one with the direction in Charlie's sprawling hand. She put it to one side to read later and reached for Lady Winslow's missive—correspondence from Charlie was rare enough to be savoured at leisure.

Bother. Her knife was covered in butter. Marina put it, and the letter, down and looked around for a clean knife. Justin had obviously sorted his post as she had, but under his long fingers was a quite different letter addressed in a looping hand on fine paper. As his hand shifted on it a faint, sickly, scent of lily reached her nostrils.

As though he felt her eyes on it, Justin pushed the letter into the pile of business correspondence and tapped them all together. 'I shall be in my study this morning, Hearnshaw. I do not wish to be disturbed.'

With a slight bow in her direction he had gone, off to his

study as he said. Off to his study to spend the morning alone with estate business and a letter from a lady.

With a letter from the exquisite Serena, Marchioness of Andover. His love.

Chapter Twenty

Alone in his study Justin tossed the pile of mail on to his desk and went and sat down. After a while he extended one finger and flicked the letters aside until the scented missive lay exposed. If he had any sense he would light a taper and burn it unopened, then go and scrub the traces of that cloying perfume off his hands.

He reached for the tinderbox, then dropped it back on to the base of the candlestick. What if she was in trouble? Justin picked up the letter. What if she was? He dropped it again. Serena had made her own bed, her own luxurious, soft bed that came with a great and ancient title and a powerful and influential husband.

But she was not happy. He had seen it in the desperation of her glittering smile, the wildness in those lovely periwinkle blue eyes as she had flirted so intensely with him on his wedding day. 'Help me, Justin,' she had whispered. 'I made a terrible mistake.'

And what had he said? Some bracing nonsense about giving it time, learning to know her husband better. And despite the fact that she had jilted him, cast him aside like a spoilt child who sees a new, shiny toy and instantly discards the old one, he had felt the old, familiar protectiveness for her, a trace of tenderness.

Oh, no, not love though. Justin shifted in his seat, tapping the still-sealed letter with his fingers. She had cured him of that, or whatever it had been. Infatuation? Probably. Desire, certainly. Pity, in large part. It seemed he had always been able to see the unloved little girl behind the frantic gaiety, the pouting demands for attention and presents and constant re-assurance that she was the most beautiful, the most desir-able, the most enviable young lady in society.

Damn it. Justin reached for the letter opener and slit the fancy sea-green wafer that sealed it. Serena's letter was like her conversation—undisciplined, self-obsessed, words tumbling over each other as she covered the sheets of expen-sive paper.

Justin, I do not know what to do...Adrian is so strict...he does not understand me. He says I am extravagant, that I must learn economy and restraint. Justin, it is no fun and when I tried to persuade him to let me go to more parties he was so angry.

He shook his head at the trivial list of complaints, his mouth twisting wryly at the account of a heedless girl suddenly finding herself expected to act as a grown-up person with dignity and a sense of duty. As he turned the page the smile froze. *...and then he struck me! Just because I said he was mean and too old to have fun and that I would go out and flirt with men who were more amusing unless he was nicer to me—he slapped me!*

The letter rambled on, five pages of shock and complaint. Justin let it slip from between his fingers on to the desk. If ever there were two people more unsuited to each other, it was those two. The middle-aged aristocrat used to obedience and dignity and order and the spoilt, heedless little madam who had been indulged with everything, except her father's love.

How could Andover hit her? Only too easily, probably—a slap to discipline a foolish wife would seem a mild rebuke to a man of his upbringing and generation. Would he beat her? Justin's fingers cramped on the paper, then relaxed. He doubted it—it would be below the Marquis's dignity. No, Andover would simply grow colder and stricter, and if Serena continued to defy him she would find herself packed off to the country to cool her heels and learn obedience.

What does she expect me to do about it? Rush to her aid on a white charger, probably. It would never occur to Serena that a man whom she had hurt and rejected, and who was now married, might not instantly forget both her betrayal and his new ties and compromise himself for her. Get himself killed most like! Justin was aware of the Marquis's reputation with pistols, and so was most of society. Serena was going to find herself sadly disappointed if she expected a host of men to gallantly rescue her from a stifling marriage.

Not like Mari. She had made a bargain, and she was sticking to it, whatever she thought of her new husband. Was she any less unhappy than Serena? She had a thousand times more courage. His vision seemed to have blurred suddenly and he rubbed at his eyes. His hand came away damp.

How did you win back the love of a woman who seemed to despise you? Justin struck a light from the tinderbox and held it to the corner of Serena's letter, letting it crumble into grey ash on the pewter dish that stood on the desk. The first thing was to stop being angry with her—which was easier said than done. It might help to accept that the love he felt for her was more important than the wounding of his precious honour, and infinitely more important than his pride.

* * *

Marina dropped her post on her desk and took the family letters outside. Mr Sheffield had set men to scythe paths through the rank grass and had placed benches under the trees. It could hardly be called a garden yet, but it was a soothing place to sit.

She found a seat close to the largest mass of roses and sat while her distress ebbed a little. How could Justin calmly receive letters from another woman—*that* other woman? And he had the effrontery to pretend to be bemused by her accusations that he had lied to her!

This was no good, she was stoking her own anger when she should be learning resignation and acceptance. Marina sighed and broke the seal on Lady Winslow's letter.

Mama was in the country with Lizzie and Giles. The weather was clement, Hector had killed two chickens and was in disgrace, Giles had commenced lessons with the Rector and Lizzie had broken out in spots.

…at least it is not freckles, spots will cure in time. How does the work at Knightshaye go on? I still find it most odd of dear Justin to take you to such a tumbledown place, but there is no accounting for men as I have so often observed…dearest Charlie is giving me much cause for concern, Marina. Have you heard from him? He seems to have some scheme that sounds most dubious and unlikely, but will not tell me any details. And I am so afraid that he finds himself in difficulties again—not that he will confide about that either. I live in dread of hearing he has been taken up as a debtor. I cannot tell you, Marina dear, how glad I am that you have such a reliable and fond husband…

Oh, dear. At least Mama and the children were financially secure, whatever wild flights Charlie got up to.

She turned his letter in her hands. Dover? What on earth was the letter franked from there for?

…and so Crispin Devlin—you must recall him, Marina, best of good fellows and a real head on his shoulders—has got a lease on this hell in the Palais Royale and we are going to run it.

The Palais Royale? But that was in Paris!

I think this might be just the thing for me, Marina. I'm fed up with losing money, it isn't as though I ever won. Got thoroughly drunk the other night and woke up feeling like death and along comes Cris with this proposition, and I thought, Why not? *He's got a legacy from his godfather and I know every game of chance ever invented. We can't fail. So we sail tomorrow. Thought I better let you know, because Mama is bound to have the vapours when I write from Paris…*

'Oh, Charlie!' *How could you?* And, of course, he expected his long-suffering sister to calm Mama when she realised that her elder son had set up as the proprietor of a gambling den in the wickedest city on earth.

'Good news from your mother?' Justin was watching her from the edge of the grass path. Marina folded the letters to give her time to compose herself and nodded. 'They all seem to be well, I think. Mama worries about Charlie, although he seems intent on doing some travelling, so that might account for it.' How still and watchful Justin seemed, those hazel eyes resting on her face as though searching for something.

'I must go and see Mrs Faversham—we are making plans for the dining rooms next.'

'Do not go just yet, Mari.'

Marina sat down again, clasping her hands over the letters in an attempt to still them. A lock of hair had fallen over Justin's forehead—in fact, it looked as though he had run both hands through his hair. She knew how it would feel under her palms if she stroked it back, knew how it would slip through her fingers if she let them stray. The crackle of paper in her hands jerked her away from the fantasy.

'Was there something you wish done?' The physical ache that had racked her had ebbed; now she was stiff with it again. Was it not enough that her mind hurt? Why did everything she feel have to be echoed, magnified by her body? *Everything*, from the pain of betrayal to the surging longing of love.

'I wish to apologise.' Justin seemed wryly amused at the startled glance she shot him. 'I allowed myself to feel jealous of our curate yet again. But most of all, I need to tell you that I never, for one moment, thought you might be unfaithful to me. I should not have said what I did.'

'You trust me?' The accusation had been so wild, so wide of the mark that somehow it had failed to hurt. Or perhaps there was no spot on her aching mind where another hurt could be inflicted.

He was so close all of a sudden. How had he managed to move so silently to her side? 'I trust you, Mari. I trust you with my honour.' The brush of his fingers against her cheek was so soft; with a murmur Marina turned her face against his palm and found it gone. 'But then, you do not think I have any, do you?'

His mood had changed abruptly. She was half out of her seat to catch his arm, to try to recapture the olive branch he had seemed to have offered. Then the lingering scent from his fingertips halted her. Castile soap, fresh on hands that were barely dry, but under it, the faint, lingering rumour of lilies.

A week passed, uneventful, drowsy in the late June sunshine. For hours at a time Marina lost herself in the task of reviving the great house, in meetings with Mrs Faversham and Hearnshaw. There were conferences with Mr Sheffield over his suggestions for the gardens and discussions over the more minor repairs that she found. There was the satisfaction of being greeted, if not with pleasure, at least with civility, by the tenants and of seeing the start of the improvements that Justin had set in train. And there was a gradually widening circle of social acquaintances to distract her.

'We have been invited to Lady Barton's supper dance next Wednesday.' Marina glanced up from her post. Justin was immersed in the newspaper. 'Do you care to attend?'

'If you do, certainly.' Justin seemed perfectly amenable to the idea, folding the paper so he could listen to what she had to say. 'I imagine our neighbours have decided we are now past the honeymoon stage and will be open to invitations.'

'Indeed, that must be it.' Best not to dwell on the thought of honeymoons. 'There is another invitation—no, two more—in my post this morning.' And nothing from Charlie. Perhaps he had thought better of his Paris scheme, or perhaps the post was unreliable. Or, more likely, writing to his anxious sister was far from his mind. Marina passed the invitations across the table.

'Accept what you like. Just remind me what we are doing and when, or I'll come wandering in from a day inspecting dung heaps or something equally salubrious only to have you ring a peel over my head because we are due at a dinner party.'

'I will give Shepton a list. I am sure he will organise things most efficiently and warn you not to be late when laying out your dung-heap inspecting outfit.' Justin seemed more approachable than he had since that odd morning in the garden. Marina ventured a teasing question. 'Are you spending much time on the subject?'

'Manure? It seems so, although less than Sheffield would wish me to. Apparently he has been reading up on the latest theories for crop raising and is convinced that we must dung the field more regularly. Why he does not carry this out without expecting me to view the process at close quarters I cannot imagine.

'But it is not a topic for the breakfast table, my dear. I can't think why I am boring you with it.'

'Because I asked. I am interested,' Marina said placidly. 'Although I must confess, something less *basic* might be more enjoyable to discuss.'

'And how does your work go? I looked at the dining rooms last night—they are both looking remarkably handsome, if a touch bare at the windows.'

'I know.' Marina was rueful. 'I have now learned from experience never to trust the fabric warehouses, but always to insist on a good size sample first. I ordered twelve ells of leaf-green brocade to set off the sapphire and rose hangings in the large dining room on the basis of a small cutting, and it arrived positively pea green. I sent it back, for I could not imagine any room in the house that would be enhanced by that colour. I do not think we will be able to hold a dinner party for at least three weeks unless I take down curtains from elsewhere.'

This was all quite pleasantly domestic, amiable and comfortably dull. Marina shot a sideways look under her lashes. Was it worth trying to prolong the moment, or would the mistrust flare between them again?

'I thought I should prepare some of the spare bedchambers next. I would welcome your opinion on which ones, Justin.'

'Of course.' He tossed down his napkin and stood up, suddenly overwhelmingly male in the intimate breakfast parlour in his buckskin breeches and dark brown riding coat.

How long his legs are. Marina let her gaze flutter down to the tight breeches and the glossy boots and gripped the table edge as she stood.

'Are you all right?' The pressure of his hand on her elbow,

steadying, was shockingly intimate after days when neither had touched the other. A shaft of desire flashed through her.

'Oh, yes, my foot has pins and needles, that is all.' The warm pressure vanished, leaving her short of breath.

'I thought the rooms in the east wing.' Hopefully, climbing the stairs would account for her difficulty speaking. What on earth possessed her to think of asking for Justin's company in a tour of bedrooms?

'I agree, that does seem best. I cannot recall how many there are, though. As a child, guest chambers were hardly of much interest.' Marina hung back as he pushed open the first door. 'Hmm. A bit small.'

'Yes.' She followed him in. 'But suitable for a young person or a child. It would do for Giles when he comes to stay.' She moved on to the next room, opening the door and entering before Justin's closeness in the doorway made her feel any more flustered than she was already. 'This one is much the same.'

'Then the next should be a sizeable suite, if my memory serves me right. Yes.' He strolled into the big, darkened room and threw back the shutters. 'And in reasonably good condition—having these closed must have helped.'

Indeed the hangings were largely unfaded, although dirty, and there was no damage from birds.

Justin stood, looking out over the parkland. 'I wonder if introducing deer might not be the best way to get the park under control.'

'Umm? I do not think there are any leaks in the ceiling either.' Marina tipped her head back to gaze up at the smooth surface above her. It was greyish, to be sure, but there were none of the brown stains she was coming to expect, charting the damage rain had done and boding ill for the state of the rooms above.

What was that? A crack or a stain... Straining eyes still fixed on the ceiling, Marina began to trace the course of the blemish.

'Oh!' The impact as she walked back into Justin, who was shifting away from the window, knocked her off balance. Marina reached out a hand and caught the bedpost as Justin caught her other arm. But her momentum simply swung her round it and she ended up on the bed in a breathless tumble, Justin on top of her.

'Ough!' Dust rose around them and he sneezed, making Marina giggle. Then the laughter drained away as their eyes met. So green, so dangerous. So very dangerous when her heart was beating as though she had run a mile and her whole body ached for him, yearning up to crush itself against his hard weight without any conscious action on her part.

'Justin—Justin, I have missed you so—'

His mouth took the words from her lips, the breath from her lungs. Hard and desperate it plundered and ravished and she was as hungry, as fierce as he, her fingers tight locked in his hair, her tongue answering the challenge of his, goading him, desperate for him to take her beyond anywhere she had been before.

How had their clothes come off? She could not recall the feel of cloth under her hands, yet now they were flesh to flesh, hot, slippery skin sliding over each other's aroused bodies.

'I love you,' she gasped, but the sound was lost in the force of his kiss. He was speaking too, words she could not hear either as they strained and arched together on the dusty coverlet.

Chapter Twenty-One

Oh, please, please... Nothing mattered any more except that Justin was making love to her at last, that she could show him how much she loved him, despite everything.

Hurry, hurry. Urgent fingers at his waist, wriggling to try to find the fastening of his breeches, her mouth frantic on his as the wonderful weight and strength of his body enveloped hers, the sound of his gasping breath filled her ears.

Then his weight was gone and the hot, trapped air was drying the sweat-slicked skin of her exposed breast. Disorientated, Marina blinked into the shaft of sunlight. Justin was standing, surrounded by swirling dust motes, dragging on his shirt.

'Justin?'

The harsh panting breaths rasped his throat, the light dazzled him as he tried to look at her, his body screamed its protest at what he was doing.

'Justin?'

No self-control, no damned self-control. When they had fallen on to the bed he should have helped her to her feet and calmly gone on with inspecting the rooms. But the moment his arms had gone round her, the moment that slender body had been pressed under his and the sweet scent of her, warm and female, had filled his nostrils, he had been lost.

He was mad—mad to have ripped away their clothing until he could caress the wonderful weight of her breasts, mad to have gasped out his love for her against the wet heat of her mouth.

Thank God, she could not have heard him, added that burden to the sense of duty she already carried. He jammed his shirt tails into his breeches, not daring to unfasten the fall to do it properly in case his will-power utterly deserted him.

'Justin!' Mari was kneeling up now, clutching the bedpost as she stared at him. He shut his eyes and turned so that he did not have to look at her, with her hair half-down, her bosom rising and falling with her panting breath, the globes of those lovely breasts, crowned by peaking, aroused nipples. 'Why did you stop?'

'Because we both know where it would end, and I will not do that to you, Mari.'

'Even though I am willing?' She was scrambling off the bed; he heard her stumble as her feet hit the boards and forced himself not to turn, stooping instead to pick up his waistcoat which had somehow been flung half across the room.

'You would walk over hot coals if you felt it was your duty, I know. And I would stop you from doing that as well, believe me.' She was close behind him now, he could sense her, even though she had moved silently to close the space. 'Do not touch me, Mari.'

'But you want me.' It was as much a question as a statement.

'Yes, I want you.' He swung round so fast she froze, then gasped as he caught her right wrist and brought her palm flat against the undeniable evidence of his arousal.

She stood there, her grey eyes huge. Then, to his utter shock, closed her fingers. 'Do you not want children, Justin? Do you not want an heir?'

He wrenched back from her, ignoring the pain as her fingers loosed. 'This is not a stud.' Her flinch at the crudity stung. 'I do not insist on love—that, we agreed, was not there from the start—but I do insist on at least some mutual respect and trust, not just a wife who is eager enough for caresses and who is prepared to grit her teeth and endure the outcome for the sake of her duty.'

'Well, you can insist on trust all you like, my lord—until you learn to do without what you cannot have and have not earned.'

The vehemence of her attack rocked him back. 'Mari—'

'Oh, go away! At least you are decent now—or are you going to stand there and watch me dress?'

Marina waited until the impact of booted heels died away down the corridor, then began to drag her clothing back into place. Her body trembled. It must be a sort of shock, for it was most certainly not desire. That had died like a fire quenched by a bucket of water. In fact, soggy grey ash summed up how she felt perfectly.

At least she could not fool herself that Justin might be coming to love her, for if there had been a time to confess it, surely that desperate, urgent coming-together was it. Bundling her hair up into a rough chignon, Marina closed her eyes and recalled the moment she had cried out those betraying words, thankfully for them to be swallowed by his kiss.

This is not a stud. Those brutal words showed just how determined he was—surely any man was going to want children, at least an heir? That had been her only, faint hope that Justin would relent.

* * *

For two days the June weather broke and seemed determined to express in rain the tears Marina was resolved not to shed. Cooped up with a husband she was set on avoiding, Marina threw herself, and her domestic staff, into completing the east-wing guest rooms.

By ten on the second morning she pushed the damp hair back from her forehead and looked around her at the maids, dogged in the sticky humidity, rolling up the carpets in the main suite.

'I do not know where we are going to lay all of these, Lady Mortenhoe.' Mrs Faversham shook her head as she contemplated the heavy rolls waiting for the footmen to lug them downstairs and lay them out for the wet tea-leaf treatment before beating. 'I had been using the drying yards, but none of them are covered, and just look at this rain!'

She was being perfectly reasonable, but somehow stripping the rooms—this room in particular—was urgent. 'Well, just have them stack them up until the weather turns again. This cannot go on much longer.' Marina looked around. The curtains were down, the bed hangings were being unhooked by a footman perilously perched on top of a ladder—that just left the bedclothes before the room could be thoroughly cleaned.

'Tsk! Look at the state of this.' Mrs Faversham waited until the footman had descended safely with his arms full of hangings. 'Take that down straight away please, Peter. Harris, lend him a hand.' As soon as the servants were out of the room, the housekeeper waved a hand at the bed.

'Someone has been…romping on this! I would not have thought it of any of our staff—now I shall have a maid in the family way before I know where I am!' Still clicking her tongue in exasperation, Mrs Faversham poked a long finger into the screwed-up bedcover and rucked blankets. 'And that is a very nice piece of brocade as well. I just hope someone has not put a heel through it.'

Feeling as guilty as if she had been found *in flagrante*, Marina reached over to help fold back the cover. Something stuck in her palm. There, snagged in the thick weave, was a pearl-topped hairpin, one of the half-dozen or so she had used in her chignon that day. A pretty ornament—and an expensive one that no servant could hope to own.

'My lady, are you unwell?' Mrs Faversham hurried round the bed and took Marina's arm, steering her towards the nearest chair. 'There now, sit down a moment—you went quite pale.'

'I…I am fine, truly, Mrs Faversham. Perhaps I bent over rather quickly.' How to get the housekeeper out of the room so she could search the bed for any more betraying pins? She had a perfect right to make love to her husband in any room in the house, and if everything between them had been as it should for newlyweds, Marina realised she might have been embarrassed, but quite prepared to blush and let Mrs Faversham think what she might. As it was, discovery was intolerable.

'Lady Mortenhoe, forgive me if I am speaking out of turn, but your mama is not here—are you perhaps increasing?'

Increasing? What did she mean? Then the older woman's meaning sank in. 'Pregnant? No, good heavens, no, of course not…I mean, I am sure not. It is just the heat.'

But I might be. Justin made love to me twice just before that dreadful quarrel. Could it be possible?

'My lady, you are positively white. I will ring—no, the bell cord is broken—I will go for your woman, now just sit still and rest.'

She was hardly out of the door before Marina was on her feet, searching the tumbled bedclothes for any more betraying pins. But there were none. Just the one tiny ornament to mark all that passion and anger.

Slowly she went back and sat down. No. It was too much to hope that she was with child and, anyway, surely she would not be feeling anything yet, even if she were.

If only Mama was here. But she would sense something was wrong as soon as she had spent a day in the house and if I write she will come at once. It was something she could write to Pris about. Pris had delighted her husband with twin boys the year before, but had been surprisingly discreet in not regaling her unmarried friend with all the details. Well, now she could.

Jenny came flying in, sal volatile in one hand and a damp cloth in the other. 'My lady, just lie down on the bed here and—'

'No! Not here.' The girl jumped at the vehemence and Marina softened it with a smile. 'So dusty. I will walk back to my room and have a little rest. I think it is just the heat.' Just the heat, just the strain, nothing more.

The rain lasted for another night before finally moving on, leaving the roses brown and sodden and the whole house feeling warmly damp.

'Ugh!' Jenny threw open Marina's clothes presses and began to pull things out. 'I am going to air all of these or they'll be getting mould spots.'

'Well, find me my stoutest boots and an old walking dress before you do.' Marina began to unbutton the delicate lawn morning dress she had been wearing. 'I am going for a walk.'

'But your hem will get soaked my lady—and the ground is all muddy.'

'Which is why I am going to change. I really need some fresh air, Jenny.'

A long trudge through the park and into the beech woods, that was where she would go. The memory of Justin recall-

ing those woods stirred in her mind and she found she was
smiling at she stepped over the bridge and took one of the
overgrown tracks leading towards the billowing green edge
of the trees.

They were as he had described them. Marina ran her
ungloved hand over the smooth grey trunks, soaring upwards,
kicked up the fallen leaves that filled the hollows, still crisp
where they had drifted when the new growth burst out.

She jumped as a pheasant shouted its alarm call almost
under her feet, and laughed to see squirrels playing tag in the
branches, rust-red tails twitching as they flew backwards and
forwards. Almost she could hear the sound of other feet,
lighter feet, running behind her, scuffing the leaves, scrambling over the fallen branches. The sound of a small boy with
his dog in his own magic kingdom.

There—she could see him. But it was only the speckled
rump of a fallow deer, veering away from the human intrusion,
not the spirit of her husband as a child. The mud was clogging
her boots and her legs felt weary suddenly. Marina sat down
on a tree stump and began to clean away the mud with a sharp
stick. She tossed it away when she was finished, sending a jay
panicking through the bushes with a harsh scream.

Silence again. The woods were still. No breeze penetrated
here and the animals and birds had calmed down now she was
sitting. Would that little boy of twenty years ago be the last
child to run from the big house to play in these woods? She
found her palm was pressed to her belly, as flat as ever under
the straight, simple lines of the old dress.

What had Justin asked for? Mutual respect and trust. She
had shown him she did not trust him, had partly told him why.
And had then gone on to show him the greatest disrespect one
could show to a gentleman: she had attacked his honour.

Because he had married her, loving another woman while

swearing that was not so. Because even on his wedding day he was flirting with that woman. And now she knew he was corresponding with her. But Justin did not know that she knew these things. Was she being fair to him to hide her knowledge? Should she give him the chance to explain?

And suffer even more humiliation? Marina got to her feet and began to make her way back out of the wood. What could he say? That he loved Serena, but she had jilted him, married someone richer with a greater title? And now—now what? That they were carrying on a clandestine relationship because he had married only for Knightshaye and she was bored with her middle-aged husband?

But at least the truth would be out in the open and Justin would know what she was accusing him of. That was only fair. It was her duty not to hide things from her husband. Marina came to a halt at the edge of the wood and leaned on a tree while she looked at the warm brick of Knightshaye in the afternoon sunshine.

It was right that she was honest with the man she loved.

The sound of carriage wheels made her turn, her introspection forgotten for a moment. She had slipped out without telling Hearnshaw that she would not be at home for callers that day, now here she was, muddied just as Jenny had predicted, her hair bundled into a net at the nape and her face doubtless flushed with exertion.

It would be better to slip in through the kitchen door and make her way up using the back stair, rather than risk an undignified encounter with the callers on her own front doorstep.

The visitors' carriage passed her as she made her way over the footbridge that led from the park across to the rear of the house, and something familiar about the coachman caught her eye. Fulbright! What on earth was Justin's second coachman doing driving someone else's carriage? Only it was not someone else's—the now familiar crest on the door of the carriage as it rumbled past was unmistakably that of the earls of Mortenhoe.

Marina caught up with it as the coachman jumped down from the box, followed more stiffly by Martin the groom, his blunderbuss tucked securely under his arm.

'Fulbright! What are you doing here?'

'My lady.' He tugged his forelock. 'We're earlier than you expected, I've no doubt—we made good time, for all that his lordship's message must have gone astray.'

'His message?' It would not do to be making a mystery in front of the staff. 'To be sure. Well, your speed has certainly caught me out, Fulbright—I must hurry in.'

Marina whisked past her rather startled kitchen staff and up the small flight of steps that led off the butler's corridor to the green baize door under the stairs in the front hall. Changing out of her muddied clothes could wait, she was too curious now.

The door opened almost in her face. 'My lady! I beg your pardon, I was not expecting anyone to be there.' Let alone his mistress looking like a hoyden, that was for sure. Marina managed to look as though careering through the servants' quarters in muddy boots was normal behaviour.

'We have a visitor, I gather, Hearnshaw. Who is it?'

'I could not say, my lady.' Hearnshaw was looking decidedly uneasy.

'Why ever not? Surely you announced them to his lordship?'

'It must be a relative of his lordship.' The butler hesitated, then, obviously put out, added, 'Just sailed in as though she owned the place. She's in the Chinese room with his lordship. Didn't give me a chance to ask if I should serve refreshments.'

Oh, dear, this sounded worryingly like a family crisis—but Justin did not have any family, unless of course one of his elderly guardians was unwell. 'You had better warn Cook to lay an extra place for dinner. How lucky we did so much to the guest rooms,' she added, half to herself, as she pushed open the baize-covered door and emerged into the shadows under the stairs.

Go upstairs and change, or go in as she was? If this was a crisis, then she should not delay. If it were not, then she could excuse herself. Whoever was in the Chinese room with Justin was being very quiet, no voices could be heard through the thick panels. Marina turned the knob and walked in.

Her husband was standing in the centre of the room, locked in a deep kiss with a slender woman, her bonnet tumbled down her back on its wide satin ribbons, her body pressed close to his, her gloved fingers tangled in his hair.

Serena, Marchioness of Andover.

Chapter Twenty-Two

'My lady?' Hearnshaw was standing in the hall, staring at her with as much surprise as a well-trained butler might show as she closed the door softly behind her. 'Are you unwell, my lady?'

'What? No.' There really was no doubt about it. That had not been a peck on the cheek, an embrace between old friends. That had been—in fact, probably still was!—a full-blooded sexual kiss. And she was not going to stand for it.

Marina realised that she was angry. Furiously angry. The tears would come later, she was hazily aware of that. The disgust and the betrayal and the misery of having her unspoken love rejected—all that was to come. Now, she was quite simply livid.

'Hearnshaw.' Her mind was speeding, planning. 'I have had worrying news. My mother is not well and I must go to her at once. Unfortunately his lordship must deal with an urgent matter concerning the Marquis of Andover—please make sure he is not disturbed—and cannot accompany me.

'I wish to have a carriage readied for me to leave within fifteen minutes. Have it wait in the stable yard.'

The plan was unfolding in her mind as she ran upstairs.

Jenny, as little packing as possible and money. Not only had she a full quarter's pin money in the pretty little safe in her dressing room, but she had a month's housekeeping too. And the careful notes Mr Sheffield had given her to explain how she could draw more money if she happened to find herself in London.

'Jenny?' The bedchamber door banged back under her thrusting hand.

'Yes, my lady?' The maid popped her head out of the dressing-room door. 'Oh, lud, look at your hem with all that mud.'

'Never mind that.' The old dress fell to the floor in a heap and Marina began to tug off her boots. 'Jenny, pack the absolute minimum for two weeks—no ball gowns, no jewellery, only my pearls and the diamond set. And hurry, we must be away in fifteen minutes.'

'But, my lady...where are we going?'

'Paris.'

Justin dragged himself free of Serena's grip at the painful cost of strands of his hair. 'For God's sake, Serena! What are you thinking of?' Hell, she was wearing some sort of lip paint; he dragged his handkerchief across his mouth in disgust.

'Do not shout at me!' The smeared lips pouted. Her voice trembled, threatening tears.

'I am not shouting!' Justin took a deep breath and lowered his voice. 'How do you expect me to react? You arrive unannounced, you throw yourself into my arms before my butler had scarce got the door shut and you kiss me so I had to damn near break your arm to make you let go.' Resentfully he rubbed the sore patches at the side of his head.

'But I wrote to you!' Serena cast off her exquisite bonnet and collapsed on to the *chaise longue* with the grace of a tragic muse. How on earth he had been such a fool to have fallen for her playacting and airs he could not imagine. Possibly because he had not then had the bracing experience of living with a woman of backbone and character.

'You wrote me a long farrago of complaint against your husband. How am I to deduce from that your intention to visit?'

'He *hit* me, Justin!'

'Did he?' She had the grace to blush and look conscious. 'Are you sure he hit you, Serena?'

'He said I ought to be beaten. He said if I called him such names again he would slap me.'

'So Andover did not actually hit you?'

'No.' The full lower lip of that gorgeous Cupid's bow mouth was stuck out now like that of a thwarted toddler. 'But he threatened it. That is just as bad.'

'He has my deepest sympathy,' Justin retorted. He regarded her, hands on hips, while she sniffled prettily into a lace hand-kerchief. 'I am deeply tempted to carry out his threats myself.'

'Justin!'

'Stop crying, Serena, I am not the idiot I used to be. And I am not going to mop up your tears and make it all better. Now, we are in the devil of a fix and I'm dam— if I know how to get us both out of it with whole skins. Where is your maid?' One look at her face had his heart sinking even lower. 'Don't tell me you ran away without a maid, Serena?'

'Adrian employed her, she spies on me. I didn't want her running off and tittle-tattling to him.'

'And how the devil did you get here? What tale did you spin Andover's coachman?'

'Um…' She was wriggling under his interrogation now, unable to meet his eyes. 'It wasn't…I mean, they would have been just as bad…'

'How did you get here, Serena?' he asked wearily.

'In…in someone else's carriage.'

'Whose?' A cold finger was running down his spine. She wouldn't have done anything so bloody stupid. Would she?

'Yours, Justin.' She would. He was a dead man. Vaguely Justin recalled bringing his will up to date. That was one mercy. 'I went to your town house because I know you've got lots of carriages. And I said that your wife was ill and wanted me to come to her sickbed. But my husband was away and the carriage was being repaired…'

'And they fell for it?' Fulbright was not going to hear the last of this.

'They were very nice, Justin. Not like you,' she added, with a burst of spite.

He walked away from her and placed both hands on the mantelshelf, bracing himself so he could stare down into the hearth, look at something other than the pretty little madam who was apparently set on destroying his marriage and having him shot by her outraged husband, all out of sheer selfish thoughtlessness.

'And what exactly did you think coming here would achieve?' Amazing. His voice was quite calm.

'Oh, Justin darling, don't be cross with me.' Serena was trying wheedling now. 'I know I was horrid to you when I married Adrian and you went and married that plain old maid in reaction because you love me so much. I didn't mean to break your heart. But now I know I made a mistake, we can both get divorced and you can marry me and…'

There was a charming Dresden shepherdess on the mantelshelf. Justin picked it up and quite calmly dropped it on to the hearth where it shattered into a mass of shards. Serena gave a little scream, which died on her lips as he turned to face her.

'I love my wife. I do not deserve her, but I love her, and if you say one more disparaging word about her I will have you put out of the house. I do not think I was ever in love with you Serena; if I was, it died when I discovered what a selfish, fickle, self-centred child you are.'

'You—'

'Be quiet!' She closed her mouth with a startled squeak. 'You have just about gone your length in compromising both of us and if your husband chooses to call me out I cannot say I would blame him. Where is he?'

'Away. On business. He is due home again the day after tomorrow. Justin—'

'Well, thank heavens for small mercies.' Justin tugged the bell pull. 'Dry your eyes, pick up your bonnet and try to look worried.'

'I *am* worried, you horrible, horrible—'

'Silence!' The door opened. 'Hearnshaw. Please send Mrs Faversham to me at once.'

'Yes, my lord. My lady—'

'No, not now.'

'But, my lord—'

What the devil was the matter with the man? 'Mrs Faversham. Now!'

The sound of coach wheels brought him to the window, but it was only the rear view of a travelling carriage vanishing down the drive. It looked vaguely familiar. Justin shook his head and turned as the door opened.

'My lord.'

Thank goodness for Mrs Faversham. Justin thought he had never seen a more formidably respectable-looking woman.

'Mrs Faversham. This is the Marchioness of Andover. Regrettably she has made an error and had believed she was expected here to stay with Lady Mortenhoe. She has just arrived in my town carriage and without a maid. Understandably the Marquis is likely to be much exercised when he hears of this and may put a most unfortunate interpretation upon her innocent actions.'

'Indeed.' The housekeeper bent a long, unsmiling stare on Serena, who wilted under it. 'One can quite see the danger.'

'Precisely. Therefore I would like you to leave immediately with Lady Andover and a maid and escort her back to town, where you will stay with her at her house. Upon the Marquis's return, you will present him with a letter I shall give you in a moment. And, naturally, answer any questions he might have about the, shall we say, timing and duration of her ladyship's visit.'

'Go back to London now? But I am tired and hungry and thirsty and—'

'And no doubt in need of the picnic we will eat on our way, after which you will doubtless wish to sleep as we travel. Come with me, my lady,' said the housekeeper firmly. 'I will find a maid to wait on you while I pack a bag and order a hamper for the coach.'

Borne along by a harder will than she had ever encountered, Serena let herself be led from the room. 'Mrs Faversham.' The housekeeper turned in the doorway. 'I do not need to tell you how very sensitive this matter is, and how much I rely upon your discretion and good judgement.'

'Thank you, my lord. You will not find your trust misplaced. Her ladyship—'

'Her ladyship is not to be worried by this until Lady Andover has gone. I will have the letter ready in a few minutes.'

The blank piece of paper stared at him mockingly. Just what could one write to an outraged peer of the realm? The truth would have to do.

My lord. I regret to say that Lady Andover, finding herself in distress over some misunderstood words that passed between you, sought refuge with my wife and I...

Justin sucked the end of his quill contemplatively. It was a nice balance between calling Serena a foolish chit and presenting a picture of her behaviour that her fond husband would instantly recognise as a whitewash. One could only do one's best and meanwhile practise one's swordplay. It was a slight comfort that as the challenged party he would have the choice of weapons. On the other hand, Andover was a fair man, and he must know his own wife by now. *Naturally, I shall make myself available to your lordship to discuss this matter further should you have the slightest concerns about her ladyship's well-being during the course of this unfortunate adventure.*

Now, what the devil was he going to say to Mari? It was a miracle that she had not come in yet from the walk she had taken. Hearnshaw materialised at the doorway. 'My lord, the carriage is prepared, but her ladyship—'

'Her ladyship is not to be bothered by this. Here is the letter for Mrs Faversham.'

The butler bowed himself out. Justin pushed his chair back from the desk and sat drumming his fingers slowly on the desk. Eventually he fished the old lustre out of his pocket and turned it over and over, letting the light catch its facets, sending rainbows darting over the walls.

When the carriage disappeared from sight down the drive he stood up, stretched and strolled out into the hall, mind made up. He could not expect Mari to believe him about this unless she also believed he loved her. Whatever the risk, he was going to tell her today.

'Hearnshaw, where is her ladyship? Is she back from her walk yet?'

'But, my lord, that was what I was trying to tell you—she left over an hour ago.'

'Left? You mean she has taken the gig out?'

'No, my lord. The other carriage. It was fortunate that we had two full carriage teams well rested in the stables, for the ones that have just come from London are in no state to—'

'Why has her ladyship gone?' The ice in his stomach was like nothing he had felt since his parents had died, a paralysing, creeping dread that seemed to drain the blood from his muscles.

'Because of the message about Lady Winslow, my lord. I thought you had given it to her. She came in and went to the salon and then came out, almost immediately, very pale and upset, and said her mother was unwell and she must go to her. She left within the quarter-hour with her woman.'

She had seen them. The only moment that Mari could have come into the salon without him noticing her was when Serena had his hair in her determined little fists and her mouth fastened on his like a limpet. She had seen her husband in a passionate embrace with another woman and drawn the obvious conclusion.

But why had she fled? That was not like his Mari—she would have stood her ground and confronted them both. Or was it that underlying mistrust that he could not get her to explain? Was this the last straw for her?

'Have my curricle harnessed with the greys and send my valet to my room immediately.' She had an hour's start on him—perhaps two by the time he left. He would find her and bring her back and there would be no more secrets between them.

Half an hour later he was running down the stairs, his fingers turning the lustre over and over in the old familiar gesture of comfort. Why had he still got it in his pocket? Justin stopped in the hall, the fragment of glass in his palm, staring at it.

He had been waiting to return it to its place when Knight-shaye had felt truly his home again. How had he not noticed that happening? How had he failed to see that anywhere with Mari in it was home? Impulsively he spun round and strode off down the corridor towards the ballroom.

When the greys spurted into a canter across the bridge the chandelier on its stand in the gloom threw back shimmering hints of light from every single prism, even from the one with worn edges, which still swayed from the touch of Justin's fingers.

Chapter Twenty-Three

Justin forced himself to a steady pace despite the urge to whip the horses up and gallop. Two hours was enough of a start that even his greys could not hope to overtake the travelling carriage over the relatively short journey from Knightshaye to the Winslows' country seat near Egham.

The long summer afternoon meant, he supposed, that Mari would try to make the journey in one stage. Would she stop to eat? He doubted it—whether it was anguish or anger that was driving her away from him, she would hardly be in the mood to stop in a strange place to dine. And if his own internal state was any clue to hers, hunger was the last thing she would be feeling.

His eyes were steady on the road between the flicking dark ears of his leaders, his hands were light on the reins as he guided the high-mettled team along the busy pike road, but his mind was an undisciplined turmoil as he tried to understand what Mari must be feeling and what he was going to say to her when he found her.

Would she believe the truth, or would that deep mistrust make it impossible for her to accept anything he told her now?

* * *

His mother-in-law rose with a delighted smile on her face as he was ushered into the dining room of Lark's Acre House just as she and Elizabeth were taking their places. The cold feeling gripped his gut again as he realised that the table was laid for two only. Mari was not there.

'Britton, set two more places. Justin, my dear, what a lovely surprise! Now, where is Marina? Freshening up?' Something in his expression must have warned her. Her smile became brittle, but Lady Winslow maintained an admirable calm as she turned to her butler. 'No, just the one place, Britton, and then leave us. I will ring.'

Justin sat. 'She is not here then?'

'What has happened? Has Marina run away?' Lizzie's voice was a squeak.

'Be silent, Elizabeth. Serve the soup, Justin will be in need of sustenance.' She was showing more resilience in the face of what was obviously more a disaster than he had imagined. He had expected vapours—instead, he began to see where Mari had come by her backbone.

'Lizzie is correct. Marina has left home because of a mis-understanding. I have every confidence that when I am able to explain it she will return.' Actually he had no such confidence, but now was not the time to voice that. 'I believed that she had come here; apparently not.'

Lizzie passed him a bowl and he took it with a murmur of thanks, passing Lady Winslow the bread as though this was a normal family dinner. Without thinking he dipped his spoon and drank, barely registering that he was consuming cold watercress soup.

'No, she is not here,' Lady Winslow said slowly, her grey eyes resting on him with a familiar hard-won calm that he recognised from her daughter. 'Do you think she might have had an accident on the road?'

'I believe not. I followed only two hours behind. Marina was with my coachman and he would not have taken a back road. She told our butler that she had been called here because you were unwell, and the stable-yard staff heard her give the coachman instructions; she must have changed them once they were out of sight of the house.'

'But why did she run away?' Lizzie demanded, braving her mother's glare of disapproval.

'Because she found me kissing another woman,' Justin snapped, suddenly too exasperated by the whole wretched coil to pussyfoot around it any longer.

'Justin!'

'It was an old friend of mine who was in distress. In so much distress that she clutched at me in a way that must have looked deeply compromising.'

'Marina would not have left you just because of that,' Lizzie declared dogmatically.

Justin met his mother-in-law's eyes. 'No. It is not easy being married, Elizabeth. It takes a while to get to know each other—and sometimes things are misunderstood. I made mistakes. Marina is angry with me and this was the last straw.'

'More like a log than a straw,' she observed, her brow furrowed. 'Will it be all right, Justin?'

'If I have anything to do with it, yes.'

'Good.' His sister-in-law had touching faith in him. 'Shall I ring for the next course, Mama?'

They spoke of indifferent matters while the servants were in the room, then, 'Where do you think Marina has gone?' Lizzie demanded over the saddle of mutton, which Justin had carved somewhat erratically.

'Our house in London, I hope. Or possibly to your town house if Charlie is at home.'

'You will stay the night?' Lady Winslow was biting her lip thoughtfully.

'If I may. My team is tired and I do not think there is any point in driving through the night. Marina will be safely asleep before I get to London.'

Later, after Lizzie had gone to bed, his mother-in-law sat in the drawing room and regarded him steadily. 'What is wrong between my daughter and you?'

'She discovered the bargain Charles and I had struck over the marriage and the house. After that she has found it difficult to trust me.'

'And I imagine the state of the house has not helped?' She saw his surprised expression. 'I read between the lines of her very tactful letters and made Charles tell me exactly how Knightshaye had been neglected.'

'Marina has managed the house magnificently. It was a shock to me to find it in such a condition and, of course, the history does not make it any easier for her. I believe she finds it hard to believe that I do not hold her in some way responsible for it.'

'For her father's sins and her brother's negligence?' Lady Winslow's lips twisted wryly. 'Have you told her the reason for the feud between your fathers?'

'You know it, ma'am?' He was surprised, and knew that it showed. 'I did not feel I could while any of those affected were still—'

'While I was alive, you mean? I do know, and you may tell her if you wish. I have long since come to terms with it. He was not a bad husband and father, you know, but he had a devil in him that would not let go.' She shook her head regretfully, her eyes unfocused, perhaps seeing back into the past. Then she gave herself a little shake. 'Marina will not find Charles at home—he is in Paris.'

'*Paris?*' What was his erratic brother-in-law doing there?

'He is running a gaming hell in the Palais Royale with Crispin Devlin,' said his fond mother-in-law calmly.

'Rochford's son? Does Marina know?'

'I am not sure. Possibly. He would confide in her before me about something like this, and I received a typical letter from him yesterday. He appears to hope I will think nothing more of it than if he had gone to Brighton for the week.'

'I will retire now.' She stood up, suddenly looking weary despite her elegant evening dress and carefully maintained poise. As he stood she leaned up and kissed his cheek. 'I expect you will be gone before I rise tomorrow. Find her, Justin, make her understand how much you love her.'

Lady Winslow was gone before he could react. Did his feelings for his wife show so very clearly? He hoped so.

In a bed in Brown's Hotel Marina lay staring up into the darkness and listening to the traffic on Albemarle Street. She had arrived in London, thankful that her ruse must have succeeded and Justin had not overtaken her. Now she was wondering if he had followed her at all. What if he had found her departure highly convenient? The scandal of Serena leaving her husband for another man was going to be frightful enough, without that man's wife being upon the scene as well.

What was I thinking? That he would forget her once he found I had gone? That he would rush after me, begging my forgiveness? She was probably entirely safe from pursuit and could have gone to their London house without the slightest danger.

Still, being here made her feel independent. Frighteningly alone, but independent, a state she must rapidly become accustomed to. Grandmama always stayed at Brown's and the manager's welcome had been gratifyingly respectful. Nor did he seem to find it the slightest bit strange that she should confide in him her need for a reliable courier to escort her to Paris in the unavoidable absence of her husband.

'He is buying horses in Ireland,' she improvised glibly. 'You may imagine my dismay when I received a letter this morning telling me that my brother was ill in Paris.'

Mr Turnstall tut-tutted over her ladyship's predicament and assured her that a most reliable courier was known to him, having just returned from escorting the Dowager Lady Foxton home from the French capital. A note from the hotelier that evening would bring Mr de Claireville to wait upon her ladyship at ten the next morning.

Giving up on sleep, Marina slipped out of bed, lit a candle and began to make a list. *Passport*—dear old Lord Whycliffe in the Foreign Office could be relied upon for that—*money, shopping.* One day in London if Mr de Claireville proved as efficient as his reputation implied, and then she would be on her way to Paris.

As she climbed back into bed, leaving a carefully detailed list of additional items that needed to be purchased lying on the table beside the inkwell, it occurred to Marina for the first time that she did not know what she would do once she reached Charlie. When she had run away, it had seemed an end in itself to escape from Justin. But it solved nothing, she realised, curling up into a miserable ball.

She still loved him, he had still betrayed her. Distance changed that not a jot or tittle, and, for the first time since she had seen those two figures locked together in each other's arms, she wept.

* * *

Mr de Claireville either did not notice his new employer's red eyes or was too tactful to appear to do so. He was also quite amazingly organised, first whisking Marina to Foreign Office. Their old family friend Lord Whycliffe was only too happy to oblige her when he heard her story of Lady Winslow's concern over her son's new venture and her desire that Marina visit and ensure all was well.

'Young devil! Burning the candle at both ends, I'll be bound,' he chuckled, fixing his seal on the crackling parchment. 'You'll soon have him sobered up and considering his position again, I'll be bound. There you are, my dear. *His Britannic Majesty requests and requires* and all that. Seems odd to be giving out passports for France again, damme if it doesn't.'

Then into the bustle of the City and Justin's bankers, who seemed quite sanguine about handing over two hundred guineas to her ladyship and providing her with references to their agents in Paris.

Marina put the money into her reticule, clutching it tightly and resolving to pay as much as possible back to those same agents as soon as she arrived in Paris. Running away using Justin's money seemed morally dubious to her, even if it was all his fault.

And finally back to the hotel to meet Jenny who had taken the shopping list and now had enough clean linen, toilet articles and luggage for both of them for the journey. With Mr de Claireville making intelligent conversation about life in Paris since the restoration of the monarchy in one corner of the carriage and Jenny sitting wide-eyed in another, they rolled over London Bridge and took the Dover road. The sight of the Thames glinting below them brought a lump to Marina's throat. Everything familiar was about to vanish. And where was Justin?

* * *

Her husband reached his own front door shortly after Marina's party caught their first glimpse of the sea. He was tired, wet, dirty and, as his butler observed once safely below stairs, in as foul a mood as a blind badger at a baiting.

The day had started badly with one of the leaders casting a shoe just outside Staines. The nearest blacksmith had proved to be visiting his daughter in Kingston, which meant proceeding at a slow walk for seven miles into Bedfont. This had been enlivened by Knapton, his senior groom, muttering gloomy prognostications about the likely damage to the animal's hoof as a result.

The Bedfont blacksmith was in his shop and willing to oblige his lordship, but not until he had completed the task of fitting a new set of shoes to Squire Walker's prize-winning team of plough horses.

Knapton pointing out that he was keeping a peer of the realm on important business waiting was met by an amiable nod of acknowledgement and the information that important as his lordship might be, he, Jack Hawkins, would never set eyes on him again, but it was more than his business was worth to upset the Squire.

The local ale shop produced a turgid brew, which Knapton lost no time in describing as ditchwater, with the result that the brewer—and his two hulking sons—took exception, and it cost Justin ten minutes and several shillings before he could extract the fulminating groom from the threatened punch-up.

Taken all round, Justin would have been happy never to set eyes upon the Hounslow road again, and the onset of a sharp thundershower as they passed Holland House set the crown on his mood.

His wife was, patently, not at home and his butler enquiring respectfully after her ladyship's health proved, without him having to ask, that his staff had no idea she was in London.

Tuckworth expressed his stately pleasure that his lordship was gracing his town house again, yet still managed to exude a faint air of reproach that there had been no warning, and very definite disapproval that his lordship was without his valet.

'Never mind that, I need a hot bath and a message taking to Lord Winslow's house in Cavendish Square.'

'Lord Winslow is from home, my lord.' Tuckworth clicked his fingers at a footman. 'Hot water and a bath for his lordship immediately and send Cranborn up to see to his lordship's clothes. Tsk, this coat is wet through, my lord.'

'I am aware of that, Tuckworth; I am soaked to the skin. It rained. And how do you know of Lord Winslow's movements?'

'Mr Bunting, his butler, is a member of my club,' Tuckworth confided, removing the offending coat and urging his employer towards the stairs. 'Lord Winslow has gone to Paris, I understand, in company with another young gentleman and with the aim of setting up a gambling establishment.'

'I was aware of Lord Winslow's movements. Is the house shut up?' As they reached his chamber Justin tugged his neckcloth open and began to unbutton his shirt.

'I have no information upon that, my lord—I will ascertain immediately. If it is not, is there any message?'

'No, I only wish to establish whether any of the family have called, or are staying in Lord Winslow's absence.'

Tuckworth's eyebrows rose infinitesimally, but with two footmen upending hot-water jugs into the slipper bath and Cranborn standing by to receive his wet clothes, Justin did not intend to expand any further.

Now what? The water was blissfully hot as he slid into it, waving away the footman's offer of back brush and sponge.

'That will be all, Cranborn, just find me some evening clothes, I will be dining out this evening.'

He could not believe that Mari had met with some accident. Not with an experienced coachman, a groom and her maid with her. If she was not at Cavendish Square, then all he could think was that she had followed Charles to Paris.

By herself? With no passport? Probably she was sitting in a harbourside inn in Dover, realising too late just what was entailed in such an expedition and all the things she should have seen to before leaving London.

Justin hauled himself out of the bath and stood dripping on the carpet before absently reaching for a towel. The anxiety he had been controlling ever since realising that Mari was not with her mother threatened to sweep his control away. His hand reached for the bell pull, then dropped. No, wait and see what the news was from Cavendish Square; it would be ridiculous to go haring off to Dover when she was comfortably settled in her old rooms.

And if she was? What then? Striding in and announcing that it was all a mistake and he loved only her was unlikely to receive a very positive response, coming from a husband who had never mentioned the word *love* once to her.

It occurred to Justin, as he shrugged into his dressing gown and began to pace up and down the length of the bedchamber, that he had never courted Mari. He had done his damnedest to persuade her to marry him, but that hardly counted—and she now knew his motives only too well. And he had made love to her, with disastrous results. But he had never wooed her. Would that work? It might surprise her, and it seemed the only tactic he had left.

A discreet tap on the door broke his train of thought and he looked up from his contemplation of the cooling bathwater to see Tuckworth.

'There is a skeleton staff at Lord Winslow's house, my lord. None of the family is in residence, nor have been there since his lordship left.'

So, that answered that. Justin dressed himself with more speed than his valet would have believed, twitched his cravat into order, and threw an evening cloak around his shoulders, forcing himself to concentrate on choosing which club to dine at. Mari was doubtless sitting in frustrated comfort in a private parlour in the Crown and Anchor, picking at her dinner and wondering what to do next.

Somehow, despite that comforting picture, Justin did not seem to have much appetite. Probably the excellent dinners at Watier's would be wasted on him. White's it was, then; at least he could be assured of some peace and quiet to think about tomorrow's tactics.

Handing his hat and cloak to the porter, Justin made his way up the shallow sweep of the club's staircase deep in thought, heading for the seclusion of the library. A tall man was coming down, but stopped at the turn of the stair.

'Ah! Mortenhoe. How very timely, I was just thinking how much I would value a word with you.'

The chilly drawl cut through Justin's preoccupation. He halted, looking up, alert and suddenly very wary.

'Andover.' The Marquis himself, with his errant wife returned to him and apparently in a temper for a confrontation with the man she had fled to. Instinctively Justin's right hand clenched at his side over the weapon that was not there.

Chapter Twenty-Four

Four days after she had watched the white cliffs vanishing into the haze over a choppy sea, Marina rested her chin on her cupped hands and looked out over the pleached limes that lined the long inner court of the Palais Royale.

It seemed hard to believe she was here, waking in a bedchamber high in the roof of one of the long wings, peeping out through the balustrade down to where the garden, which had thronged with noisy revellers late into the small hours, now drowsed in its short period of early morning peace.

Two days ago Mr de Claireville had delivered her to the door at five in the afternoon with the same courteous efficiency he had shown throughout their journey. Assured that she was now quite safe, he bowed over her hand, accepted the discreet package of notes for his agreed fee and departed with the coach, leaving her explaining to the large and dubious doorman that she was, indeed, Monsieur le Baron's sister.

C. et C. read the newly painted and gilded sign over the smart black door: *Charles et Crispin*, no doubt.

'Où est Monsieur le Baron?' After three days, even with

her courier making all the arrangements, her French was coming back to her. She stepped forward with determination and, to her relief, the hulking figure backed away to allow her entrance, Jenny on her heels.

'Doesn't he speak any English?' the maid demanded. 'I don't know how I'm going to get on if they all speak foreign.'

'Speak it better than you,' remarked the doorman in unmistakable East London accents.

'Then why didn't you say so?' Marina demanded in some exasperation, peering past him into the gloomy entrance hall. She was tired, grieving over Justin and, if the truth be told, somewhat daunted to find herself in the middle of Paris. The war was over, the monarchy restored, but even so, she had spent most of her life regarding the French as the enemy.

'Mr Crispin said I was to practise. My gentlemen never said nothing about some gentry mort coming to stay.'

'Please fetch in my luggage. They are not expecting me, and you may address me as La…as Miss Winslow, if you please. Now, where is my brother?'

'Asleep, a'course.' The man regarded her as though she was simple, then turned and yelled down the passage, *'Jean, allez, vite!* They didn't get to bed until well past five this morning.'

'Well, when do they get up?' Marina stood aside for an undersized youth to get past and start collecting up their bags.

'Another hour or so, then they'll have something to eat.' He stood there stolidly, watching her.

'Then please take me to a bedchamber and find a suitable room for my maid. I will need hot water at once and then tea and bread and butter for both of us. I will dine later with my brother.'

The porter looked at her for a long minute, then turned and started to stomp up the stairs, the youth following him. Jenny picked up Marina's jewellery box and a hat box and followed. As they climbed, the stairs constantly turned and Marina realised that the wing of the Palais was only one room deep with perhaps a passageway running along the back. After what seemed long minutes and hundreds of stairs, they arrived on a landing and the man pushed open a door.

'Will that do, Miss Winslow?'

'It will if someone dusts it and makes up the bed,' Marina said tartly, trying to regain her breath. 'Please send a maid up when the water is brought. I will take my refreshments up here.'

By seven that evening, when her heavy-eyed brother wandered into the private salon on the first floor, Marina had established herself as a force in the household. Startled maids used to the laxity of a bachelor household were set to dusting, the chef had received a visit that quite clearly established Miss Winslow's preferences for her meal times and menus and the huge porter had confided not only that his name was Jem Hunter and he was a retired prize fighter, but also much of the routine of the house.

Lord Winslow blinked at the unexpected figure who rose as he entered, then staggered as she threw herself into his arms. 'Oh, Charlie! I am so happy to see you!'

Marina clung to his neck and found she was crying. It felt remarkably good, a relief after days of controlling herself and her emotions, and even knowing how much her brother hated weeping females was not enough to stop her.

'Marina—what the devil are you doing here? Now, now, don't do that! Hang it, you are making my coat all soggy. What's wrong?' He patted her shoulder ineffectually, looking up with a hunted expression as his friend came in.

'Excuse me.' He began to back out, only to be arrested by Charles's imploring cry of,

'Cris! This is my sister, don't know what she's doing here. For God's sake, man, haven't you a handkerchief or something?'

Young Mr Devlin rose to the occasion with a large, clean square of linen. 'Here you are, ma'am.' Marina accepted it gratefully, blew her nose and released her brother.

'Thank you. Charlie, I am sorry, I did not mean to cry all over you, only I am so tired and it is such a relief to get here and find you.'

'But why are you here? Nothing happened to Mama, has it? Or the children?' She shook her head and his face cleared. 'Just fancied a holiday, then, did you? I can't do much to take you around, you know, we're run off our feet here.'

'Is it a great success, then? I am so pleased for you.' Marina took a deep breath. 'I have left Justin.' Crispin Devlin got to his feet and began to back towards the door. She waved a hand to him, 'No, Mr Devlin, if I am going to stay here, I ought to tell you too, but, please, promise me you will be discreet.'

He nodded, colouring with embarrassment at being on the receiving end of some intimate revelation, but sat down again.

'It is Lady Andover. She…he… Charlie, I think they are lovers. She writes to him, and then she turned up at the house and I found…I found them…'

'Damn it!' Charlie roared, leaping to his feet, fists clenched. 'He told me that was over, the double-dealing bastard! I'll kill him, that's what I'll do. I'll get the first boat back to England and I'll call him out. Cris, you'll stand with me—now who else can I trust to keep this quiet?'

'No, Charlie, I don't want you to kill him—'

'No need,' Cris observed from the depths of the sofa. 'Andover will do it for you as soon as he finds out. He's the devil of a shot, never misses.'

'That's true.' Lord Winslow calmed down a trifle and went and poured three glasses of brandy, handing them to his sister and his friend. 'We'll watch the London papers for a couple of weeks; if he doesn't do it by then, I'll go back and see to it myself.'

Marina set the unwanted brandy down and took her brother's arm. She had come seeking sanctuary and had plunged into even more of a nightmare. 'Charlie, stop this. I love Justin, I do not want you to kill him, or wound him or anything else. I just do not think I can live with him any more.' She looked at him anxiously. 'Do you really think Lord Andover will call him out?'

'Sure to. Might not kill him, though. Andover's a crack shot, so if Mortenhoe's got any sense he'll choose rapiers. Nothing for you to fret over, though, it'll all be over by now, I would think.'

Cris Devlin was thumbing through the pile of newspapers by his side. 'Nothing in here, but these are almost a week out of date.' Marina stared at the two men, wondering if she was going to faint. How could they take it so calmly? Why had Lord Andover's reaction to this never entered her head? Justin could be dead or maimed even now.

'I must go back.' She was halfway to the door before Charlie caught her arm.

'What good would that do? Andover's not going to pay you any attention.'

'If I was there, I might have been able to cover it up, pretend Serena was there at my invitation. It never occurred to me... I was so angry and upset I just wanted to run away...'

'Too late now, and anyway, no one would have believed you,' Cris said firmly. 'It was all round society about Mortenhoe and Miss Henslow—everyone knew.'

'I didn't,' Marina said sadly. 'I had no idea until my wedding day and I heard people talking.'

Her brother came and put an arm round her shoulders. It

felt so good. Marina leaned into him, finding strength from his anger and concern for her. 'I thought it was all over, that he didn't love her any more,' he said awkwardly. 'I'd never have agreed to the marriage if I'd known.'

Later they had eaten a meal, conversing about careful nothings until the two young men began to forget her predicament in their preoccupation with their business venture. Marina could hardly blame them—they simply did not understand her feelings.

'Is the gaming house proving successful?' she asked, expecting a worrying degree of vagueness, or for Charlie to be evasive about costs and debts. But, no, they were clear about their profits and outgoings, about which tables were seeing the best takings and even how the decision to purchase slightly better champagne for the suppers was proving a good investment.

'And are you winning much yourself, Charlie?' That would be the fatal flaw of course—any amount of profit could slip through his fingers in an evening.

'I'm not gaming.' Her astonishment must have been plain, for he grinned and explained. 'I don't want to. Amazing, I know, but the buzz of running the house is so much better than playing myself, and seeing all those fellows playing and losing and knowing the profit is ending up in our pocket— now that's what I call satisfying.'

'Goodness.' Marina had never believed that Charlie would be able to do more than control his gaming. Now it seemed he had an outlet for his energy and risk-taking. 'I will keep house for you,' she decided. 'If I can stay for a few weeks until I know what is happening.' Until she knew whether she was a widow or simply a betrayed wife.

Weary by now, she had let the men show her round the gaming rooms, blinking in the light as the footmen lit the mass of chandeliers and wall brackets that illuminated the two long rectangular rooms on either side of the front door. One was almost filled with the *rouge et noir* table with its coloured cloth and cut-in bay for the dealer to stand. The other had the buffet table and numerous smaller tables for cards and dice.

Then she had stumbled upstairs to bed, bone tired and filled with nightmarish anxieties about Justin. Somehow she had slept, tossing and turning and half-waking sometimes when the shouting and singing from the gardens below reached her high window.

And had woken that morning refreshed and with a sense of calm which surprised her. Somehow during her sleep her mind and emotions had been working. Justin was young, fit and would have the choice of weapons in any duel. However enraged the Marquis was, he was unlikely to want to kill and find himself having to flee the country. And he was highly unlikely to want a divorce and the resulting scandal.

When the news finally reached her, Marina reassured herself, she would find that she was still married and that Lord Andover had retrieved his errant wife. *And then what? Justin does not need me now he has Knightshaye and he will not want me back after this. I love him, I should be happy if he is safe and that dangerous liaison has ended.* But it seemed that happiness was not something so easily come by; she would simply have to become accustomed to living with this aching sense of loss.

It also seemed that she had moved from the restoration of one house to another. Charlie and Crispin had expended their time and investment on the public rooms, but behind the scenes was a different story. Mentally and physically Marina rolled up her sleeves and went to work.

Her brother came downstairs at six that evening to find her in the *rouge et noir* room, showing Hunter the best way to brush baize. 'Taking over the housekeeping, Marina?' He grinned and kissed her cheek.

'If you'll let me.' She smiled back, surprised at how it made her cheek muscles ache. How long was it since she had produced more than a social smile? 'Do you employ women at the tables?'

'Certainly not! This is not that sort of house, and if you think I would let you…' Charlie looked positively stuffy.

'I was only teasing.'

The knocker sounded and Charles looked at the clock in surprise. 'Who can that be? We don't open until nine. You stay out of sight, Marina, I'm not having the randy bucks who come in here ogling my sister.'

Justin stood on the threshold, distracting himself from his anxiety about Marina by assessing his first impressions. Well-polished brass, trim paintwork, a discreet sign—Winslow and his partner knew how to make the place look the part.

He glanced up and down the arcade at the respectable late shoppers looking in the windows of the jewellers and other purveyors of *objets de luxe* who lined the garden front of the long wing. Behind the metal grilles the pleached trees and neat box hedges were well kept and the parterres showed no signs of last night's revelry. If she was here, then it was a far cry from the disreputable den he had feared. If she *was* here. His fingers sought the comfort of the talisman lustre, but his pocket was empty. It was hanging in the dark, at home, waiting for Mari to come back.

The door was opened by a hefty individual who bore all the hallmarks of an ex-prize fighter. *'Nous sommes fermés,'* he announced with the air of a man rifling through a mental phrasebook.

'I am not here to play,' Justin said firmly in English. 'I wish to see Lord Winslow.' There was a movement behind the porter, then his brother-in-law came out onto the threshold. 'Charles, is Ma—?'

'You bastard!' The blow took him neatly on the chin and completely by surprise. Justin landed on his back on the paving and lay, staring up at the vaulting above his head, his predominant emotion one of relief. If Charlie was that angry, it meant that either Mari was there, or he knew where she was.

'Get up, you philandering coward!' Justin raised his head, rubbed his aching jaw and got to his feet warily. 'You don't treat my sister like that and get away with it! Come here and I'll break every bone in your body.'

'I'll do it, guv,' the bruiser offered, flexing fists like hammers. 'She's a nice lady, Miss Winslow, I don't hold with flash culls upsetting nice ladies.'

'He's mine.' Charlie shouldered past the man and swung at Justin. This time, he saw it coming, sidestepping and catching his infuriated brother-in-law a blow on the cheek that sent him reeling back against the doorframe.

'Charlie, I really do not want to fight you. If you will just let me explain… Hell.' The doorman squared up, narrowed eyes sunk between pads of scar tissue, and let fly. Justin dodged, but at the cost of a long scrape down the side of his face. He retaliated, got in a handy blow to the man's belly and thought for a moment he had broken his fist.

'Stop it this minute! Jem, help Lord Winslow up and no one is to hit anyone else—do you understand?'

His heart thudded in his chest; one hammer blow of relief and delight at hearing her voice. 'Mari.' She stood on the doorstep, an apron round her waist, some sort of brush in her hand and dust on the end of her nose, and glared at him. He had never loved her more. 'Mari, are you all right?'

'Of course I am. Do you think I am so feeble that I would

be cast into despair by my husband's infidelities or too foolish to travel abroad alone?' She turned to her brother and ran her hand gently over his reddened cheek. Justin recalled the touch of those long fingers and ruefully applied his own pocket handkerchief to his bleeding face. 'And poor Jem—how could you hit a man who was only defending his master's household?' she added reproachfully.

Justin flexed his hand. It would take an iron bar to do *poor Jem* any damage.

'I need to speak with you.'

'No.'

'Mari, we cannot have this discussion on the doorstep, we are attracting attention.'

'We do not have to have this discussion at all.'

'Mari, you cannot—'

'I can do anything I choose, my lord. You have forfeited my trust.'

'I thought I had done that weeks ago.' He saw her flush and catch her lower lip between her teeth. 'Mari, give me fifteen minutes; if, after that, you wish me to leave and never come back, then I will make financial arrangements for you that will ensure your complete independence.'

'Don't listen to him.' Charles snapped. 'Name your seconds, Mortenhoe.'

'Certainly, but only after I have had my conversation with Marina.'

'Oh, let him come in.' She sounded weary. Her anger was easier to accept 'I will talk to him. Alone, Charlie.'

Reluctantly the two men on the doorstep moved aside and he took a step forward to follow Marina into the hallway and up the stairs. Then he stopped. His head was telling him that this was the sensible, prudent thing to do—sit down with Mari, explain it all in a civilised manner, persuade her he was telling the truth and return things to the way they were before. He was sure she would see it as her duty to return to him.

But his heart was telling him something quite different. Talk to her, yes. Explain it all honestly—but then gamble. Gamble that if he told her he loved her she would believe him. Gamble that she would return his feelings and not add a dutiful affection to the other duties he knew she expected to fulfil. Gamble his entire happiness on this throw, because if she could not love him he knew they could not go back to the way things were.

Justin Ransome did not do things on a whim, he did not gamble on what was precious, he planned and acted rationally. *To hell with that.*

Justin held out a hand to his wife. 'Come and walk with me. Have supper with me. Trust me.'

The steady grey eyes regarded him, shadowed underneath with faint smudges. 'Come with me, Mari,' he repeated. 'Please.'

Chapter Twenty-Five

Marina did not hesitate, shocking herself quite as much as Charlie. 'Yes. Just wait while I change.'

'You look perfect—although perhaps the apron—'

'Justin, this is *Paris.*' She had found her sense of humour again somehow. Bruised and wilting, true, but there still, able to flash amusement at a man who expected her to go out into the fashion capital of the world without a thought to what she was wearing.

'Very well, I will resign myself to waiting. Winslow, may I come in?'

Charlie stood aside reluctantly, still deeply suspicious. 'You can wait in the *rouge et noir* room.'

Marina turned back at the foot of the stairs and regarded her husband. The skin under his eyes was smudged with tiredness. The graze on his cheek was red and angry, a fine bruise was developing on his chin and the elegant coat was smudged with dust from where he had landed on his back. But his eyes were not tired. They blazed with something that made her breath catch in her throat.

Her love for him made her abrupt, 'Come here.' He stood obediently while she wielded the baize brush over his abused coat.

'Very wifely,' he murmured as she straightened his cravat.
'I have missed that. And other things,' he added in an outrageous undertone, making her blush and run quickly upstairs.

She came down half an hour later, more composed in an elegantly simple evening gown of amber silk caught high under her breasts with the plainest of ribbon trims. Her evening cloak was thrown over her arm.

'Ah!' His expression made her heart thud, but she managed to place a non-committal smile on her face.

'Is this suitable?'

'Perfect.' If Justin was attempting to cozen her into forgetting why she was here and what had caused her to flee England, he was doing a very good job of it. Marina made herself recall the scene that had greeted her as she walked into the salon to find Serena in his arms and hardened her heart. 'If you are ready, I thought a walk before we ate?'

Marina contented herself with a nod, trying to ignore the expression on Jem's face as she left on her husband's arm. He began to stroll through the gardens, which ran the length of the Palais. They were becoming populated now with men on their way to the hells, late shoppers returning home and couples strolling, as they were, arm in arm. It was still not so crowded that one could not have a private discussion.

'Justin, if you are going to tell me some tarradiddle about my being entirely mistaken in what I saw—'

'You saw Serena Andover in my arms with her lips on mine. There is no mistake about it.' She had expected him to deny it, had been braced for that argument. This frank admission forced a gasp from her lips and she felt the blood ebb from her cheeks.

'Marina!' He caught her against him as she stumbled and for a moment she clung to him, eyes closed, drinking in the familiar scent of him, the sensation of the strong muscles holding her.

So tempting to sink into the warmth and the familiar strength and to forget what had happened. Marina forced her eyes open and found Justin watching her closely. 'Are you unwell? Was the journey exhausting?'

'No.' How to explain that she had been expecting a fight, for him to deny everything? Somehow she had hoped he would and could prove her wrong. His easy admission had been like a blow above the heart. Marina kept her voice calm and matter of fact. 'I am quite well. I hired a most competent courier for the journey so that was not in the least tiring.'

'But your passport, money—?'

'We have family friends in the Foreign Office. I went to your bankers as well.'

Justin grimaced. 'I was comforting myself with the thought that you would arrive at Dover, realise you had neither the paperwork nor the resources to continue and I would find you sitting in comfort in a respectable inn. It was only after I had scoured Dover that I could believe you really had made the crossing.'

Something in the chill around her heart melted a little. He had been worried about her. But then, she had never thought him unkind or uncaring. Simply unfaithful and untrustworthy.

'I am more competent than you think, obviously. Before you ask, I stayed at Brown's Hotel in London and the manager recommended the courier.' Her eyes searched his face. Had he fought Lord Andover? If he had, was he unhurt? It had seemed so, from the easy way he had moved on the doorstep. A tiny part of her, wincing with shame at itself, had been excited by the sight of him fighting. Best to get this over with now before she weakened completely.

'If you and Lady Andover are lovers—'

'We are not. We never have been.' His eyes were steady on hers, his voice quite even.

'But—' Marina stilled her instinct to push him away and pace angrily across the crushed limestone path. 'You had better tell me exactly what it is you would have me believe, Justin.'

'I would have you believe the truth,' he said quietly. 'I met Serena in Brighton, quite by chance. I was there to look at property I was thinking of buying; she had been sent away to recover from some ailment or another. I was quite simply dazzled. I thought myself in love.' He smiled, 'If I had spent my youth falling in and out of infatuations, I might have recognised it for what it was, but I was star struck.

'The more she told me of herself, the more I was drawn in. She is the only child of a wealthy man and her mother died when she was just six. Always beautiful, she became her father's pet, but looking back now I can see that he gave her everything except his love and affection. She was showered with every toy, ponies, lap dogs, servants, pretty dresses.

'Aged seven she would be brought out at parties to lisp through a song, be cooed over and sent off to bed. It was much the same by the time she was seventeen. I pitied her so much.'

Marina made a bad job of suppressing her murmur of disbelief, but Justin shook his head. 'Think about it. I grew up without parents, but with loving guardians who taught me, listened to me, helped me find my purpose in life, chastised me and praised me. You had a family, affection, a role in life. My mistake was in thinking that if I loved her she would become less spoilt, less heedless, less grasping for pretty things and caresses.'

'You were wrong?' Maria tried not to sound uncharitable, however much she felt it.

'Her protestations of love for me lasted just as long as it took her to return to London and flutter her lashes at Andover.

He fell for her at least as hard as I had, and had the advantage of a loftier title, greater wealth—and immediate access to her father. By the time I got back to London a week later she was betrothed.'

'You must have been heartbroken,' Marina said politely. Did he really think this was an explanation likely to placate her?

'No, I was not—to my own surprise. My pride was hurt, I was confused that someone could apparently change so overnight, I was anxious for her. But after the first shock and one long, sleepless night, I realised I was seeing her all too clearly as she was and that what I was feeling was anger and wounded pride, not heartbreak.'

'Oh.' Marina strove to make sense of this. Justin was close and warm by her side and she had received an explanation that ought to satisfy her. *But...* 'But...on our wedding day, I saw you together. I saw the way she looked at you, the way she touched you. And I saw you look at her. Your face.'

'Damn.' She could see him wrestling with the shock of her words. They had reached the end of the gardens, passed through the grille and gained the great court. 'I said I did not love her, but that does not mean I do not worry about her and pity her. Andover is a hard man, a dangerous one to cross; and while I had no doubt he would be the most indulgent of husbands to a wife who obeyed him in all things, I had my doubts how he would deal with Serena's wiles and tantrums.

'Her nose was out of joint because I had married, and Andover was putting his foot down. She wanted to be petted and flirted with. I was concerned that she was on a very dangerous path.' His eyes narrowed as he watched her face. 'There is more, is there not? That alone was not why you mistrust me so?'

Talking of it after so many weeks of silence was like swallowing a stone. Marina gulped. 'I heard people at the wedding talking about you. They said you were still in love with her, that she had jilted you and you were marrying me on the rebound. And when you asked me to marry you, Justin, I had asked if there was anyone else and you had denied it.'

Her voice was running away with her and the tears were pricking at the back of her eyes. Marina took a breath and went on, more steadily. 'If I had not seen with my own eyes, then I would not have believed them, or at least,' she added honestly, 'I might have been suspicious, but I *would* have asked you. But I had just discovered from Charlie that you had only married me for the house, and I saw how you looked at her. And when I asked about her on the journey you said nothing. I did not feel I could trust anything you told me.'

'So we began our marriage with you thinking that I had married you on the rebound from Serena, that I still loved her and in any case I only proposed because I wanted Knight-shaye and could get it no other way?' She nodded mutely. 'And then I make love to you, hurt you physically and receive a letter from Serena? I suppose you guessed it was from her.'

'Yes. And then I find you kissing her! Justin, how can you explain that?'

He did not answer at once, looking round as though he had arrived where they stood without his knowledge. 'Lord, we're almost at the Louvre. I don't expect you want to see that now.' She shook her head, so he turned and began to pace back the way they had come, his voice slow as he found the words to explain.

'I had no idea she was coming, although given her outpourings in her letter about how foul Andover was being to her I might have suspected. She was in the room before I could properly take it in and threw herself weeping on my chest. When I bent my head and put my arms around her to try to find out what she was sobbing about, she took hold of my hair and pulled my head down until she could kiss me. It hurt like the devil,' he added with feeling.

'In a word, you were assaulted?' Marina found that her lips were twitching. Under any other circumstances his description conjured up a hilarious scene.

'I only managed to free myself with the loss of a clump of hair on either side. Look.' Gingerly Justin pushed his hair aside close to his right temple.

'Oh. Poor thing,' Marina put up a finger and lightly touched the reddened patch.

'You are laughing at me.' His eyes were green and a spark of humour to match hers was dancing in their depths.

'Just a little. You must admit, it is preposterous, a large man rendered helpless by a chit of a girl. What did you do with her?' A surge of some emotion was building up inside her, making her feel quite light-headed. What was it? Relief, she realised. Relief and hope and love and, quivering into flame, desire.

'I sent her packing back to her husband in the custody of Mrs Faversham at her most severely respectable—I am afraid our housekeeper knows rather more about our intimate affairs than one might wish. Plus a maid and a polite letter explaining that Serena had unfortunately misunderstood matters and had arrived for a visit when she was not expected.'

'Will he not want to call you out?' That terror was lurking just below the surface of her thoughts.

'Apparently not. We had a most amicable, if cool, conversation at White's the evening I arrived in London. I was not called upon to meet him at dawn, nor to show him the wounds on my scalp received while defending my virtue. Andover seems to have the measure of his bride now—she is about to spend a long three months with his mama in the country.'

'Charlie said he would call you out and…and kill you.' Her voice shook.

'Would you have cared so much, Mari?' Justin turned and at last, at long last, took her hands in his, ignoring the growing throng of strollers around them. 'You must have been very angry with me.'

'I was. I was furious.' She was clinging to his hands now, afraid he would let go and it would be a dream.

'That gave me some hope, oddly enough. I thought—when I could think straight for worrying about you—that you must have been very hurt to have run away like that. And if I had hurt you, then perhaps it meant you cared for me a little.'

'I have always cared for you.' There, she had said it—no, almost said it. *I love you.* The words trembled on her lips.

'I care for you too. Very much. It was not like losing Serena when I realised you had gone, Mari. It was as though part of myself had been cut away.'

She had been so very sure he was going to say that he loved her that when he did not her lip quivered, despite her best efforts to maintain her poise. He must have noticed. With a soft exclamation he guided her into the shadows of one of the arcades, deserted now the little shops had shut. And finally Justin did what she had been wanting him to do ever since she had seen him on the doorstep: he kissed her.

He kissed her very slowly, very thoroughly and as though it was an end in itself to reduce her to a quivering wreck in his arms. Night after night since she had run away Marina had been conjuring up the memory of his mouth on hers. Had her memory been so poor or was there something new here? Hazily she wondered if this was a claiming, a marking of her as his again after she had flaunted her independence and fled.

But it was no punishment for an erring wife, this slow slide of his mouth over hers, the pressure of his lips, the heat of his mouth or the demanding thrust of his tongue with its promise of another, utterly intimate, intrusion.

Marina wriggled until her body fitted closely against his, then gave up thinking and wondering and simply let herself slide into the luxurious surrender Justin was demanding.

She came to herself to find they were clasped in each other's arms not feet from the chattering, strolling multitude who were filling the gardens, that she had apparently not taken a breath for about ten minutes and that if her husband did not make love to her here, now, this second she was going to…

'I missed you,' Justin said simply, turning her carefully so he could step out into the lantern light and resume their walk.

'I…well…I missed you…of course…I mean…' Her body was screaming at her, all she wanted to do was to make love with him, show him that she trusted him now utterly and that nothing stood between them. She wanted him to tell her he loved her. But he did not.

What was he doing? This man, who had just reduced her to helplessly stammering at him, was setting his disordered clothing to rights and running a hand through his hair without the slightest sign of demanding to take her straight back to her bedchamber.

'These last few days have changed everything, would you not agree?' Justin shot a cuff with critical attention. 'We need to re-evaluate the whole basis of this marriage for, after all, we have both got what we wanted when we went into it, have we not? I have Knightshaye, you have a title, independence, financial freedom.'

Is he suggesting we separate? Or that we lead some kind of independent lives? Marina swallowed the hurt words that sprang to her lips and fixed an expression of polite indifference on her face. 'But of course, let us have a civilised discussion. And give up all pretence,' she added with rather more emphasis than she had intended.

* * *

Justin quietly expelled a long pent-up breath. Relief fought with arousal as his body throbbed with the memory of Mari's passionate response to his kiss. She trusted him again, she desired him. Did she love him?

He looked at his wife's face. It was still pale, the lovely grey eyes dark and troubled. And he saw too the courage of the smile she found for him, despite his cool, testing words.

Going slowly, being careful—that was not what she needed. His wife needed certainty and she deserved his passion and his love. And he was going to give her all those, now, tonight.

Chapter Twenty-Six

'Charlie worries about me,' Marina said tentatively as they stepped out into the balmy, torch-lit evening, trying for a more neutral topic. Her whole body ached again, as it had in those hideous days after Justin had discovered her true response to his lovemaking. 'Did he hit you very hard?'

'No harder than I deserved.' He guided her aside to sit on a bench under a linden tree, wafting its subtle fragrance into the warm evening. 'Mari, there is one more thing I must tell you: the reason why my father gambled with yours and lost Knightshaye.'

'You said you could not tell me.'

'I know. It affected someone still living, but she thinks I should.'

'Who?' Marina twisted round on the bench, trying to read his face in the shadows.

'Your mother.'

'*Mama?*'

'Yes. Your parents were betrothed when my mother first came to London. My father, and yours, both saw her for the first time at a ball and both fell in love with her. But she spurned your father, an engaged man—and, in any case, my parents were already falling in love.

'But Lord Winslow was obsessed, it seems. He pursued her, fiancée or no fiancée, and would take none of her rebuffs as an answer. Then he went too far—one evening as she was travelling out of London to visit a relative he abducted her and carried her off. It seems his intention was to take her over the border, by which point she would be so comprehensively ruined that she would have no choice but to marry him.'

'Papa? Papa would do such a thing?' Her every instinct was to protest, to disbelieve Justin, but in all honesty, she found she was not surprised. Shocked and horrified, indeed, but not surprised. Papa had always taken what he wanted, done what he wanted, with a smiling face if he was getting his own way, with complete ruthlessness if not. She knew now she had never loved him, shocking though that was to admit about one's own parent.

'What happened?' She knew Justin could read her belief in her face.

'My father pursued them and caught them up the next day.'

'The next… He was too late?'

Justin nodded. 'I only found out because my mother left me her diaries to be given to me when I was twenty-one. My father called Lord Winslow out, of course—in fact, he tried to fight him there and then, but my mother pleaded with him about the scandal. So he made another one and simply carried on with the elopement. There was considerable talk, but it died down.' He broke off, twisting a fallen twig between his fingers. 'She miscarried two months later.'

Marina could think of nothing to say. Instead she reached out a hand and took Justin's. His fingers spread, linked with hers and squeezed.

'Papa should have known that Winslow would never be bested. He married your mother and for years all was well. Then, one night, on who knows what whim, he challenged my father to cards, naming Knightshaye as the stake. When Papa refused he asked if he wanted the truth about the already notorious elopement to be made public. My father was no gambler, but he would hazard anything for Mama. You know the rest.'

'How could you risk marrying me? What if I turned out to be like that?' She shook her head at her own stupidity. 'But of course, you are like your father—only you would risk anything for Knightshaye.'

'No. If I had not realised who and what you were from the moment I saw you, I would never have done it.' Justin read the hurt behind the defiant words. Now he was sure, even if she was not. Mari loved him. 'I would have refused Charlie and I would have found enough money, somehow, so that he could not deny me. It might have taken a long time, but I had already waited years. I could wait again.'

Now, he had told her all the secrets, all the past. It was time for the future. 'Are you hungry?' In the light of the nearby *torchère* he saw the indignation that he could think of food after the events of the past hour fill the candid grey eyes. And then with disarming honesty she nodded.

'Yes. I suppose I should have more sensibility, but I am starving. I cannot think when I last ate with any appetite.'

'Come along then.' Justin stood up, a feeling of calm washing through him. It was the effect Mari had had on him from the start and it made him want to laugh out loud.

'There, will this do?' They had done no more than walk along the arcade to the end of the Palais furthest from the Seine, then turn the corner past the entrance to the theatre, which somehow squeezed itself into the narrow building.

He had seen the place earlier and had been instantly attracted to it. A door stood open, light spilling out onto the pavement. Beyond one could glimpse a large, low-ceilinged room set with tables. Around the walls were little booths for greater privacy and the space was beginning to fill with couples and small parties intent on an early supper before the theatre or other entertainments.

Mari was looking intrigued, as he thought she might—she would never have seen anything like this in London, and it would certainly be considered scandalous for her to set foot in such an establishment if it had existed.

The waiter greeted them, took their cloaks and showed them to a booth. Mari sat looking around her discreetly while Justin consulted the waiter about their meal. When the man had gone he sat back, simply enjoying watching her.

She caught him out and smiled suddenly, her face lit with pleasure at their mild adventure. 'Why are you looking at me like that? Do I appear such a Country Mouse, peeping out at the sophisticated French Town Mice?'

'You appear enchanting.' He reached for her hand, then sat back as the waiter brought a bottle of wine and a trencher of bread. Mari blushed. He waited until the man turned away and this time caught her hand.

'Justin!' she whispered. 'People will see.' He found her agitation charming and set out to tease her just a little, lifting her hand to kiss it. *'Justin!'*

'May I not kiss my wife's hand?' A platter of Bayonne ham appeared, along with olives and a mysterious small dish. Justin kept a firm grip on Mari's hand until they were served.

'I thought you just said you did not want a wife any more.' She shot the challenge across the table, tugging her hand free and pretending to give her attention to the food. 'What are those in that dish?'

'Anchovies. Very salty. I did not say I no longer wished to

have a wife. I said we should re-evaluate our marriage.' *Was this the moment? Here and now, without any of the things he had meant to say to lead up to it? Should he chance everything over a platter of ham?* 'I no longer want a marriage of convenience. I want a love match.'

Marina dropped her fork with a clatter, the slice of strange ham dropping into the bowl of anchovies. 'Love?' she faltered. Justin was looking as though he was about to face a firing squad: pale, grim and determined. 'You want a love match?'

'Yes.' He retrieved her fork and placed the slice of ham on her plate.

'But you do not love me.' Marina glanced round, appalled that she could have been overheard, and realised that amidst the babble of French conversation they could have been plotting to assassinate the Prince Regent without attracting notice. 'You were quite clear about that when you proposed to me.'

'I was. I was determined to tell you the truth.' Justin nodded. 'I liked you, I admired and respected you—and I desired you far more than it was possible to tell a respectable single girl. But then I married you. Bread?'

'Yes, thank you.' Marina took the slice blindly, feeling as though she had been mesmerised. 'You married me and found you loved me? Is that what you are saying? When did it happen? Why did you not tell me?' *It could not be true, it was impossible.*

'I realised when I discovered I was jealous enough of that young pup of a curate to throttle him for even being alone with you. And I did not tell you because you very firmly reminded me that we had a marriage of convenience. I had too much foolish pride to simply throw my feelings at your feet and risk you trampling on them.'

'Oh.' Breathless, unable to speak, she simply stared at him. They might just as well have been alone instead of in the midst of a crowd of cheerful strangers. 'And then I…we…oh, Justin. It all went so very wrong.'

'Mari.' He was white now, the bruises on his face standing out as though they had been painted there. 'Mari, I do not want you to be anything but honest with me—I would rather be hurt now, with your honesty, than harbour any more false hopes. But do you think you could ever love me?' His eyes, green and intense, locked with hers and she realised that against all hope this was the truth and that her husband loved her.

'Hell, now I have made you cry.' He sounded appalled. Shakily she raised a hand to her cheek and found it damp.

'Of course you have.' Her hand, wet with her tears, found his across the table. The bowl of anchovies fell, unregarded, to the floor. 'I love you. I loved you from before we were married. I never thought I would ever hear you tell me you felt the same way.' He turned her hand in his, kissing her palm until her breath became uneven. 'Justin, stop it, people will see.'

'I don't care.' His eyes, lifted to hers across their clasped hands, were triumphant, dangerous. 'Shall I stand on my chair and tell the room that my wife loves me? I would like that.'

'No!' She held on tight, half-laughing, half-convinced he meant it. 'Look, we have got olive oil all over the floor!'

'Never mind, I shall tell the waiter we are in love. Now, eat.'

'Eat? I thought that you would want to go back—' Marina broke off, blushing fiercely. Her pulse was racing, she could hardly know what to think.

'I want you to eat your supper and drink your wine. I want to watch you across this table, knowing that you are mine and that in a little while I am going to make love to you, slowly and carefully and until you melt in my arms. I want to make up for every moment of pain you have suffered and I want to savour the anticipation.'

'I do not think I *can* eat.' Her heart was filling her chest.

'Yes, you can. Now drink this.' Justin pushed a glass of wine across the table and nodded at the food on her plate. 'Come on. I promise I will not insist on dessert.'

Laughing helped. And the charm of the busy restaurant, full of people all intent on their own rendezvous, amorous or otherwise, somehow made her less shy. The waiter swept away the wreckage of the anchovies with nothing more than an expressive roll of his eyes to show he had noticed they were foolishly engrossed in each other, and perhaps the wine Justin was filling her glass with helped.

They arrived back at the door into *C. et C.* arm in arm and, in Marina's case, rather inclined to giggle. Hunter opened the door to Justin's knock, a wave of warmth and noise from the gaming rooms flooding out into the night. Marina found herself subjected to the same sort of scrutiny Bunting gave the young ladies of the Winslow household when he suspected they had been up to mischief. The expression sat oddly on the burly doorman.

'Good evening, Hunter. Please tell Lord Winslow that I am safely back.'

'Yes, Miss Winslow.' He glared at Justin.

'Lady Mortenhoe,' Justin said firmly, stepping over the threshold so briskly that Hunter had to step backwards.

'I'll tell your woman you are back, shall I, Mi—my lady?'

'No, thank you, Hunter.' She smiled sweetly. 'Goodnight.'

They hurried past the open doors into the gaming rooms and almost ran up the staircase. 'This feels very clandestine,' Marina confided.

'I know—it adds a surprising *frisson*.' Justin grinned at her as they rounded the next turn of the stairs. 'Is it much higher? I'm going to need my breath to kiss you…'

'Here.' Marina threw open the door, the giggles suddenly quite vanished. The room was lit fitfully by the reflection of the flambeaux in the gardens on the whitewashed ceiling and Justin picked his way through the furniture to find the tinderbox and branch of candles. The light flared between them and she slowly shut the door behind her.

'Mari.' He held out his hands and she went to him, all her doubts gone. She felt so much in love as he held her that she trembled.

'Sweetheart?' He tipped up her face. 'Are you frightened? I will be so careful—'

'No!' She was vehement, standing on tiptoe to clasp her arms around his neck and find his lips. 'No. Love me, Justin, love me, do not treat me like porcelain. I want you so much.'

The narrow bed creaked alarmingly as they tumbled on to it, clothes half-gone, but Marina hardly noticed, intent on the hard, hot flesh under her palms, the miracle of rediscovering her husband's body when she thought he was lost to her.

She spared a moment's thought for her lovely gown as a ripping sound marked its passage to the floor, then wreaked as much havoc on the buttons of the fall of Justin's trousers. Finally, they were naked, entangled on the bed and she could hear the echo of her own panting breath in his as he struggled for control.

There was a moment, a tiny flicker of anxiety as the long, lean body fitted itself so naturally into the soft curves of hers, then she arched up to met his thrust, gasping, not with pain, but with the shocking pleasure of it. It was so right, so overwhelming, so consumingly intimate.

'I love you.' Justin was murmuring the words as he stroked gently within her, turning her initial awe into a spiralling, demanding, tightening surge of pleasure. It seemed impossible to endure it and yet she wanted more, wanted more of him, of the hardness that possessed her, gasping his name as the world imploded around her and the flambeaux outside seemed to light up the room.

'Mmm?' Justin shifted a little so Mari's head fitted more comfortably on his shoulder as she moved in the narrow bed. He waited for her to wake up fully, curbing his impatience for her to look at him so he could see again that light which turned the serious grey eyes silver and sparkling.

What time was it? he wondered, watching the sky through the billowing gauze drapes. In answer a clock chimed sweetly, somewhere below. Six. Far too early to get up. Not too early to make love to one's wife. Again.

He was feeling quite ridiculously smug and almost laughed at himself for it. Still, to make a woman as happy as Mari had assured him—shown him—he had made her several times last night…yes, a man was entitled to feel just a little smug about that.

'What are you smiling about?' She had woken up without him realising and was regarding him with a twinkle her eyes.

'Last night,' he admitted and enjoyed watching the rosy colour staining her face. 'Did I tell you I loved you very much?'

'Once or twice,' Mari admitted, delighting him with her attempt to sound nonchalant. 'Justin, do you want to stay in Paris?'

'If you do. Would you like to? I am sure the Ambassador won't mind me bringing you back to stay.'

'Only…' She dropped her gaze, running one finger through the hair on his chest in a deeply distracting manner. 'Only I think I would like to go home.' She looked up and smiled. 'Home to Knightshaye.'

'Yes.' He pulled her tight against him, revelling in the feel of the long, slender flank pressed against him. 'Yes. And we will have the chandeliers cleaned and the ballroom prepared and have a house party.'

'Chandeliers? That is not a very flattering thing for you to be thinking about just now.' She was exploring with her fingers under the sheets.

'I will show you when we get home—' Justin broke off with a gasp. 'If we ever get out of this bed, you minx. I suppose you want me to make love to you all over again?'

'No, thank you,' Mari said demurely, spoiling the effect by running the tip of her tongue along the curve of his ear. 'I want to make love to you instead. And then we can make love to each other again.'

'I shall buy my brother-in-law a very superior walking cane from the shop next door,' Justin observed a few minutes later, desperately trying to keep his mind off what his wife was doing—a futile attempt to keep control of the situation. 'I feel I owe it to him in thanks for a quite outstanding piece of matchmaking.'

'I know.' Mari stopped what she was doing and wriggled up the bed to plant a kiss on his lips. 'Do you realise that for the only time in his life Charlie has backed a winner?'

FALCON'S DESIRE
by Denise Lynn

Emboldened by grief, she had ensnared the infamous
Rhys, Lord of Faucon. Now, imprisoned in her castle,
Faucon posed an even greater threat – not to her
defences, but to her heart. They established an uneasy
truce. But would that be destroyed when she learned a
new-found alliance bound her to him as his bride?

THE HORSEMAN
by Jillian Hart

Dillon Hennessey was a man like no other. Strong,
yet caring, determined, yet kind. But he was still
a man, Katelyn Green reminded herself, and therefore
not to be trusted. Dillon could see the sadness at
Katelyn's core. He wanted to help her, *would* help
her, if he had the words and the ways. But would his
tenderness be enough to win a woman who had
been robbed of her faith in love?

On sale 6th October 2006